SLOW RIDE

POWERTOOLS: HOT RIDES, BOOK #2

JAYNE RYLON

HAPPY ENDINGS PUBLISHING

ABOUT THE BOOK

When tragedy struck, the loss of Jordan and Wren's shared lover ripped them apart.

Guilt and shame made it impossible for Agent Jordan Mikalski to look the love of his life in the eye. If he couldn't face her, he sure as hell couldn't live with her or make love to her or even be the man to comfort her in the depths of her grief.

Wren Asbery's mourning threw her into a deep depression she wasn't sure she'd ever climb out of, made worse by Jordan's abandonment in the time of her greatest need. For that she'll never forgive that bastard.

After years of slow healing they realize they're both attracted to the same man, which means they have some things to figure out fast. Will Kason Cox be doomed to lust after two people who can't stand each other or will he be able to become the glue that sticks them back together?

This is a standalone book in the Hot Rides series and includes an HEA with no cheating. The series is part of the greater universe where both the Powertools and Hot Rods books are also set, so you can visit with many of your previous favorite characters and see what they're up to now!

ADDITIONAL INFORMATION

Sign up for the Naughty News for contests, release updates, news, appearance information, sneak peek excerpts, reading-themed apparel deals, and more. www.jaynerylon.com/newsletter

Shop for autographed books, reading-themed apparel, goodies, and more www.jaynerylon.com/shop

A complete list of Jayne's books can be found at www.jaynerylon.com/books

1

———

FIVE YEARS AGO

Wren kicked back in her favorite leather recliner. Sure, the thing was beat up to the point of leaking stuffing. Worse because she never remembered to take her work boots off before sitting in it. But it was comfy and still smelled faintly like the two guys she'd been missing a hell of a lot, more every day they were gone.

Of course, she couldn't be too sad since they were off saving the world or some shit while she was stuck in Middletown, living her boring barely-getting-by life, and working as a roving specialty welder. If Jordan and Johnny weren't so damn noble, she probably wouldn't love them half as much as she did. Yet even a portion of her admiration and lust would still be more than she'd ever conceived was possible until she'd experienced it herself.

She rubbed her chest and thought about rubbing other stuff too. Just the idea of Jordan and Johnny could turn her on. And it had been too damn long since they'd been home—in her bed—to do something about it. Going cold turkey after being spoiled by *two* of the world's finest lovers wasn't easy.

Wren had already burned through the entire stash of batteries they'd left her as a parting gag gift when they'd gone on this latest assignment to who-knew-where. Jordan and Johnny were special agents for ICE. That meant they traveled frequently and did stuff they didn't like to talk much about when they came back, though she'd deduced they were focused on smuggling operations at the border. She respected their desire to leave that heavy shit at work, as there was plenty of stuff in her past she didn't care to rehash or dwell on either.

Usually their job wasn't too dangerous, according to what they'd divulged, but lately...well, things had been changing in the world.

Wren took a gulp of the chilled white wine she'd poured herself and closed her eyes. She pictured her boyfriends' faces the last time they'd all lain in bed together, tangled in the sheets, their grins and bright eyes proof that they'd enjoyed what they'd shared as much as she had.

People assumed that just because she looked one way —like a blond-haired blue-eyed angel or, god forbid, a beauty queen—that she had to act that way too. Fuck that. She'd never been one to use the right fork at a fancy dinner or dress as prim and proper as her mother had wished.

So why should it be any different when it came to her love life?

Jordan and Johnny had made her see that there was nothing wrong with being greedy in bed. They hadn't said so yet, but they both loved her. Nearly as much as she adored them, she was sure. They worked together, as a team, to make sure she knew it even without exchanging those three little words that too many people said without really meaning.

It had started out innocently enough. Johnny had hired her to fix a crack in the hull of his aluminum fishing boat last spring. She remembered how he'd insisted on helping her carry her gear down the weathered dock. Not because she was a woman, but because he was a gentleman and would have helped anyone who'd come out there that day. His favorite country singer, Kason Cox, had crooned about secret love from a dusty old radio in the corner of the shed near the no-frills cabin situated on massive Lake Logan, about fifteen miles outside of Middletown.

They had been joined shortly by Jordan. Wren had been grateful for her face shield, which had kept them from seeing how her eyes bugged out while trying not to stare at two of the most gorgeous men she'd ever seen right there, side by side, in one place.

After her work was finished, they'd shared a few beers, some flirtation, and then several kisses, each of the guys taking turns blowing her mind and all of her preconceived notions about what a romantic relationship should look like right out of that cool lake water.

From the moment they'd met, there had been no resisting the attraction between them.

They'd spent the entire summer together, rivaling the scorching sun with the heat that radiated from them whenever they collided. After months of showing her exactly how much he appreciated her strength, passion, and independence, Johnny had finally convinced Wren that wearing one of the sexy dresses he'd spotted in the back of her closet didn't make her a vapid woman. It took longer than it should have because of the associations she'd formed between clothes like that and the socialites who wore them to her mother's parties.

Wren rolled her wineglass over her forehead, but it was too late. Her mind was already reliving that night. The one that had altered something inside her. The one that had made her sure they belonged together. For good.

Johnny had talked her into trying on that fiery red dress. When she'd emerged from her bedroom draped in the bold silk, Jordan had dropped his beer. None of them had bothered to wipe up the spilled liquid or the shards of green glass.

Instead, both men had moved as one, closing in on her.

Johnny had twirled her, dancing around the living room to the Kason Cox song that had come on again—the same one from the boathouse, "Secret Love". And she'd taken that as an omen. They were meant for the everlasting bond the singer was searching for in his heart-wrenching song.

Remembering the way they'd kissed her—Jordan with fierce urgency, and Johnny with aching tenderness—she nearly sank through their favorite recliner. They satisfied both halves of her. The rough-and-tumble tomboy side and the more girly facets she'd always been afraid to embrace for fear they would make her weaker.

Jordan was never afraid to give her what she needed, even if he was sometimes coarse or rough. He knew she could handle his blunt desire. His confidence inspired her to let loose and embrace the parts of her she'd been told were too brash, too bold, and too rugged.

But Johnny... He was always there to make sure she was safe. He coddled her and tended to the parts that needed nurturing no matter how much she wished they didn't. Johnny made sure that if she and Jordan got carried away, she had somewhere to recover after the storm. He was her shelter and the man who grounded her while passion whipped around them all.

Wren was no blushing virgin. Still, she'd never experienced anything like what Jordan and Johnny could heap on her, fucking her all night long, refusing to stop until she had run out of orgasms and was too exhausted to try for more. She shifted in the chair, rubbing her thighs together as if that would help.

She certainly hadn't set out to have two men in her life. It had just happened that way. She'd met the partners, both special agents, who were so much more than coworkers. They were two halves of one sexy, tempting whole. Friends and both her lovers.

And now she couldn't imagine her love life any other way.

Well, that wasn't exactly true.

She took another sip of her wine as she thought about the possessive desire she'd seen in Jordan's eyes. Aimed not only at her, but also at Johnny. At first, she had thought she'd imagined it. Over time, his hunger had grown undeniable. At least to her. Johnny seemed oblivious to Jordan's heated stares and how hard he got every time they accidentally touched while making love to her. Ignoring the truth any longer could cause a rift in their relationship. Wren wasn't willing to risk losing the best thing she'd ever had over some dumbass misunderstanding.

She had been close to broaching the subject or maybe facilitating something forbidden and naughty between the guys in bed, bringing the two men closer.

Their triad didn't yet feel perfect, or complete, with them paying all their attention to her and ignoring the bond between themselves. Right before she'd worked up the courage to press the issue, her men had been shipped off on this assignment without any warning at all.

So she'd spent the few months apart practicing her speech. The one she intended to give when they returned, to hopefully bond them together as strongly as the chassis she'd welded for a specialty auto restoration shop—Hot Rods—earlier that day.

Yes, you guys are partners at work, but you're so much more than that here. You're my best friends, my lovers, my whole world. And I want you to be as happy as I am every day that I get to spend with you. You need to be as honest as you've forced me to be about who I am and what I like. I think you owe that to yourselves.

Hopefully that would be all it took to nudge them together. It would be so sexy to watch them make out with each other and to fuck the way she knew they wanted to deep down.

Jordan would probably cave first. He'd wrap his hand around the back of Johnny's neck and draw the man to him before devouring his lips in a frantic kiss. Eventually, they'd break apart panting, and Jordan would order Johnny to undress while he ripped his own clothes off. Soon he'd have Johnny bent over the nearest piece of furniture while he—

A knock at the door startled her from her daydream. She cleared her throat and fanned her face a few times as she stood and straightened her jeans and ripped T-shirt. The knocking became a banging that kind of pissed her off. Who the fuck could be out there at this time of the evening? The mailman had delivered her supplies hours ago.

Whoever was out there had nothing more important to tell her than how to be saved by their god or the cost of their cookies. Mmm...cookies. If she couldn't have sex, she might as well have dessert.

Wren strode for the entryway of her modest one-bedroom apartment. It wasn't much, but it was hers. No, *theirs*. The guys had moved in a few days before they left on their assignment. It didn't make sense to pay rent for two places when theirs would only sit empty.

Besides, they'd been spending all their nights in her bed anyway. It had been another of many steps in the right direction as far as she was concerned. A smile stretched across her face at that thought. Wren was still grinning when she whipped open the door.

Instead of a cute kid peddling snacks, she was met with two very serious men in uniform. Their mouths were set in grim slashes that had nothing in common with her rapidly fading smile. "Are you Ms. Wren Asbery?"

She nodded.

They say life can change in an instant.

Wren's shattered between one heartbeat and the next, when she learned that Johnny was never coming home.

She didn't hear the exact words. Not through the buzzing that had started in her brain, but she felt them. Direct impacts to her chest, every one. As surely as the bullets they told her Johnny had taken earlier that day.

How could he be gone? How could she have not felt it the second his spirit left the world?

He'd died, and she hadn't even gotten to say goodbye.

It was already over. Done.

The officers stayed long enough to make sure she

understood and that she survived the initial shock. Then she was on her own. And would be from there on out. The more minutes passed, the more it hurt.

"I'm sorry, ma'am." The officer or whoever the person was, she couldn't remember, nodded then turned to go.

"Wait…" she called out until he looked back over his shoulder with pity in his gaze. "What about Jordan? Is he okay? When is he coming home?"

"Jordan?"

"Special Agent Jordan Mikalski. Johnny's partner." She stood as straight as she could, her fists clenched, braced for the worst news possible—that she'd lost both of the men she loved at once.

"Oh. Our records said…" The guy trailed off as he glanced at his partner, who shrugged.

"I love them both." Fuck anyone who had anything to say about that. Especially right then.

"Agent Mikalski sustained minor physical injuries. He's being debriefed. I would expect he'll be home within the next twelve to twenty-four hours."

Wren deflated, air rushing from her lungs in a whoosh.

Immediately, she felt guilty for her relief. Johnny had sacrificed everything for her, for Jordan, and for a better world. But at least she hadn't lost them both. She never could have survived that.

"Thank you," she muttered, her hands shaking uncontrollably as she clutched the door and stepped backward into the shadows. She hoped the officers wouldn't see the tears pouring down her cheeks faster and faster as the terrible news they'd told her began to sink in.

"Do you want us to call someone to be with you?" the agent asked.

"Just Jordan. I need him. And...I think he's going to need me." Wren hated it that her voice cracked when she rasped, "Please."

"I'm sure he'll be here as soon as possible, Ms. Asbery."

Wren nodded, then shut the door, spinning around to lean her shoulders on it. There was no other way she could stay upright. Her lower back slammed into the fiberglass as her knees buckled and she slid down to the floor, sobbing.

Agony only continued to grow as hour after hour passed, turning into days, and still there was no sign of her other lover.

Dread sprouted from the dark nothingness of her grief.

Just because Jordan was alive didn't mean she hadn't lost him in this tragedy, too.

2

———

Jordan had put it off as long as he could. There was nothing left to do but go home.

And face Wren.

It was easily the hardest thing he'd had to do in his life, including watching Johnny die in his arms. Because even though Johnny had accepted the inherent risks in his job and mercifully hardly realized a gunshot wound had clipped his carotid artery before bleeding out, Wren was going to have an entire lifetime to suffer.

If she hurt even a fraction as bad as he did, it was going to be hell on earth. Pure torture.

Which was why he'd been wandering aimlessly for... days, probably, though he'd lost track for certain. He'd ridden out to the cabin at the lake, paced the shore, screamed into the wilderness, and cried until he'd made himself physically ill. Stayed awake for days on end then slept for what seemed like a few more, unable to get out of bed. None of that had changed the numb dread inside him.

His entire core was frozen.

Jordan was more scared than he'd been when he'd realized they'd walked into an ambush near the border. Because he wasn't sure that even Wren could thaw him. He sure as hell wasn't going to be able to comfort her either, not when he felt like an emotional zombie.

It was a disaster waiting to happen.

He put his key in the lock and paused, wondering if he should knock. Technically, he lived there. But it was Wren's place and he couldn't imagine how he'd be welcome ever again. Not after he'd failed her. He'd promised to keep Johnny safe. To bring him home for her to love and be loved by in return.

Now she'd have to settle for only him.

Jordan knew he'd never be enough to fill both their shoes. Besides, he didn't have the gentle touch his partner had. Without that to soften his sharpness, he wouldn't be any good for Wren.

It was a pointless exercise. He stood there long enough that he thought he might be better off tucking the key in the mail slot and walking away, leaving everything of his old life behind in that quirky, cozy apartment with Wren, and starting over as the entirely new and foreign person he felt like.

Except right then the doorknob was snatched out of his grip.

Wren stood there, gaping at him. Extremely bloodshot whites surrounded her irises, making them seem even bluer than usual. Her long blond hair was kinked and matted as if she hadn't brushed it in the entire week since...*the incident,* as he'd started thinking of it to himself.

For a moment, they simply stood there, staring at each other in shock.

Then she screamed and flung herself at him. "Jordan! Son of a bitch, Jordan!"

At first, he couldn't tell if she was trying to pull him closer or beat him up as her fists pounded his chest and she buried her face against his shoulder. Probably it was a bit of both.

He had no choice but to catch her or let her fall on the busted concrete sidewalk. No way would he ever let that happen, so he wrapped his arms around her and held her close as he half-dragged, half-carried her inside. Every blow she rained on him he absorbed, wishing it hurt more. Maybe then it would drown out the pain coming from within him for a moment or two.

It felt wrong to hold her, to smell her, to cradle her so close to his heart when he knew he didn't deserve her. Whatever had been between them had died as surely as Johnny. Grief, anger, betrayal, shame, outrage—all of it was too intertwined with his feelings for Wren and the man he'd lost before he'd ever found the guts to admit that he loved him.

No, Johnny had known that. He just hadn't understood that Jordan was *in love* with him, too.

Now it was too late.

He couldn't fix any of it. Neither would he take it back.

The past summer had been the hottest time in his life. He planned to hold it as close as he was hugging Wren right then. He'd relive it in his memories as often as possible to erase the despair that had nearly driven him to join Johnny. He wasn't sure exactly how long he'd sat at their cabin, with his service pistol on the table, pointed in his direction, but it had been long enough to drain every drop of liquor they'd stashed in the cabinets there.

He'd felt the weight of the icy steel in his hand, and had tested the feel of it against his temple.

But as his finger had tightened on the trigger, he'd imagined he heard Johnny outside, singing along to Kason Cox as he worked on the outboard motor that was always quitting on them, forcing them to row their way home with the sunset glinting off the mirror-calm surface of Lake Logan before it dipped behind the majestic mountains on the opposite shore.

Jordan had put the gun down and gone to look out the window, finding only leaves blowing past in the brisk autumn breeze. No Johnny. No Wren.

Only the memories of brighter days had saved him.

That didn't mean he could keep the best part of his life all to himself now that Johnny was gone.

"Where were you? Are you okay? Of course you're not, but..." Wren was running her hands all over him then, as if trying to verify that he was in one piece. Jordan tried to ignore the way her touch electrified his skin. Even then, in the depths of his grief and guilt, she had the power to move him. "Jordan! Talk to me, damn it!"

"I'm sorry," was all he could say.

Wren paused then, blinking up at him as though she didn't recognize his monotone voice. Hell, he didn't either. Neither did he recognize the distance that wedged between them, tearing them apart.

"This wasn't your fault..." she began.

"It should have been me," he told her, refusing to lie.

"He knew the dangers. He did this job anyway." Wren sniffled. "That's what makes both of you heroes."

"I'm no hero." Jordan put Wren to the side. He paced the entryway until she grabbed his hand, tugging him toward the kitchen. More memories assaulted him, reminding him of the nights they'd danced, joked, and fucked in what should have been their home.

Wren shoved him into the recliner he and Johnny had rescued from the side of the road one night before garbage pickup. Then she climbed into his lap. She smothered him in hugs and gentle kisses that felt like the ultimate betrayal to Johnny, who'd been the seductive one in their duo.

"Wren, don't." He clasped her narrow waist and set her away from his chest, hoping he could draw in the breath required to make her understand.

"I needed you. Didn't you need me?" She bit her lip as if she could keep the words from flying into the gap he'd deliberately put between them again. It would be too easy to erase that space. To give in. To make things worse.

How could he admit it without harming her further? He couldn't so he didn't. "I was lost."

Still was. Might always be.

Wren nodded slowly, her hair falling forward to frame her gorgeous face. "Can you tell me...anything? About what happened?"

Jordan winced. He could, but he didn't want to. Unless that's what it would take for her to get it. To understand why he didn't deserve her. Why he couldn't do this anymore. He drew in a shaky breath past the iron bands that had been constricting his chest since he'd witnessed the light going out of Johnny's green eyes.

"If it's too hard—"

"There was a double agent. He told the smugglers where we'd be." Jordan spit out the details in staccato blasts that reminded him of the shots that had rained down on them. "I went in first. Something tipped Johnny off. He roared. Dragged me back and threw himself over me."

Wren's lip quivered between her teeth. Her chin wobbled. Then tears dripped off her cheekbones as she began to shake all over.

"They got him here." His fingers touched the spot where blood had sprayed from Johnny's neck like the garden hose Jordan had run over with the lawn mower last summer. He'd never seen so much blood. So fast. There hadn't been anything they could do to stop it. "It was over in a matter of seconds."

The longest damn seconds of his life.

Jordan could swear he and Johnny had an entire conversation in the glance they'd exchanged. But he hadn't so much as whispered the only words that had mattered in his best friend's dying moments. *I love you.*

He hadn't realized he was crying too until Wren leaned in and kissed the trail of his tears, attempting to take away his pain as easily as the moisture there. Impossible.

But her touch did dull the ache a tiny bit. So he gave in and let her hold him, and let himself embrace her, too. He rocked her against his chest until she shifted, her long legs overflowing the recliner. Then he stood, holding her as he moved without thought, carrying her toward the bedroom.

He'd only meant to make her more comfortable. To put her somewhere she didn't have to be scrunched up and awkward.

Except, when he set her down and she refused to unwind her arms from his neck, he went with her onto the soft, warm bed where they'd made love so many times that his body responded with muscle memory.

It was impossible not to mix up the past and the present, to recall how much hope and joy he'd had a week ago. He wanted to be that man again, if only for a moment.

Wren, never a passive lover, was thrashing beneath him, kicking off her sweats and wriggling out of her shirt. Thankfully, she hadn't been wearing anything beneath her clothes. He paused to drink in the sight of her pale skin and the flush of her nipples before ripping his own shirt off as she unfastened his jeans.

It was rushed. Hurried. With no time to think or regret or second guess.

With a few more brusque motions, he was naked and they were pressed together skin-on-skin from their collarbones to their ankles. He nearly rolled to his side, giving Johnny room to spoon her from behind, to wrap her in his arms as Jordan filled her again and again. Until he realized that wasn't how this was going to go.

Not tonight. And not ever again.

Jordan hesitated, but Wren didn't allow him to disengage. She wrapped her fist around his cock and pumped it until it was fully hard. Then she guided him between her legs and lifted her hips up, working him the barest bit inside her.

Jordan groaned. His muscles flexed of their own accord. He buried himself in her pussy, trying to warm himself in her heat. Wren slung her arm around his shoulders and held him close. She screamed his name and clutched him to her heaving chest.

It was primal. Raw. Ungraceful. Everything they were on their own, without Johnny's suave influence or his finesse.

Wren met him thrust for thrust, rocking upward to

absorb his frantic fucking. She growled and bit his shoulder, as if that would be enough to stake her claim on him and hold them together when they were so close to flying apart.

Jordan tried to show her his wrecked heart with every lunge. He balled his fists in the sheets on either side of her and unleashed all of his pent-up agony, fear, and disappointment.

She took it and turned it into something beautiful, moaning as he impaled her.

Somehow, she transformed his grief into bliss, if only temporarily. Her eyes flew open and she stared deep into his as she lost control. She surrendered to the relentless pistoning of his cock and the smack of his flesh against her clit.

Wren came, wringing his dick with every contraction of her muscles.

She clawed his back as she did her best to hold him to her.

He reveled in every scratch that reminded him he was still there. Still alive.

And when she rose up and latched onto his mouth, feeding him a series of moans, he joined her. Jordan spilled deep within her, his ass clenching in time to the spasms that launched his come from his balls.

It was a release, yes. An epic one, even. But it wasn't the same.

Johnny wasn't there to appreciate their show or to take Jordan's place while he recovered enough to have another go at bringing Wren rapture. They were reduced to being ordinary.

It wasn't what they'd had before.

Jordan had lost more than his best friend that day, even if Johnny hadn't known how he'd felt.

Wren opened her eyes and the sadness in them hadn't vanished. In fact, it seemed to have amplified. "How can he be gone? Is he, really?"

Just like that, reality came crashing in. Jordan nodded, unable to let her believe even for an instant that they were going to get that part of their souls back. Johnny was dead. Only his ghost would ever join them in this bed, and in their relationship, again.

No matter how desperately Jordan wished it could be different, he was never going to have the opportunity to come clean with his partner. Or become more than the other guy's friend and co-worker.

Wren reached up and touched his cheek lightly, caressing him with the pad of her thumb as if *she* was trying to comfort *him*. How much had those piercing eyes of hers seen? Everything, her touch told him.

"You knew?" Jordan asked on a wheeze.

"That you were in love with Johnny?" She smiled faintly around a stifled yawn. The past week had obviously exhausted her. "Of course. I thought there was time...that we'd work things out."

Except there hadn't been and they wouldn't.

Jordan should hate himself for what they'd just done. He hadn't meant to give in, but clearly he had no willpower when he was near Wren. He already despised himself so much, what was one more sin on the pile?

Besides, the single orgasm he'd given her had seemed to settle her.

When he slipped from her body, they both sighed. He reached over to the night table and took the brush there. As gently as he could, he began combing her hair, untangling the mess it had become at least partly because of him. If only he could fix the rest of their relationship as easily, he would gladly do it.

There was no hope for that except to cut it off.

Wren must have felt it too, deep down. She was dozing off, clutching him to her so tightly he couldn't slink away or pack his shit or do any of the other things he should. So, instead, he lay there next to her and watched her sleep for most of the night.

Only when the first glimmer of dawn began to turn the sky from ink to the deep blue of the lake on a stormy day did he shake himself. What was he doing? Making things more difficult, that's what. He had to go before he forgot to do what was right. He had to make a clean break and let Wren go, free to find what happiness she could after this.

He gently unwound her limbs from his body. Even in sleep, she'd wrapped around him as if that could keep him by her side when they both knew love wasn't strong enough for that.

Jordan rolled from the bed and stood.

"Where are you going?" Wren mumbled groggily, and reached out. If her fingers so much as grazed his, he wouldn't be able to do what he had to. For both their sakes.

He might not have died, but he'd been irreparably damaged.

It wouldn't ever be possible for him to be so reckless and uninhibited with his heart now that he knew how bad it hurt to lose a part of it.

"To the store..." He was a coward. So much so that he couldn't tell her the truth and listen to her fight for something they'd already lost. "Go back to bed, Wren. Have sweet dreams of how things used to be."

She looked up at him, blinking sleepily in the darkness. He thought she saw a flicker of resignation in her azure eyes. Did she know this was goodbye for good?

"Just remember, I love you. Always will."

He couldn't say it back. Because it wouldn't be fair and he wasn't sure he even had a heart anymore. It had been ripped out the day Johnny had died. Instead, he lifted her hand, kissed her knuckles, grabbed his clothes off the floor, then turned and locked the door before he walked out.

He refused to look back in case he caved again and ran to her.

3

———

FIVE YEARS LATER

Wren rubbed her stomach as she leaned back from the break room table at Hot Rides motorcycle shop and belched. She hoped her friend Devra took that as the compliment it was. "Damn. If my assignments had tasted this good when I was in school, maybe I would have given a fuck about them."

Now that the fall semester had begun at their local college, Devra had restarted her coursework, double majoring in culinary arts and restaurant management. Being one of the woman's designated taste testers was another unexpected perk of the employment agreement Wren had finally caved and signed about three months ago.

Quinn, one of Devra's two husbands, had made Wren better offer after better offer until she literally could not refuse his generosity. Secretly, she hadn't wanted to either. It felt nice to have some stability and a core group of people surrounding her again. Though she tried desperately to think of her employer, co-workers, and their zillions of friends and extended family as mere acquaintances, it was all a bunch of bullshit.

Despite her bad manners and social awkwardness, they'd gradually taken her in and made her one of them, for which she would be forever grateful.

"Oh, come on. You're telling me you weren't a straight-A student?" Trevon, Devra's other husband, laughed at Wren. His golden eyes sparkled against the backdrop of his rich, dark skin. "You're too much of a perfectionist to have been anything else."

"Ah, well. Busted. But just because I did well in school didn't mean I liked it." She shrugged one shoulder. "More like it had been unacceptable to my parents for me to be any less than a model student. They still haven't forgiven me for leaving home at eighteen, turning down acceptance letters to all the colleges they'd made *generous donations* to, and paying my own way through trade school to be a lowly welder instead. Can't say I've ever lived up to their expectations, especially not by being independent, which meant they couldn't use their money as leverage to run my life anymore."

"Yikes. Sorry." Ollie, who was also newish to Hot Rides, knocked his shoulder into hers. The salvage man was cute, funny, and sweet. He hadn't tried very hard to hide his interest in her either. If she were smart, she'd be attracted to him as more than a co-worker or a garage buddy.

Clearly, she hadn't aced any relationship tests.

Despite the fact that Wren hadn't returned his flirtations, Ollie hadn't let things become weird between them. He was one of her favorite people to hang out with and ensured that she never felt like a third—or was that fourth?—wheel in Trevon, Quinn, and Devra's powerful relationship.

Okay, so if she was being totally honest, some small part of her was jealous of their insane chemistry and the fact that Devra was living Wren's fantasy life. Still, the trio never made her feel unwelcome. Besides, with Ollie around, plus the Hot Rods and their ladies coming over to talk shop or non-shop with her, she didn't seem out of place. Even more than that, with their kids to play with and the warm welcome from Tom and Ms. Brown, who were quickly becoming like surrogate parents to her, the Hot Rides felt like family even more than friends.

Yeah, Wren wasn't sure why she'd waited so long to become part of this gaggle of misfits. For the first time in her life, she really felt like she'd found her place. That had made the decision to give up her apartment in Middletown and move into the empty tiny home next to Devra, Trevon, and Quinn's on the Hot Rides property that much easier.

Especially since Ollie had agreed to Quinn's proposal that he scavenge parts exclusively for Hot Rides and their sister-shop, Hot Rods, down the road for a premium and the same shares in the garage that the rest of them got, too. Since then, he'd been parking his van in the grass near their tiny homes, camping out overnight before hitting the road again early the next morning, en route to whatever junk heap turned gold mine he wanted to explore next. They hadn't realized at first that Ollie was a card-carrying member of the van-life club. She'd always assumed he used his rig for hauling his treasures home after a successful salvage. In actuality, he had a trailer for that.

The inside of his long white van was an immaculate

tiny home, not so different from Quinn's or the one she now occupied. Unlike her parents, everyone at Hot Rides was making it clear that having what made you happy didn't have to mean having a lot of fancy shit.

The simple life was the best.

With the awning and propane barbeque Ollie had built into the exterior of the van, he had no trouble expanding his living space during the summer. Hell, he even had a pet hedgehog that was the cutest damn thing she'd ever seen. Now that they were heading into the cooler part of the year, he appreciated a spot complete with hot water showers and an electricity hookup to hunker down in.

And they all enjoyed having him around more.

No doubt about it. Ollie was exactly the kind of guy Wren should be looking for *if* she was ever going to admit she might be ready to move on from the glorious disaster her love life had been for five no-fucking years. Unfortunately, no matter how hard she tried to feel something for him below the belt, it just wasn't happening.

Maybe she wasn't as healed as she'd hoped.

Ollie mistook her extended silence for introspection about her parents instead of him and what might have been if she wasn't so damn damaged. "Your folks obviously made you feel like your dreams weren't valid— or that you weren't as kickass as we know you are—if you didn't do what they would have chosen for you, but at least they cared enough to try to help you in their own way. Maybe?"

He tried to put a positive spin on things, which was something she really appreciated about him. Nothing ever got him down, and he was willing to raise the people around him up when they could use a boost.

"I guess." Wren cleared her throat. Someday she should probably attempt to smooth things over with them. She'd tried once, after things had imploded with Jordan and Johnny, making her realize that if she didn't tell people important stuff when she had the chance, she might live to regret that decision.

It hadn't gone well. The rumor mill had carried hints of her bad behavior back to her parents, disgracing them when she was romantically linked with two different men at the same time. She hadn't had the guts to tell them that they had it all wrong. That she wasn't frivolous or some kind of slut. She should have made them understand that she'd loved both men, even if she'd ended up with neither in the end.

Wren was different now. Stronger, she hoped.

That didn't stop her from leaping up when the roar of two engines echoed up the long, winding driveway to Hot Rides. Small doses of this friend shit were enough for her right now. She was still getting used to opening herself up again, even if these men and women would never judge her for the things she revealed to them.

Considering their propensity for acceptance and the ménage Quinn, Trevon, and Devra had going, she might even get up the nerve to unburden herself about her past relationship...eventually.

For now, she was glad for the perfect excuse to slip away from their conversation.

It was dangerous, working here. Coming to care for the Hot Rides.

But she hadn't been able to stop herself. She'd fallen in love with being part of their not-so-little family. Wren hoped they couldn't tell how desperately she needed them.

"You guys keep eating. I've got this." She had nothing else to do since the shop was still building their clientele and had only recently added her services to their menu of offerings.

Despite both Gavyn, the shop's owner, and Quinn, the head mechanic and shop manager, telling her to call it quits early, she hadn't gone home. Mostly because it didn't sit right with her to take advantage considering the beyond-generous salary they paid her. Partly because she lived right out back so she was sort of home already. And a little bit because she was pathetic enough to crave her co-workers' companionship given that she had essentially been a hermit these past five years.

"You sure?" Quinn asked around a mouthful of falafel.

She laughed and flashed him a thumbs-up, happy to help.

If Wren had only known what was coming, she might have changed her mind. In hindsight, the gut punch caused by meeting the man about to stroll through Hot Rides' door would make the uncomfortable discussion they'd been having seem like Welding 101 versus TIG-welding aluminum.

Fortunately, she was a master of her craft and had a lot of experience suppressing her emotions.

4

Kason hooted as he took the sweeping curves through the woods leading to Hot Rides faster than he ought. Not because of the rush of adrenaline, though he'd be lying if he didn't welcome that taste of the forbidden. He did it because he knew his bodyguard—Van Hernandez—would be scowling fiercely in his fancy black pickup truck with heavily tinted windows, which trailed the purple-and-orange customized Ducati Diavel power cruiser Kason was hoping to have enhanced and fine-tuned while he was in town.

Fortunately, Van had never yet kicked his ass, though he'd threatened to when Kason's thrill-seeking tendencies had gotten out of hand with excessive drinking, drugs, and gambling in the past year or two. His friend's concern had convinced Kason to take some time off, ground himself, and get help.

For some of his problems, anyway.

So far no one—not even Van or his counselor—had

figured out the real reason he'd done all that dumb shit. And Kason was planning on keeping it that way.

Van would have to deal with Kason's minor rebellion.

Hell, he'd even worn a helmet. How much more could the man ask of him even if it was his job to keep Kason safe?

Too soon, the winding country road led him to a painted sign. It was black with flames in the background and the silhouette of a motorcycle up front. *Hot Rides* was lettered in silver inside the shape of the bike.

Kason deliberately signaled before making the right into the long driveway that led to the specialty shop, which was gaining quite a reputation for the quality of their work. Hopefully his adherence to the road rules would be enough to appease Van.

Even better yet would be if Hot Rides lived up to the things people were saying about it.

Kason had amassed a pretty significant collection of motorcycles. He had tons of ideas for upgrading his current fleet and things he'd like to buy or build to expand it even more...*if* he could find the right partners to do the work.

One downside to being famous was that everyone thought you should have a rich-guy tax applied to work you hired out. Either that or you should be excited to take freebies for publicity instead of paying for what you'd really like best and enjoying it in private instead of as some glorified circus animal. He shook his head at his admittedly first-world problems.

Still, if the mechanics at Hot Rides were both high-quality and fair, he'd be back. Over and over. They wouldn't be able to get rid of him.

When the garage came into sight, Kason revved the

engine and zoomed ahead. He parked and climbed off the bike before Van could catch up, eliminating his opportunity to deliver a lecture. Van was too damn careful to break the speed limit or do anything even a little naughty.

That's probably why he kept striking out with Kason's drummer, Kyra.

Which was none of Kason's damn business. He was their boss, not their nosey neighbor. So he pretended not to notice whatever the hell was—or wasn't—going on between the two, whom he considered friends in addition to employees.

Kason had enough to worry about keeping his own life in order. One way he did that was by immersing himself in non-damaging hobbies, as his therapist referred to them.

Translation: buying more motorcycles and fancying up the ones he already had was A-OK.

He strode to the office portion of Hot Rides and went inside, amused by the mini-rev noise that replaced a standard tinkling bell to announce his visit. At about the same time, a woman emerged from the garage, which he glimpsed through a large plate glass window.

The space was immaculate. Workstations were laid out neatly and the equipment was all top-brand stuff. Photographs of past builds wallpapered the office and he found himself drooling over nearly every one. Though not as much as his mouth watered for the Hot Rides receptionist.

The tall, willowy blonde behind the counter tempted him to throw away his new rule. The one about meaningless sex going on the no-no list. Maybe that had been a stupid restraint to place on himself, but the truth was he hadn't been enjoying his hookups any more than he had the endless shots and thousands of dollars he'd wagered—and lost—on dumb shit.

When he'd overindulged, he'd gone numb to the thrill of things that used to excite him.

Even music had become a chore. The thing he'd dedicated his whole life to being his best at. The career he'd fought for since he'd run away from home at sixteen. He'd never forget forging that shitty ID so that he could play in bars and earn enough for a hot meal or two, even if it wasn't enough for a place to stay, before moving on to the next town. Those fast-food dinners had tasted better than some of the exclusive chef specials he'd eaten since.

It was all a matter of perspective, and with success, he'd completely skewed his own.

He'd gotten spoiled.

Kason wasn't about to throw away all that hard work and a decade of dreams just because he couldn't have *everything* he wanted. There was still plenty of stuff he could enjoy.

He leaned in and very deliberately took off his sunglasses, prepared for his new obsession to shriek and fawn over him.

Except she didn't.

Instead, she arched one perfect brow and asked, "How can I help you?"

By coming for a ride with me. On my bike, and in my bed.

Kason might have been asshole enough to say it if she'd been one of those people who was impressed by his fame. A woman he knew would get off on telling her friends she'd fucked him as much as she did on how well he pleasured her.

"I brought a modified mid-nineties Ducati Diavel with

me today. I wanted to see about customizing it further. Increasing the horsepower, dropping the handlebars, maybe changing out the rims and tires. Basically, whatever the mechanics think would enhance its performance or its style." If he was doomed to strike out with the gorgeous shop assistant, he at least tried to focus on his excitement over the bike.

That's what his therapist had recommended, anyway. That he concentrate on the things that sparked joy in him instead of his disappointments or his anxiety about losing the fame and fortune he'd amassed. Little did she know that one of the things he craved most was at the root of his fears.

Don't think about that.

Instead he studied the fine bones in the woman's long fingers as she took notes to show her boss. They matched the rest of her, tall and thin. She didn't look like the women he usually found himself attracted to—or sleeping with, rather, since he hadn't had to pursue a woman in forever. For one, she wasn't wearing makeup. Her pale hair was naturally glossy and framed her gorgeous face where it hung straight and unstyled. The T-shirt and ripped jeans she wore weren't curve-hugging women's cuts. Even the boxy clothes couldn't hide her feminine appeal, however. She was raw and honest, daring him to take her as she was. And he wanted to, desperately. He usually picked from the fans who threw themselves at him simply because of the image he portrayed when he was onstage or because they thought they knew him after watching interviews he'd done.

This woman was something completely different. Kason found himself craving a new flavor. Wasn't that part of what his whole crisis had been about? Maybe he could find less risky ways to satisfy his desires.

Before he could think of something clever to say, to make the woman look up with her bright blue eyes and maybe laugh or talk to him about something more personal than motorcycles, she finished writing and asked, "Could you leave the bike here for a few hours so Quinn—our head mechanic—can do a thorough evaluation of what's already been done to your ride, some research about what's possible, and brainstorm new ideas no one's tried yet? He'll put together his recommendations along with some sketches, if that's okay."

"Sure, that's fine." Kason tried not to sound too sleazy when he said, "I'll be in town until the end of the week. After that we'll have to work things out over email until it's ready for pickup."

"Don't you want to wait for an estimate before deciding to go ahead with the work? I'll be honest, our rates are about ten percent higher than industry average due to the specialized experience of our team. Plus we mandate a certain level of quality in terms of the brands of components we install, in order to ensure you get the best we can deliver. You won't find bargain basement price here, but you will get more than your money's worth, I can promise you that." The woman impressed him with her knowledge and her directness. It wasn't often someone was that honest with him.

It was exactly what he'd been hoping for.

"Don't worry, I can afford it," he promised, unsure if he was irritated that she didn't know it or grateful that for the first time in a long time, he was being treated like a normal human being. He'd nearly forgotten what that felt like. "And I've heard your guys know what they're doing. So I want to see for myself. Let's consider this a test of their skills. If they pass, I have other bikes I have big plans for."

Now why the hell would she scowl at that? It was supposed to be a compliment and a promise.

The faux engine revved again as Van joined them in the shop. His friend might blow his cover if he kept standing there, in the corner, with his arms crossed and his dark glasses still in place. He looked every bit like a bodyguard instead of some random guy's ride home.

That didn't stop the receptionist from blasting him. "Oh, you'll see. Hot Rides is the best at what *we* do, even if not all of us who work on the bikes have dicks."

Oh shit.

From behind him, Van was attempting to disguise his laughter with a fit of coughing every bit as fake as the mini-engine door chime. That was okay, Kason deserved to be embarrassed.

He'd earned this extra-fine woman's annoyance.

He hoped there was some way he could make it up to her. Because more than her striking looks, he liked her fire and her take-no-shit attitude. Imagining her working on his motorcycle guaranteed it would become the new favorite in his collection.

Riding usually made him hard. The next time he climbed on the Ducati would be no exception.

5

———

"I'm sorry. I'm an idiot," Kason Cox said with a disarming smile as he raised his hands, palms out so Wren could see his calluses, earned by playing guitar. "I shouldn't have assumed... I apologize."

"Thank you." Wren believed he was sincere, so she let him off easy. After all, Johnny would have wanted her to give his idol a second chance before ripping his man-parts off and stuffing them down his throat.

It had been a while since she'd seen a picture of the country star, but Wren had recognized him immediately, even before he'd come inside the shop's office.

It was almost like seeing a damn ghost.

Her heartbeat pounded double time and her hands trembled, making her handwriting shaky as she took notes for Quinn and the rest of the team. Not because Kason was famous, but because his voice was inextricably entwined with so many of her sensual memories that she could never separate the two.

Parts of her body that had been dormant for years stretched and took notice every time Kason Cox opened his wickedly fine mouth. She pasted on her most blasé expression and said, "What's the best way to get in touch?"

Yet somehow her question seemed suggestive, even to her.

When she glanced up, really allowing herself to take him in for the first time, she realized that Kason was even more handsome in person than on billboards and TV shows.

Damn, no photoshopping necessary for him.

He was tall, with chestnut-colored hair. Colorful tattoos hugged his biceps, enhancing each of the cut lines on his sculpted arms. And when he took off his sunglasses and held her gaze, his emerald stare threatened to set her panties on fire. Or would have if she'd been wearing any.

All of the sparkles she'd thought were gone forever when other guys—even ones she liked and respected, like Ollie—couldn't bring them back for her floated through her veins as if she'd mainlined happy glitter.

What. The. Fuck.

It must be because he reminded her so much of Johnny. Especially those captivating eyes... Damn!

That had to be it.

As he leaned in closer, she realized he smelled as good as he looked. Like leather and motorcycle oil and the outdoors. "The shop can contact me via email."

He rattled off an address and she jotted it on the top of the sheet where she'd taken her notes.

Then he said, "But you can call or text me if you like. My number is—"

Wren couldn't believe he'd slipped that offer in there. She was so stunned, she didn't even catch his phone number. And she sure as hell wasn't going to ask him to repeat it. There was no way she was about to dial him up so they could chat about...what exactly? Where to meet up to fuck? Because surely he couldn't be interested in more than that.

Maybe it would make things easier. To be with someone just for the sake of sex and verifying her lady parts still worked like they should. It would be a relief to discover she could find some sort of release with a partner, even if it was temporary and only a physical reaction compared to the profound connection she'd had with her two ex-lovers.

Wren hesitated too long, though.

With a sad smile toward her still pen that promised he didn't hold it against her, Kason asked, "Is that all you need from me then?"

He was probably suggesting she take down his name and a credit card number or some other professional junk like that. Unfortunately, she didn't exactly know what they required. She wasn't really an office worker. Besides, no one could be expected to think straight with Kason Cox standing less than two feet in front of them.

Quinn and Gavyn would forgive her if she messed up a couple of details.

Because there were a hell of a lot of other things she could have used from Kason, except she wasn't going to cross that line. Not with someone she met at work. And especially not with someone who made her body react so strongly for the first time in forever.

It was too dangerous, no matter how much she wished she could.

Wren gripped the pen she was holding so hard it broke with a very audible crack.

Kason grinned, as if daring her to deny he was having some sort of effect. He couldn't understand the reason behind her attraction and wouldn't be pleased if he knew she was thinking of someone else. That had to be why he had this significant an impact on her.

Thinking of Johnny gave her an idea. Before she could talk herself out of it, she said, "Actually. If you don't mind..."

"I don't," he rushed to reassure her with a wink.

"Then, yes, there's one other thing." She tried to remember her manners, but they were rusty. Hopefully Gavyn or Quinn wouldn't mind her momentary lapse in professionalism. "Would you autograph something for me quick before you go?"

"So you *do* know who I am?" he asked, his smile curving up on one edge. She wished it made him seem conceited or smarmy instead of so damn sexy.

There was no denying it anyway.

"You were my boyfriend's favorite singer." Wren sounded like she'd chewed on that broken beer bottle from the night she'd danced with Johnny to Kason's song when she admitted it.

"Let me guess, because of the gap between my last album and now, he found someone else to sing along with on the radio?" Kason's smile morphed into a grimace. Then he joked, as if his ego could withstand the blow, "It's not Taylor Swift, is it?"

"Actually, no. He's dead." *Way to be weird and abrasive, Wren.*

It was just that anything more than that was still too hard to even say out loud.

Devra gasped from somewhere in the back of the room, making Wren aware that they had an audience. Where Devra was, her two guys wouldn't be far behind. Ollie was probably there too, witnessing this shitshow.

Maybe even Gavyn had poked his head out from the stock room to see who had come in.

Great, that was going to force another conversation she wasn't sure she was quite ready to have. Definitely not while in the presence of Johnny's idol. So it would be wise if she scared him off. The sooner, the better.

"Ah, shit. Sorry. Again." Kason winced, sliding his sunglasses lower so that she could see the earnestness in his gaze. "I wasn't trying to be an asshole. It comes naturally. As you've seen, twice now."

At least he owned it. Besides, there was no way he could have known he was wandering into a minefield when he'd attempted to flirt with her.

Ollie—yep, there he was—cleared his throat and stepped closer. It had been a hell of a long time since Wren had a man to protect her. Even then she hadn't needed one. Still, it felt kind of nice to have his support anyway.

Wren wouldn't have thought it possible, but she laughed a little despite the conflicting emotions threatening to rip her apart. Five years was long enough to be too sad to appreciate all the things she did have even if it meant smiling through her pain. "You couldn't have known. It's been years. Anyway...If it's not too weird, would you mind signing something to him?"

"I'd be honored." Kason smiled then, a genuine thing that warmed his whole face and did curious things to her inside. This time in the vicinity of her heart. Huh. "I have an idea."

He looked over his shoulder at the man who was obviously his bodyguard. The dude hadn't moved an inch since he'd come inside, but he'd positioned himself between the door and his client, ready to swing into action if necessary. "Hey, Van, hand me some of those backstage passes the promoter gave us earlier, would you?"

The serious guy, who still hadn't said a single word, reached into an inside pocket of his leather jacket and withdrew a rectangular clump of cardstock, rubber-banded together.

Kason must have noticed her eying the man. "That's Van. He makes sure none of the hillbillies get too rowdy and shoot me when I sing off-key or some shit."

Wren jerked. She imagined his face splattered with crimson like she'd seen Johnny's so often in her nightmares, blood bubbling out of his neck. She clutched the counter to keep herself upright.

"Bad joke. Sorry." Kason accepted a wad of tickets from Van and put them on the counter. He signed one, then scooted the entire pile toward her. "Despite the fact that I seem to say all the wrong things around you, it would be great to see you there. I'll try to stick to my lyrics, which I actually put a lot of thought into, instead of running my fool mouth. If you don't already have plans, and it's not too...difficult..." Of course Kason had to be sensitive to write and sing those romantic songs. Damn him. "I'd really like it if you'd come to my show in Middletown on Friday night."

"She'd love to," Devra said over Wren's shoulder with a friendly smile that belied the solid jab she delivered to Wren's spine out of Kason's view.

"Bring your friends backstage with you." Kason looked to Devra, Ollie, and the rest of the small crowd that had gathered. "There will be an after party, too. It'll be fun. I promise."

"I'll think about it." Wren swallowed down her bile and terror long enough to let Kason's easy smile settle her.

She was off balance. Her emotions running wild. And she didn't care for that one fucking bit.

Not after she'd spent so long getting them under control.

Kason Cox had waltzed into Hot Rides and erased five years of mourning in an instant. He'd turned her on, scared her, reminded her of good times, insulted her, and made her want to hug him in the span of a few minutes. How the hell could that be possible?

He was trouble, and she'd be wise to rip up every one of those tickets the moment he was out of sight. All of them except for Johnny's, of course.

They sat there on the counter, tempting her.

"Fair enough." He tipped his head, making her think of old westerns. Though he wasn't wearing a fancy hat, he had the makings of a cowboy—a honed body, denim and leather, classic maleness, chivalry, and sex appeal for days. "Either way, I'll see you when I pick up my bike. I appreciate you giving me a tight turnaround on the proposal since we're only in town until the end of the week, and I've heard you guys know what you're doing."

"Of course." Wren wasn't sure if it was a good or bad thing that he'd be coming back. She'd make sure to note when his appointment was so she could take a sick day if needed.

It wasn't like her to hide.

Then again, she hadn't met a man who did what he did since that afternoon when she'd fallen in love at first sight with a man humming one of Kason Cox's songs.

Yep. She was fucked.

"It was nice to meet you...." He held out his hand. His eyes danced with mischief as he dared her to touch him, even that little bit.

Not one to back down from a challenge, Wren took it and shook, immediately regretting her impulsive decision. Those sparkles he'd ignited turned to full-on fireworks. They jolted her so badly, the only thing she could do was blurt her name. "Wren. Wren Asbery."

"Pretty. Not as pretty as you, though." He had to be smooth, too, didn't he?

"Thanks. I'd better get back to work." Of course everyone in the room knew that was a whopper since she'd told them she was finished for the day. Theoretically, though, she could scrub the equipment or spend some more time arranging her bay in the garage. Anything but stand there and be caught up in the laser beam of Kason Cox's all-too-knowing stare.

"Right." He stepped away, toward Van—whose smirk did a lot to erase his badass vibe—before Kason spun around. He took two long strides, returning to the counter, selected a pen from the metal can there, and jotted something on one of the backstage passes. "In case you change your mind or feel like...whatever."

She blinked at him.

Did *whatever* mean a quickie in some Middletown hotel? Probably, if she was up for it. Which she definitely was not. Dinner? Long talks about nothing late at night? Nah. A man like Kason Cox wasn't the conversational sort.

He was a man of action.

Kason did that nod thing again, then he was striding out the door.

Van muttered, "You're rusty, Cox."

Then he was cracking up as his boss, and apparently his friend, punched him in the shoulder. Not that the tap would do any harm to the bodyguard. Kason's poor knuckles were in greater danger.

Wren stayed planted there, staring as the guys piled into a sleek black truck with dark tinted windows then drove away. She could still smell Kason and hear the rich tone of his voice in her mind.

Devra charged her, squealing, and threw her arms around Wren. "Damn, girl! He's fine. You're going to that concert and you're taking me with you, right?"

"I'm not sure it's a good idea for the two of you to go alone," Ollie grumbled.

"Volunteering to chaperone, buddy?" Trevon asked with a grin as he threw his arm around their garagemate to ease the sting of the truth. "I don't think you'd like that any better."

Devra reached for the tickets and counted them out. There were enough for all of the Hot Rides, including Gavyn and his wife Amber, plus some of the Hot Rods, to have a night out if they wanted.

Did Wren want to?

Hell yes.

Would she?

Hell no.

"You should go, Devra. Take whoever you want." She carefully tucked Johnny's backstage pass into her pocket, then pressed the rest of the tickets into her friend's hands. "They're yours."

Ollie winced. "Hey, sorry. I shouldn't have said that. You obviously liked the guy... Go."

"Thanks." Wren tried to smile through the confusion of emotions slamming into her now that the sparkles were fading and only the painful things were left behind. "You didn't change my mind, though. I just...I can't."

That last bit came out as a whisper. Wren knew she only had a few moments to escape before making a spectacle of herself in front of her new friends. So she said, "Excuse me."

Then she dashed through the break room to the bathroom, slammed the door, used her boot to shut the toilet lid, then slumped onto it, burying her face in her hands. She began to shake all over and tears leaked through her fingers.

It turned out that despite what she'd thought, she hadn't cried them all out yet.

Damn it.

6

A few minutes later, a soft knock came on the steel door of the bathroom, startling Wren. She furiously swiped the moisture from her cheeks before patting her face dry with her sleeves. Bawling in the bathroom wasn't going to help her reputation as a badass welding bitch.

Fortunately, when Wren unlocked the door it was Devra who peeked in sheepishly. "Do you want me to go away and forget I saw any of that?"

Because she asked, Wren knew it wasn't necessary. It was new and fresh to have someone, especially a female friend, she could open up to about some of these things in her past that had been weighing her down for far too long. "No. Would you sit and talk with me for a minute?"

"Of course. But come on out of the bathroom, okay? I don't know you *that* well...yet. And let's be honest. The guys aren't always the neatest." Devra wrinkled her nose, succeeding in making Wren laugh, which was a miracle in itself.

Wren blew her nose on a scratchy brown paper towel

before emerging into the break room. Devra rushed to her side. Before Wren realized what she was about to do, she'd wrapped her arms around Wren and squeezed. "I'm sorry you're hurting."

Was she, though? Not really. Not in the sharp and unbearable way she had in the past when something reminded her of Johnny or Jordan and the time they hadn't gotten to spend with each other. It was more of a dull ache that throbbed deep in her chest now, somewhere in the area her heart had once occupied.

She ran her fingers over the autographed backstage pass and smiled, remembering Johnny dancing in only his underwear, softly singing along out of key as he cooked breakfast for the three of them after one of their wild nights together.

"I didn't mean to eavesdrop..."

Wren waved Devra off. The woman had endured enough of her own issues recently. Wren had been front and center when her shit hit the fan, so it only seemed fair that Devra knew about Wren's past, too. Especially since Jordan had been involved in Quinn, Trevon, and Devra's mess and had actually done a decent thing to help them out.

Here at Hot Rides—and Hot Rods, too—there would be no judgment. None of them had led easy lives. All of them had overcome loss, and failures, and terrible odds to be there.

"It's fine. It's old news." Wren pulled out one of the metal folding chairs and plopped onto it. "What do you want to know?"

"What you told that man, the singer, is it true?" Devra perched on the chair opposite Wren, leaning in close. "You lost someone you were seeing?"

Wren nodded.

"I'm so sorry. I know how hard it is when someone you love passes away." Devra reached out and took Wren's hand, almost certainly thinking of her own father, who had been murdered. Wren squeezed Devra's hand in return. "I know this is dumb, but for some reason, I thought Agent Mikalski..."

"Jordan." Wren tried not to snarl his name. That traitor. How could he ever have loved her if he'd simply walked away? She never could have chosen to leave him, not even after Johnny...

"Yeah. Well, I sort of thought *he* was the man who'd broken your heart and the reason you keep yourself so... isolated." Devra winced when she said it, but it was the truth.

"He did. He is. Partly." Wren looked away then. She might be making some progress, but it was still hard. Nearly impossible to express how deeply she had been scarred by loving and losing.

"You were in a polyamorous relationship, too. Weren't you?" Devra asked. "Quinn told me that you once told Jordan it was okay to be frank in front of the Hot Rods gang because they were like you two. That's what you meant, isn't it?"

Wren nodded. "I was lucky enough to find a pair of guys I thought were perfect for me. Just like you actually have."

"So what happened?" Devra bit her lower lip. "You know that's my worst fear. Ever since they tried to deport me. When I thought I'd never see Trevon and Quinn again... It was..."

Devra might be the only person who truly could understand Wren and her suffering. So she said, "Johnny and Jordan were partners at ICE. Both agents. One time, Johnny didn't make it home, and Jordan..."

She shrugged.

Truth was, she didn't know what the fuck his problem had been because he hadn't told her. Was it Johnny's death he couldn't handle? Or was it that he'd only been with her to get closer to Johnny? He'd cut her to the bone with his betrayal and it still had the power to level her. "After Johnny died, he came home for one parting fuck. But that was it. He didn't even have the balls to admit he was leaving me. Said he was going to the store. I guess he had a really big list of shit to buy since it's been five years and he hasn't come home yet."

"What? Are you kidding me?" Devra stood up then, slapping her palms on the table. "That asshole! That's not the kind of man I thought he was at all. Should I knee him in the nuts for you next time I see him?"

Behind Devra, her guys and Ollie were peering into the break room nervously.

"Uh, at the risk of getting our balls smashed too, can we come in?" Ollie asked.

Wren rolled her eyes and waved them in. There was no use hiding anything around here. She understood that when you had the kind of relationship Trevon, Quinn, and Devra shared—the kind she thought she'd had once—there could be no secrets. They might as well hear about her situation direct from her.

"Everything okay in here?" Quinn asked.

Wren nodded yes as Devra shook her head no.

Trevon propped himself up, half-sitting with one booted foot planted on the floor and the back of his opposite thigh resting on the table. Quinn came around the other side and took Devra's hand. "What's wrong?"

"It turns out Agent Mikalski isn't the saint I thought." Devra seemed legitimately angry on Wren's behalf. It hadn't been her intention to turn these people against Jordan. He'd only done good things for them.

"Who is, really?" Wren asked, her shoulders slumping further. "It just happens that the one time Jordan decided not to live up to his standards of perfection, I was the one who paid the price."

"You're defending him?" Devra stared at her with wide eyes.

Wren supposed that's what true love was. Even now, she couldn't hate him. Be angry with him? Absolutely. Hate? Never.

"I'm not saying this because of some sort of bro code. If Devra says he deserves a swift kick or three I'm sure he does." Trevon winced. "But Jordan is overall a good man. He risked a lot to help us. The only reason he would do something that hurt you both is if he thought it was for the greater good. I see that it wasn't, but sometimes men are dumb when we're in love. I made some pretty bad assumptions about what I thought Devra needed out of our marriage before Quinn helped me pull my head out of my ass."

"That's a very good point." Devra turned to Trevon and kissed him sweetly, proving that she didn't hold any grudges.

Quinn nodded. "I hate to pile on, but I think they're right. I've seen the way Jordan looks at you. And he's repeatedly told me to take care of you like he wishes he could. He loves you. I can see he did a piss poor job of showing you that and handling the shit in your past. I'm sorry. I bet he freaked the fuck out when your..."

"Boyfriend," Wren supplied. She might as well be

totally transparent. It felt good to finally have someone to talk to about this. People who could understand the complex dynamics of an even more complex relationship. It made her feel better that they didn't automatically bash Jordan. Like just maybe she hadn't been wrong to give him her heart and soul after all. "They were both mine."

"But not each other's?" Trevon asked with a raised brow.

She shook her head. "At least not when Johnny died. Maybe in time things could have been different...we'll never know."

Ollie sighed from where he leaned against the wall, one ankle crossed over the other. "Jordan flat out told me he's been in love with you forever, but that he'd ruined his shot with you. He's a hard man. The kind who might not be able to forgive himself if he thought he hurt someone he cared about."

"He *did* hurt me. He took my heart—which was broken from losing Johnny—ripped it out of my chest, and stomped on in until it exploded." She couldn't help but cry then, even if she told herself they were angry tears. "He abandoned me when I needed him most. I'm glad he stays the fuck away from me because I despise him."

Ollie cursed then and banged his hand on the wall. "Never mind. I'm going to beat the shit out of him next time I see him."

Trevon shook his head ruefully. He took the edge out of the air when he stood and rounded the table. He saw through Wren's rage to the pain beneath it. "Nah, you don't hate his guts. You wouldn't still be crying over him if you did. I think it says a lot about you that you still care about him even though he screwed up so spectacularly."

He held his arms out, open. Wren didn't think twice

before leaning into him and resting her cheek on his abs. Even he, a man she'd only known a few months and certainly had never slept with, comforted her when the one who had supposedly been her soulmate had not.

Some things were unforgiveable. That didn't mean she could change her own feelings, which had been and always would be genuine. "I wish I could hate him."

"It's hard for me to imagine the person you're describing is the same man who fought so hard to help Trevon, Quinn, and I stay together. He risked everything for us." Devra, always the optimist, acted like this was a fairytale with the possibility of a magical ending instead of real life. "Maybe he's matured. There's still hope. If you love him and he loves you…"

"Not gonna happen," Wren insisted as she pushed away from Trevon and sat up straight again. "Sometimes, love isn't enough."

That bitter truth soured her stomach.

Wren stood, fingering the backstage ticket in her pocket again. At least that made her feel better. Kason had made her smile again.

"In that case, I definitely think we should hit up that concert." Devra winked at Wren. "It's time to find someone who makes you happy, don't you think? Even if that person is yourself."

Now that Wren could agree with. It was time to stop letting the past drag her down.

"Yeah, okay. I'll go if you will. Call Kaelyn, Sabra, Sally, and Nola too." Wren shrugged at the guys. "Sorry, but I'm feeling like a ladies' night is in order."

"Don't worry about us." Quinn grinned. "We've got Kason's sweet ride to play with. We're going to do such an awesome job on it that he brings all the rest of his collection here too. I hope you end up liking the guy, because I have a feeling he's going to be spending a lot of time around the shop."

Great, no pressure.

Wren had barely found a place she felt at home and another man had the power to wreck it for her. Fuck that. She thought of his gorgeous eyes, fast smile, and his willingness—unlike Jordan—to admit when he was wrong.

Maybe she should text him once, just to let him know they were coming after all.

Maybe, if she could work up the nerve.

But first, she had something more important to do.

7

Wren hated this place. She almost never came here. Hadn't even when Johnny had first been killed. It wasn't that the cemetery creeped her out or made her even more miserable than she already was. It just seemed so cold. So quiet. So devoid of life. Everything Johnny had never been.

Usually when she wanted to feel close to him, she went for a walk at the lake. Today, she would make an exception.

She stuffed her hand in the pocket of her ripped jeans and fingered the thick paper there as she climbed up the grassy hill to Johnny's grave. It was in a pretty spot, tucked beneath a massive, gnarled oak tree that was raining crimson leaves at the moment.

Wren spent a few minutes tidying things up, dusting off the area around his headstone and tracing his name with her index finger. Eventually, she gave up as more leaves skittered around, settling over his plot like pools of blood, reminding her that she could never change what had happened. So she dropped from a squat to her ass on the ground, wrapped her leather jacket tighter around her and pulled out her phone.

She couldn't say what made her do it, but she flipped open her music app and poked the label for Kason Cox. His timeless voice rang out, chasing the chill out of the air and her bones. Maybe a few other places too.

As she sat with her back leaning up against Johnny's tombstone, her legs out straight and crossed at the ankles, the memory of Kason's intense green eyes and his easy laughter did something to her that was as potent as the effect his voice had on her. Was it because those attributes reminded her of Johnny's similar features or because she might finally be coming alive again inside?

Wren listened to the music and closed her eyes. She imagined dancing with Johnny in the moonlight while Jordan watched, which inevitably led to having sex with both of them under the stars. She knew why Jordan had been willing to share her, but what about Johnny?

He'd once said, "I love that I get to see you like this. When you come for him, you're living with abandon. Those are the times I think I know you best. This is who you were meant to be and I'd hate for you be anything less."

Wren was letting Johnny down.

These past years she'd been imposing extreme restraint on herself, her emotions, and her life. It was everything he'd tried to encourage her *not* to do. Very similar to the mold her parents had tried to force her to fit into. She'd been screwing up.

Now that her wounds were scarred over, because she couldn't imagine they'd ever heal entirely, it might be time to try again. To honor Johnny by being the woman he'd recognized within her.

Wren withdrew the autographed backstage pass from her pocket. She kissed the foiled paper, then tucked it against Johnny's stone, using a rock to hold it in place close to him or at least as close as she could get these days.

Of course that brought to mind new visions. Ones where Johnny morphed into Kason. It felt weird, but also sort of natural. She imagined what it might be like to kiss him, feeling the prickle of his scruff against her cheek while they swayed together.

It wasn't long before another vision joined the first. What if Jordan was there? What if he sandwiched her between them and finally gave her what he'd been withholding? Or better yet, what if he was the one kissing Kason?

Wren gasped as she imagined how hungry he would be.

Because if she felt like a starving woman, how much worse would it be to have never tasted what you craved so desperately?

She shuddered, hating that even now she gave a fuck about Jordan and his feelings.

This was pointless. Dwelling on the past forced her to relive her agony, over and over. It didn't bring Johnny back; it only made her miserable.

Wren bolted to her feet before knuckling away a tear. She patted the top of the marble marker, letting her fingers drag all the way to the edge before they fell away, leaving her empty handed once more. "Goodbye, Johnny. I promise I'm going to dance enough for us both."

8

—————

A FEW DAYS LATER

"Agent Mikalski, get the hell out of here already. Don't you know you're on vacation?" The director propped his hands on his hips.

Both of them knew that *vacation* was a fancy word for mandated leave. The higher ups hadn't been pleased with Jordan lately, especially given the outcome of Devra Russell's case, though they couldn't prove it had been him who'd destroyed key evidence against her. He figured it didn't really count as evidence when it had been maliciously trumped up by a bigoted asshole. Others clearly wouldn't have seen it the same way.

At the end of the day, he'd done what was right even if it had meant breaking a few rules. Okay, a lot of them. If he wasn't protecting innocent people, then what the fuck was he doing in this job? What had he risked his life and sacrificed so much for, if not that?

Things were getting muddy. He was confused.

The director was right; he needed time away.

Jordan saved the file he'd been working on, then shut his laptop. Spending several weeks out at the cabin on the lake,

59

fishing and reflecting on his priorities, might be exactly what he needed. Maybe he'd return refreshed and reinvigorated. Or maybe he wouldn't come back at all. He had some serious decisions to make about where his life was headed.

"I do, sir." He shrugged into his jacket, then brushed past his supervisor and headed for the door. For light. For fresh air and freedom. "See you next month."

Jordan wished he had a motorcycle like Quinn Daily and his husband, Trevon. Or Gavyn or Alanso from Hot Rods. Maybe he'd have to stop by Hot Rides and ask for some advice on finding a bike of his own. It would make the ride out to the lake even more enjoyable.

He wondered what Johnny would have thought of that, and chuckled. The guy wouldn't have believed Jordan capable of doing something so reckless. But times were changing and Jordan needed to learn to live more like his friend had, loving every minute in case it was his last.

Thinking of Johnny, he stocked up on his best friend's favorite beer. He piled it, along with the rest of the supplies he needed for one last visit to the cabin before it got too cold to stay there this year, into his car. Out of habit, he stopped at the cemetery on his way out of town, snagging a can out of the plastic six-pack holder before he climbed out of the driver's seat.

He popped the top and crouched down, tipping his hand to pour the beer into the dirt when something caught his eye. A black rectangle embossed with silver was wedged under a stone right on the spot he'd been about to douse in shitty beer.

"Shit!" He sloshed a few drops over his knuckles before he could stop the stream. After licking his hand, he shook it off, set the beer on the flat top of the marble marker, then nudged the rock aside.

The paper beneath blew away.

"Shit! Shit!" Jordan lunged for it, crumpling it in his fist as he caught the damn thing before it could escape for good. When he took a closer look, it seemed like a phantom fist punched him right in the gut.

It was a ticket. No, better than that. It was a backstage pass.

How the hell had it gotten there? And why?

Silver marker pen scribbled on top of the black rectangle was messy enough to be an actual signature but not so convoluted that he couldn't clearly read it. *Kason Cox.*

"Son of a bitch!" He brushed his finger over the script. Johnny would have absolutely lost his shit over the memorabilia, never mind an opportunity to see Kason Cox perform live. If he'd met him backstage, he probably would have crapped his pants. He'd adored that guy's music and...more. The sentiment behind his emotional songs had resonated with Johnny.

Jordan blinked a few times as he thought of Johnny riding down back roads in the truck they'd shared, shout-singing every word of Kason's first album into the wind whipping through the open windows. It was only when the memory faded and Jordan scrutinized the ticket some more that he realized the concert was that night. Right there in Middletown.

In fact, it started in less than an hour. Barely enough time for him to make it given rush-hour traffic and the horde of people that would no doubt be swarming the local college football stadium. If that wasn't some kind of sign from Johnny that he needed to get out more, he didn't know what was.

Jordan decided to start his vacation off right before heading out to the lake.

"I'll bring this back, I swear. Maybe I'll even get him to personalize it to you." Jordan smiled and shook his head at the weird way the universe worked sometimes. He'd learned not to question it and to be more like Johnny had been, to go with the flow every once in a while.

His gut was telling him this was one of those times.

So he turned his car around and headed back to Middletown.

9

"You're not going to chicken out, are you?" Devra asked as she clutched Wren's wrist and dragged her toward the door. "I've never been to a concert and I really want to see one. I checked out Kason's music online and it's really great. Come on, please. Trevon and Quinn wouldn't like it if I went alone, but they'll be fine if we have a girls' night out."

"The Hot Rods ladies are going. Whether or not I'm there, you won't be alone." Wren laughed despite her trepidation. "Mustang Sally by herself is enough to scare off anyone who'd bug you. Sabra, Kaelyn, and Nola are way tougher than me, too."

"Blah blah, whatever. Get your ass outside." Devra grinned. "Don't tell me you don't want to see Kason again. He invited you, not us. Besides, you look incredible in that dress."

"I still say I should wear jeans," Wren grumbled.

"No way. You look amazing. I mean you always do, like when you wore that silky jumper thing to our wedding.

But when's the last time you put on an actual dress?" Devra asked.

That was exactly the problem. "Five years ago, give or take."

"I know you're comfortable in your usual get up, but don't tell me you don't love the way you look in this. I saw your face light up the moment you tried it on." Devra shook her arm, covered in zillions of thin gold bangle bracelets. She looked pretty hot herself, sporting dark eye liner and a burgundy V-neck top over a black leather mini-skirt she had to have borrowed from Nola or Sally.

Devra wasn't lying. Wren did feel spectacular. Like she was reclaiming a piece of her she'd thought was gone forever. "It's just...kind of...freaking me out, okay?"

"I know." Devra hugged her. "It's hard to change. It's scary to stop being comfortable and reach for what you really want. But it's so worth it."

Wren smiled at her friend. "Yeah, when you end up married to two hot-as-hell men who think the world of you and shower you with love and affection."

"Is that what you want, too?" Devra wondered. "Because if it happened to me, it's possible, you know?"

"I'd settle for one guy who really loves me. But if it worked out that way..." Wren nodded. "I wouldn't say no."

Devra shot her a disbelieving glance. Thankfully, she didn't push the issue.

Okay, fine. Wren admitted it to herself. She wanted to be in another ménage relationship more than anything, she was just realistic enough to acknowledge she wasn't likely to get that lucky twice in her lifetime. She'd found her perfect matches—Jordan and Johnny—only for them to be ripped away from her.

It was terrifying to think of exposing herself to that kind of agony again.

"It's just a concert, Wren." Devra tugged her some more, dragging her toward the door. For such a small woman, she was strong as fuck. "Listen to the music, daydream a little about the hunk on stage, have a drink or two, and we'll be home, hanging around in our comfy PJs before you know it."

"Okay. You're right."

"I know I am." Devra grinned. "Nola will be here to pick us up in two minutes. Get your shit together, and let's go."

10

Kason paced his dressing room before the show. It was kind of weird doing this stone-cold sober. He remembered why he'd started drinking and occasionally doing drugs in the first place. Chemicals dulled his nerves. He wasn't scared that he wasn't a good performer or that his songs weren't up to par. He worried that people would see through him and the endless ballads he sang to women now that he suspected the reason he'd only ever found heartbreak was because he wanted something different from what he'd been singing about.

The stress of acting like someone he wasn't anymore, and feeling like a world-class liar, had eaten at him until he'd started leaning on substances, gambling, and other distractions a little too much. Okay, a *lot* too much.

He swiped his hand over his damp forehead.

"You doing okay?" Van asked from his post near the door, though his job was more like babysitter than bodyguard lately.

"I will be once the lights come up and I can sing instead of waiting."

His drummer, Kyra Koda, poked her head in the dressing room. Her pixie stature and the cute curls bobbing around her face, complete with big green eyes, were a total mockery of the beast she became when she rocked the drums for him or any other front man. He was lucky to have her.

It was Kyra's threat to leave the band, because she "couldn't stand by and watch him lose himself anymore" that had finally spurred Kason to get help. Hell, he hadn't even realized he needed it before that.

Worse, he knew that if Kyra abandoned him, Van wouldn't be far behind. His best friend might never say it, might never cross any professional lines, but the way he was staring dreamily at Kyra right then proved he was at least half in love with the woman, even if he didn't plan to ever do anything about it.

"Almost ready?" Kason asked her.

"I'm always ready, boss." She grinned. "How about you?"

"I'm good." *I think.* He'd be better if that gorgeous blonde woman from the motorcycle shop showed up backstage after the show. He might not be completely satisfied, but she would help him pretend like that was enough for a while. An orgasm or two would help even more.

"I'm going to get in place. See you out there." Kyra smiled at him. "I'm proud of you."

Why? he wondered, but he didn't ask. No matter how she responded, he was ashamed of himself.

He hadn't written a song in two years. That wasn't so long that it was freaking people out yet—other than himself, of course. He had to find his creativity again. His drive. His passion.

But what if he couldn't do it sober anymore?

Then this comeback tour might end up being a farewell tour instead. He guessed he'd had a decent career. Before the drugs and gambling, he'd been pretty careful with his money. He'd be okay if it all fell apart tonight or in the next few months. That didn't mean he wanted a life without music.

All his worries faded away when a roadie knocked on the door twice and shouted, "Kason, you're on!"

He jumped up and down a few times, his fists clenched and his arms tucked in tight to his sides before shaking them out. Van smacked him on the shoulder and said, "You can do it. You've got this. They love you. We all do."

Kason refused to let them down. Not his friends and not the people who'd come there tonight to listen to him sing. He burst from his dressing room at a run, and didn't stop until he was at center stage, all eyes and lights focused on him. Then he donned his showman persona, which cloaked his real struggles. It was easy to escape for the two and a half hours they played.

Nothing mattered but putting on a good show.

Performing itself was like a drug to him. It drove out the buzzing anxieties that nagged him when the world was quiet. Here and now, the only thing he could hear was music and the screaming of fans.

During his most popular song, Kason always picked someone from the crowd to sing to. To make a connection with. It made him feel less like a charlatan.

That night, he scanned the front row on the right side of the stage. Most everyone looked the same to him in the glare of the lights. Big hair, bigger hats, jeans, flannel, and old concert shirts were everywhere.

So it caught his eye when he noticed a man in a suit. What the hell was he doing there?

And why did that tie and steely gaze make him nearly irresistible?

Kason didn't have too long to think about it. Kyra kicked off the beat that the rest of the band followed during the intro of "Secret Love". He edged closer, trying to get a better look at the man as he began to sing. And suddenly it was more than that.

The guy brushed his hand across his eyes as if he was moved by the lyrics, or by Kason singing to him. The pain Kason recognized from within himself was painted over the man's mostly clean-shaven face. Kason wanted nothing more than to soothe him, either with his song or with his hands and his mouth and his cock.

The lyrics took on new meaning as he imagined loving the sadness out of this man in the crisp white shirt and black slacks, making them both more whole than they seemed at that moment. A flash went off from a few feet away, nearly blinding him.

It made him aware that the very last thing he needed was the camera that fed the jumbotron to zoom in on his private performance and broadcast it to a stadium full of people.

No thanks.

Kason broke their stare and jogged to the other side of the stage before he made a fool of himself and did exactly what his agent and manager had been warning him against for nearly a year and a half now.

Stupid! He had to be more careful.

As he traveled past Kyra's drum set, she shot him a

quizzical look that he flat out ignored. He never changed positions during "Secret Love". Never.

It broke the intention of the moment. Which was exactly why he was doing it now.

Fortunately, when he arrived at the opposite side of the stage, he caught the glint of platinum blond hair and a killer smile he hadn't gotten to enjoy that day at Hot Rides. There was no mistaking Wren, though. She stood out, even in this crowd. He settled into the final two verses and delivered them as though she were the person he'd written this song about.

No one had to know it was actually about a man not so different from the one he'd started singing to. The first—and last—guy he'd ever had a crush on.

He hadn't done anything about his attraction then and he wouldn't do anything about the way that fan had moved him a moment ago either.

Hopefully Wren would come backstage later and remind him that he enjoyed a good old-fashioned romp plenty enough.

Kason sang his heart out to her, even if she didn't understand what he was trying to tell her.

11

Kason charged off the stage, the rush of performing still pumping him up. Adrenaline was more powerful than any substance he could have imbibed. He went straight to his dressing room, peeled off his sweat-soaked clothes, then strode into the shower.

Stage lights were brutal. So was the amount of energy it took to put on a show like that. Thanks to his therapist-approved gym schedule and focusing on his health, his endurance had never been better. Even still, he was both amped up and exhausted simultaneously.

His cock hadn't received the message.

As always, when he finished performing, he had a raging hard-on.

In his younger days, there had been willing women waiting in his dressing room to solve that pesky problem for him. Now, though, he preferred to take things into his own hands instead of having Van or someone else on his team stock his room with very willing females like they were nothing more than the snacks laid out for him to munch on.

He must be getting old. Or maybe he was growing up.

Either way, he wasn't leaving this shower until he'd relieved some of his arousal, or he was liable to make a fool of himself. That or make bad decisions once he found himself surrounded by the fans and crew waiting to celebrate another amazing performance with him backstage.

Would Wren be there?

He wrapped his suds-covered hand around his cock and began to stroke it.

Kason imagined what it would be like if she was, if he could carve out a space for them to actually talk and get to know each other, or if she was as adventurous as he suspected and they skipped out on the after party to do more than just chat.

He would try to take his time with her, but the odds of that happening—or her even wanting something gentle and seductive from him—were slim.

They would tear each other's clothes off and burn the night down as they fucked each other's brains out. Kason pictured what it would be like to lie back and let her have ultimate control. She'd ride him, unashamed of her power and passion, using him to please herself while letting him rest up for when they changed places.

Once she'd taken her fill, he'd let himself loose, flipping her over and driving into her until neither of them could resist the temptation of succumbing to one final orgasm together.

As he pictured it, his hand sped up, jerking his hard-on furiously.

Except at the last moment, it wasn't Wren's bright blue

eyes he pictured staring into his as he exploded or her red lips he fantasized about kissing as he poured his come inside her. Instead, he imagined the man in the suit, the one with the shattered soul.

The daydream blurred and the man was suddenly there, standing beside the bed, watching.

Just before Kason came, the man fisted Kason's hair in his hand and undid his belt, then his suit pants. When Kason—still fucking Wren—turned his head, took the guy's dick in his mouth, and sucked, the guy would lose every shred of the self-control that was holding him together, despite how damaged he was inside. He'd groan and shake, rising on his tiptoes to embed himself in Kason's mouth.

Kason would suck greedily until the man couldn't restrain himself a moment longer and orgasmed, shouting Kason's name. Not someone else's. Not a woman's. No, Kason's.

What would be even better would be if Wren enjoyed it. If her pussy wrung his cock even as the man's release flooded his mouth, Kason would be in heaven.

He groaned, then shuddered and braced one hand against the tile to keep himself upright when his knees threatened to buckle. His balls drew tight to his body as he shot all over the shower walls then spilled the rest of his release down the drain.

That was the only place his lust could go. He sure as shit couldn't allow it loose outside his fantasies.

Even if his epic climax hadn't softened his cock, that thought alone would have. He finished his shower in freezing cold water, then stumbled into the main room, still drying off.

Van was guarding the door, keeping the rest of the world out until Kason was ready to face it. "You good?"

"Yeah."

"You sure? I have a secondary route. I can slip you out the back if you want to avoid the chaos and go to bed early. Or hang out at your house or whatever you need. I've got your back, Kason."

"I know you do. Thank you." He wrapped his towel around his waist and started getting dressed. "It means a lot that you've stuck by me, Van."

"You might pay me, but you're more my friend than my boss, you realize?" Van was always serious, but he was even more so when he said, "You can trust me, Kason, with anything that's bugging you."

Not everything. If Van knew what he'd been thinking of a few minutes ago, would he still be standing there? Or would simple everyday things like getting changed in front of his bodyguard suddenly become weird? He didn't need that kind of complication in his life.

So he changed the subject. "Tell me the truth...how was the show? Did it suck or was it as good as it used to be before I went off the rails?"

"Never heard a crowd scream louder." Van grinned. "You killed it, Kason. You're back."

He nodded because he believed he *was* on the right path again. As long as he didn't do something dumb, he could reenergize his career.

Kason smiled because the strains of a song began to play in the back of his mind. Faint, but the music—*new music*—was in there waiting for him to discover it. He was going to be okay. "Let's celebrate."

He exploded from his dressing room, not too proud to admit the roar of applause, whistles, and shouts still had the power to move him even after nearly ten years of working as a fulltime musician. Even better, he saw her. Wren. Right there in front of him.

His stare clashed with hers, and the appreciation written there erased the effects of the hand job he'd given himself less than ten minutes ago. He didn't even try to fight it.

The list of shit he could have was a lot shorter now than before.

Motorcycles.

Music.

~~Booze.~~

~~Drugs.~~

~~Gambling.~~

~~Sexy thoughts about men.~~

Women. Lots and lots of women.

Hell, that last vice was practically part of his job description. So he did what he was learning to do best and lived up to everyone's expectations.

He strode to where Wren was leaning up against a wheeled case the roadies were about to refill with wires and scaffolding so they could roll out of Middletown and set up wherever the next show would be. When you never stayed in the same place long, it made it tough to do things the old-fashioned way. You know, meet a girl and ask her out, take her to dinner a few times before kissing her goodnight and working your way up to spending some quality time together in bed.

Or even the less-old-fashioned way of hunting for someone on a dating app and meeting up for a good time. He didn't even have time to swipe right on someone or the guts to put himself out there knowing he'd have crazy fans show up instead of people interested in him for him. The one time he'd tried, he'd been reported for attempting to catfish someone. They hadn't believed it was really him.

So he just went for it, for Wren, the way he'd gotten used to operating.

Kason reached out and put his hands around her slender waist. When she beamed up at him instead of slapping his scruffy face, he bent down and sealed his mouth to hers.

Half the people around them cheered louder. The rest, mostly women who didn't approve of his not picking them to manhandle instead, grew quiet. But Wren, she melted.

Her tough, indifferent mask fell away at the first contact of his lips on hers. She looped her arms around his neck and kissed him without a moment of hesitation or insecurity. If she gave a fuck about what any of the hundred or so people swarmed around them thought, he couldn't tell.

This was the woman he'd glimpsed the other day. The one who'd met his gaze directly at the shop and dared him to criticize her for her hanging on to the memory of a dead lover. The one who'd done her job despite having someone famous waltz into her shop. The one who'd tried to obscure a killer body beneath work clothes that did nothing to highlight the subtle curves he was now familiarizing himself with. The one who was a mechanic of some sort and certainly not the garage's receptionist.

Kason's hands wandered from her waist, up her back, and then lower, lower to the curve of her ass. Wren didn't object. Instead she hummed and leaned into his embrace, giving him a non-verbal green light by spearing her fingers into his hair and tipping his head so she could reach him better.

She slipped her tongue into his mouth and sparred with his own, meeting him thrust for thrust.

In a flash, he realized that sex with her would be...incredible.

Wren was a wildcat. A badass in an angel's clothing.

Well, okay, an angel had never looked like her with that slinky black dress, but still.

Kason was about to signal Van to escort him and Wren to whatever secret wormhole he'd arranged when, from behind them, a man called her name. Maybe the dude couldn't tell they were busy. The equipment case was probably hiding Kason's hands, which were about to slip beneath Wren's dress in full view of anyone who cared to look.

"Wren? Is that you?" the newcomer persisted, even though he had to have figured out what they were up to by now.

Instantly, she stiffened. And not in a good way.

The heat and liquid grace she'd been as she burned in Kason's arms vanished in an instant. Tense and shocked, she jerked away looking guilty as fuck.

Kason wondered if he was about to brawl for the first time in a while. He might welcome a fight if he hadn't already been about to let off this steam in a much more enjoyable way. Wren had amped him up without hardly trying.

He'd been so intrigued by her that he hadn't even asked if she had a boyfriend. It looked a hell of a lot like she did. Kason tried not to be judgmental, but loyalty meant something to him. If she'd been cheating on someone with him, the rest of her ultra-attractive qualities didn't matter.

The other guy was coming closer now, though several

women—including the petite lady with dark hair Kason recognized from Hot Rides—attempted to shield Wren from his ire.

"You better talk to him before security tosses him out," Kason said, his desire fading.

"It's not what it looks like." Wren put her hands on his forearms and squeezed. "I swear."

"Oh yeah? Because it looks like your boyfriend—" Kason glanced up for a better view and realized the man who'd shouted for Wren was none other than suit-guy. Of fucking course it was.

"Ex," Wren hissed.

"What?" Kason asked, confused.

"He's my *ex*-boyfriend. And I fucking hate him even more now than I did before." The crinkles around her eyes and the sadness in their aqua depths called her a liar. She was hurt, but she didn't hate that man.

"I thought he was dead." Kason spoke without thinking. He didn't want to be intrigued by Wren, her handsome-as-fuck ex and whatever convoluted history they clearly shared.

"My *other* ex." She crossed her arms as if to shield herself from his reaction, though she had no idea how opposite it would be from what she expected when she clarified. "I was in love with them both. At the same time. But when Johnny died, Jordan and I fell apart. Except I can't seem to get rid of him all of a sudden. Excuse me, please. I'm going to take care of that right now."

Kason hoped everyone was too distracted by the spectacle Wren's very-alive ex, her five smokin' friends, and now Wren herself were making to notice the steel rod in Kason's pants. She'd said *what*?

Had he heard her correctly?

And just because suit-guy and someone else had shared Wren, that didn't mean they'd shared each other. In Kason's mind, though, that's exactly what he was picturing, just as he had earlier.

Had some part of his subconscious picked up on their matching sorrow?

He didn't have time to think about it more because right then Wren whirled around, and strode toward the spot where her friends were clearly trying to corral her ex.

Kason gestured to Van, then pointed to the brewing situation before diving in himself.

There was no chance in hell he could walk away now.

12

———

Jordan hadn't had any intention of actually going backstage after the concert. Yet there he stood in the security line clutching his...no, *Johnny's*... backstage pass in trembling fingers.

Did he really belong there? Probably not.

Was he going in anyway? After that final performance, where Kason Cox's gaze had snagged his as he sang "Secret Love" and appeared to stare straight into his damned soul? Hell fucking yes.

The singer had magic, that was for sure. It was what made him a star. He could connect with millions of people around the world. He was capable of manipulating their emotions in the best possible way with his voice and the stories he told through his songs.

Maybe that's all that had happened tonight. It could be that Kason had moved Jordan with those lyrics about a love so strong and forbidden that you didn't dare share it, not even with the person it was meant for. But to Jordan, it had seemed like so much more.

He hadn't felt that kind of attraction—like he'd met

and recognized a kindred spirit—since the life had poured out of Johnny onto the dirt floor of that warehouse masquerading as a corrugated metal barn in the middle of nowhere where the ambush had gone down.

Jordan thought about stepping out of line and continuing his trek up to the lake about a thousand times in the fifteen minutes it took to make it to the security team, who were vetting the people at the entrance to the after party. In the end, he simply couldn't.

It had been a long five years of living alone, of feeling like no one else could understand his anguish. Long enough that he wanted to at least talk to Kason now that he'd realized the other guy just might get him.

If he didn't take this chance, he knew for certain—since it had happened to him before—that he would regret it for the rest of his life.

When he saw the crush predominantly composed of flashy young women covered in sequins, with glossy lips, and big hair, he realized he was probably crazy. He could use a stiff drink if he was going to investigate any further. But as he pushed deeper into the throng, he realized there wasn't a bar anywhere backstage.

He'd just about given up any hope of actually seeing Kason himself when a roar went through the gathering. So he followed the shouts and whistles, assuming Kason would be at the center of attention. Fortunately, the crowd kept growing louder as he plunged deeper into it.

The very last thing he expected to see as he rounded a corner was his beautiful Wren caught up in Kason Cox's arms while they attempted to suck each other's faces off. If anything could have made the man more attractive to Jordan than the moment they'd shared earlier, that was it.

"Wren!" he shouted without thinking as he tried to

part the gawking throng and get closer. For a better look or maybe out of some crazy notion that she would welcome him into their circle with open arms.

If he'd thought about it for a half second, he would have realized how foolish that was.

She wasn't his anymore.

Never had been, really. She'd been Johnny's, and he'd elected to share her with Jordan.

None of that mattered to his instincts. They shut down his rational thoughts and drove him forward.

"Wren, is that you?" he yelled again. This time he was close enough to realize that soon she and Kason were going to need a room or risk being indecent right there in the middle of the backstage party. Maybe that's what celebrities did. He wouldn't mind staying to watch. By the way Wren froze when she finally heard his voice, she probably wouldn't approve.

"What the hell are you doing?" A familiar woman drew his attention by calling, "Jordan!"

"Devra, hey." He tried to brush past her but found the way blocked by several of the women he recognized from his visits to the Hot Rods garage as well as Devra's wedding. "Nice to see you ladies again."

He peered around Nola, trying not to let Wren and Kason out of his sight.

"Jordan, please. I know you love Wren." Sabra tried to make him be sensible. "Don't ruin this for her. She's happy. She spent the whole night singing along, dancing, and...smiling."

"I'd say that if you upset her, I'll put my boot up your ass. But..." Mustang Sally whipped her long thick black braid over her shoulder. "I think she's about to come do the honors herself."

"If you want to change your mind and leave, we'll slow her down so you can go without making any more of a scene." Devra put her hand on Jordan's forearm. "I'm trying to help you like you helped me."

"If you want to do that, let me talk to her. To them." Jordan flicked his gaze from Wren, who was indeed marching straight toward them, to Kason. Devra winced but stepped aside.

"Thanks, squad, but I've got this." Wren flashed a tight, not-very-reassuring smile at her friends, then spun to face Jordan.

He probably should have said something profound or at least apologized. Instead, the thing that tumbled out of his mouth was, "You're wearing a dress."

Immediately, she blushed. If he knew Wren, and damn he did, that would only piss her off more. Her eyes turned icy in an instant. He hadn't meant it as an accusation. It had startled him, that's all. He hadn't stalked her or anything, but especially lately—now that they had mutual acquaintances—he'd caught enough glimpses of her to realize that she'd reverted to her old habits after Johnny had died.

If it was Kason who was thawing her again and making her feel confident enough—as Johnny had before Kason—to dress like this, that was a good thing.

A *great* thing.

And here he was messing it up for her.

He really was the worst person possible for Wren.

Fuck.

Before either of them could say something, Kason beat them to it. He practically snarled when he neared and asked, "How'd you get in here?"

Funny, that wasn't how he'd looked at Jordan during

"Secret Love." Was he afraid Jordan was going to mention their eye-fucking or the intimate moment they'd shared in front of 10,000 or more of their closest friends?

Jordan tried not to look guilty as he tapped the backstage pass in the flimsy plastic holder around his neck.

Kason peered at it, his eyes widening when he realized it was the autographed ticket he'd obviously given Wren. "Where'd you get that? Did she give it to you?"

Jordan shook his head. He wasn't about to throw Wren under the bus when she obviously liked this guy, even if he was kind of tipping from hottie to jerk in Jordan's estimation. "Found it when I went to visit my partner. Well, his grave I mean."

Kason's green eyes grew wide then flew to Wren. "Partner? Your ex was his *partner*?"

Why would Cox get so bent out of shape about that? Jordan narrowed his eyes, putting his agent skills to work now that his brain was starting to reengage.

"Jordan is a special agent for ICE," Wren deadpanned. "They were literally partners."

As much as they both knew Jordan had wanted it to be more than that, working together and sharing her was all he'd been able to claim about his actual relationship with Johnny.

"Oh." Was it his imagination or did Kason Cox seem disappointed by that news flash? After the way he'd sung "Secret Love" to Jordan, Jordan wasn't sure what the man was into. He certainly had seemed to be enjoying having his tongue stuffed down Wren's throat.

Maybe he was bisexual, too. Or at least like Jordan believed himself to be even if he hadn't had the right circumstances to test that theory.

"Son of a bitch, Wren. I'm sorry, okay. I should have realized you'd be here." Jordan swallowed hard. "I wasn't thinking. I was on my way to the lake, saw the ticket, and came right over. Sorry. I didn't mean to interrupt."

No, he hadn't done it on purpose. But he couldn't say he was sorry he had. Because some base portion of his brain still thought of Wren as his.

Worse was the part that got off on watching her come apart in another man's arms.

Maybe he shouldn't have interrupted. Then he could have spied on them...

You're a sleazy fucking asshole.

"Enjoy the rest of your evening together. I mean that, sincerely." He stuck his hand out to Kason, who accepted it grudgingly. The guy had a solid grip. Even that couldn't account for the impact of his hand enfolding Jordan's. Both of them released each other simultaneously, before they could acknowledge the zing that traveled between them. "The show was fantastic, Mr. Cox. Johnny would have loved every second."

Wren didn't say anything, but Jordan saw her throat flex as she swallowed down her emotions. She nodded brusquely. When he pivoted to leave, she called out, "Hey, Jordan."

He spun around again so fast he got dizzy. It would have been impossible not to notice the protective and possessive hand Kason had on her lower back. "Yeah?"

"Make sure you put that back where you found it." Her steely stare gutted him, and he deserved it.

"Of course." He closed his eyes for a moment, then really did leave that time, stopping only momentarily to reassure Devra and the Hot Rods ladies that he was fine even if he clearly wasn't.

It was more important to him that Wren was, though. So he said to them, "You'll make sure she gets home safe?"

"Us Hot Rods and Hot Rides stick together," Sally promised him. "We'll be fine."

For the first time in a long time, Jordan wished he belonged somewhere—anywhere—too.

13

———

Wren rolled over in the lofted bed of her tiny home on the Hot Rides campus. Usually, she was the first one up, and had even started doing yoga with Sabra and Holden most mornings. Not today.

She couldn't bring herself to get out of bed.

Or at least she hadn't been able to yet by the time a series of raps echoed from the front door, not twenty feet away from where she was trying to fall back asleep so she didn't have to face the disaster the night before had turned into.

"Open up, Wren." It was Devra. "I have a pot of fresh coffee…"

Tempting.

Wren opened one eye.

"And a whole tray of pastries I made for my class project…"

How was she supposed to resist that? Wren climbed down the bookcase ladder and flung the door open before stalking the few feet to the kitchenette and dropping into a seat at the two-person table.

"I thought that might get your attention." Devra grinned as she made herself at home. Technically, this had been her house for a while, before she and Trevon had moved in with Quinn next door. She got out plates and cups. The aromatic steam from the coffee she poured into Wren's mug had her feeling slightly more human.

"What's this?" she asked as she reached for a square of dough with apples and chopped nuts on top. Whatever it was called, it was delicious. She moaned.

"Should I call it a Kason Cake?" Devra asked with a mischievous grin.

Wren choked and had to take a gulp of her still scorching coffee, which then led to more coughing. She gave Devra the finger as she tried not to die. Her friend only laughed.

"Please don't. I'm already embarrassed enough as it is." Wren groaned. "Last night was a catastrophe."

"I thought it was going pretty well right up to the point where Jordan crashed your party." Devra was quieter and serious when she said, "I thought for a moment it might end up being a party of three."

"That's because you're a hopeless romantic." Wren shook her head, then took another sip of her coffee before polishing off some more of the pastry. "Not everyone gets as lucky as you or the Hot Rods or the Powertools crew or Tom and Ms. Brown... Hell. I need some of that to rub off on me. Maybe it will eventually, but no. Nothing magical happened last night to take away all the shit that's happened between Jordan and me. And Kason...well, maybe something could have developed, but it didn't have a chance."

"You just met. Maybe on your next date..." Devra plucked a chocolate croissant from the platter and took a bite.

Wren's shoulders slumped. The truth had hit her hard this morning. She'd blown her only chance with Kason. "No. He's gone. Not that I googled it or anything, but TMZ says his bus was sighted in Indianapolis this morning. They must have driven overnight. Even if I wanted to—and damn, I actually do, Devra—I can't fix this. It's too late."

"So what if he's not in Middletown? His bike is here. He's got to come back sometime, and a man like him has the means to travel whenever and wherever he wants." Devra stabbed her croissant at Wren. "Call him. Tell him you wish last night had gone differently and see if you can have a do-over next time he's in town."

"I can't." Wren wasn't sure she was hungry anymore. She set down her apple thingy—she was definitely not going to call it a Kason Cake.

"Why not?"

"I don't have his phone number. I never wrote it down since he said it was for personal use and I never intended to use it." She looked out the window then, wondering if she'd ever find someone or if she was doomed to be alone forever. Until yesterday, there hadn't been any question in her mind. She never planned to be interested in someone again. But now that she was, it was even worse than when she'd been resigned to a lonely fate.

Now she craved more.

"You would call him if you could?" Devra asked innocently as she took another nibble off the corner of her chocolate croissant.

"Well, okay, maybe I'd start with a text. But yes, I'd

reach out. I feel terrible that I took off like I did. But Jordan...and Johnny...and the kissing and the dress... It was too much."

"I understand." Devra nodded. "It was an intense night."

"Why do I feel like there's something you're not telling me?" Wren picked up her Kason Cake—*damn it!*—and chomped into it. Sticky sweetness flowed over her tongue, reminding her of exactly how damn good he'd tasted. She'd kissed him like a woman coming off a self-imposed hunger strike. Because, really, that's exactly what she'd been.

And now she couldn't help but want more.

A grin spread across Devra's face. She looked so pleased with herself Wren didn't mention the smear of chocolate at the corner of her mouth. "I remember his number. That day when he came to the shop, I could tell you were acting weird. And I'm good with memorizing stuff for recipes. I don't really think about it, I just repeat things in my mind until they stick there."

"You what?" Wren leaned halfway across the table.

"Yup. It's stored in my brain." Devra took another sample of her baking and tapped her temple with the index finger of her free hand. "I mean, we also have his email address on file at the shop, but I know you'd never use it for personal stuff when he specifically gave you the phone number for that. Besides, my backstage pass is the one he came back and jotted that number on."

Holy shit! She'd forgotten all about that. Wren had been overwhelmed that day and it had slipped her mind. "Devra, you're a fucking genius."

"I know. So...better get those texting fingers ready."

Wren fumbled her phone three times in her

excitement. When she had it firmly in hand and unlocked, she opened a blank text. "Okay, go ahead."

Devra recited the digits, then said, "Do your part. I'll leave the rest of the Kason Cakes here in case you need them after your talk."

"I'm going to apologize, not sext the man." Wren rolled her eyes.

"I'm pretty sure he'd be glad to accept dirty pictures in lieu of an *I'm sorry*." Devra stood. "I'll be next door, studying, if you need anything."

"You're going to do great," Wren reassured her friend. "You can remember phone numbers like it's nothing, so that textbook crap is easy for you and these are the most amazing pastries I've ever had. I'm going to gain another ten pounds hanging out with you if I'm not careful."

"Thanks." Devra's smile widened. "I appreciate you saying that. We've fought so long for me to go back to school, I don't want to mess it up now that I have this opportunity."

"Make your professors some of these Kason Cakes and you'll pass with flying colors." Wren devoured the last of hers enthusiastically, making Devra laugh as she headed out.

If only it was that easy to pump herself up. She stared at her phone and typed out three or four messages, deleting each one for being too pathetic, too nonchalant, or too serious.

So before she could change her mind, she simply wrote *I'm sorry*, then clicked send. Maybe he wouldn't even bother to respond. He was famous, she didn't mean anything to him, and they'd shared one brief—if fiery— kiss with a little bonus gropage. He'd probably already forgotten her. Might even have spent the night with one of the other fans who'd made it clear they were his for the taking last night.

Wren's throat went dry at that thought.

It only got worse when he responded with *Um...what for?*

Until she realized he didn't even know who he was talking to. Oh shit. *This is Wren. And I'm sorry for bolting last night. I was really looking forward to...*

What exactly?

Her finger hovered over her phone's screen for a moment before typing *...getting to know you better.*

I'm still *looking forward to that.* He put a winky emoji after his statement, making her laugh. Both because he hadn't written her off as a pain in the ass and because she knew he was intentionally trying to put her at ease. He wasn't disturbed by the drama she'd brought to his party. How could she not think he was adorable and sweet and understanding and...extra sexy?

Wren took a long drink from her mug as she thought about what to say. She liked texting. It gave her time to consider her words and communicate more effectively than she sometimes did in person. Maybe she should have tried that with Johnny.

Then some of those difficult conversations that had been stuck inside her might have come to light. In the end, it probably wouldn't have mattered, but now she would never know.

She wasn't about to make that mistake again.

So even if it was hard, she was going to be honest about her feelings. *I'm glad. I was scared I screwed things up last night.*

You? How? You're a great kisser and you looked incredible in that dress you apparently wore just for me.

Wren laughed harder. *You wish. I wore it for* me.

That's good, Wren. Seriously. I'm glad you felt comfortable enough to stop acting like you're the one who died. Sorry if that's harsh, but...

It's fine. It's true. She couldn't say he was wrong. *So you think I'm a good kisser?*

Yes. And I'm willing to bet that you're even better in bed, without an audience.

How candid did she want to be exactly? She couldn't go back on her fresh resolution, so she laid it on the line. *Actually, I kind of like being watched. Did what I told you yesterday, when Jordan showed up, change how you feel about me?*

The wait for his response seemed to stretch for years. Maybe he was choosing his words as carefully as she was. Either that or he was debating whether to continue the discussion at all given what she'd just told him. *If by 'change how you feel about me' you mean 'turn me on even more,' then hell yes. If you're asking if I think less of you because you have a heart big enough to love two men, who also loved each other, at once then...definitely not.*

She winced. That made her seem less selfish than she had been. *I didn't say they loved each other.*

It's obvious they did. I could see it in Jordan's eyes last night. Don't try to tell me they were only coworkers. That's BS.

There was never anything sexual between them, if that's what you think. Wren wasn't sure why she felt the need to clarify. Between love and sex, one was far more important than the other, and it wasn't the physical aspect.

Oh.

Can you clarify? Texting doesn't leave a lot of room for correctly interpreting an oh. She hadn't felt this way in so long she'd almost forgotten what it was like. The anticipation and longing. The need to be accepted for who she really was.

It was official, she gave a shit what Kason thought.

A whole lot of shits, to be exact.

I'm surprised, that's all. From the way he acted when he talked about the guy, and the fact that the three of you slept together, I would have thought...

How had he figured all that out from just a few seconds with them both? Were they that transparent? Or was Kason especially good at reading people?

Hopefully Jordan wouldn't mind her being so frank. He owed her one anyway. *Jordan wanted more, except he never got the chance to tell Johnny. I used to think Johnny was oblivious. These days, I'm starting to think maybe he only acted like it since it was obvious to me and you and probably anyone else who cared to look.*

That sucks. As much as I wanted to deck Jordan last night for interrupting us, I wouldn't wish that on anyone.

Damn, and he was empathetic too? Even when it came to someone he had no reason to care for? Wren sighed. While she herself might give Jordan a hard time, she didn't want anyone else doing it.

I wonder if that's why... Wren had never voiced this thought out loud. She thought about deleting what she'd written, yet didn't. Somehow, she felt safe sharing with Kason so she finished typing and sent it before she could change her mind. *I wonder if that's why Johnny threw himself in front of Jordan that day. He literally took a bullet for him. Saved his life. Maybe even though he couldn't love Jordan back in the same way, he still felt the need to protect Jordan as if he did. Or maybe* because *he did.*

Now that she'd put it out there in black and white, Wren felt certain that was the case.

If Jordan ever came to the same conclusion, he'd keep flogging himself—even worse than he did now—for Johnny's death.

As angry as she'd been at him the night before, she debating texting him next.

Nah. Not yet and maybe not ever. He didn't want her in his life. He'd made that more than clear.

Kason's reply was slower to come this time. Then he said, *Whatever the case was, it's pretty obvious to me that the three of you had something I've never experienced. Is it too fucked up to say that, even though it ended like it did, I'm jealous?*

Nope. Because as bad as it still hurts, I wouldn't erase it if I could.

How about this... Next time I'm in Middletown, why don't we try to make some new memories for us both? Happy... horny...ones.

Wren laughed out loud. *I like that plan. I'm not sure what your schedule is like, but we're planning a birthday party for Trevon—one of our mechanics—in a few weeks. It would be awesome if you could come. There will be a lot of motorcycle riding, shit talking, homemade food, and plenty of time to get to know each other better.*

She intentionally rehashed his phrase, except instead of a winky face, she used the kissy emoji followed by the eggplant emoji. Take that.

I'm in. That time he didn't hesitate. Unfortunately those two little words were followed by, *Hey, sorry. Van says I have to go do sound check now. Can I call you later? It'll be late, after the show.*

Please do. Since it had worked out so well thus far, she decided to go for it and say what she was thinking. *I sort of figured you'd be busy partying with beautiful women.*

I'll enjoy talking to you a hell of a lot more than I would having another meaningless hookup.

Wren read his message at least ten times, wondering if he'd meant to imply that whatever they were doing wasn't meaningless, but she couldn't quite bring herself to be needy enough to ask. Damn Jordan for shaking her confidence enough that she even wondered.

Then I'll be waiting. Sing your heart out.

Even though you won't be in the front row, I'll still be singing to you. Gotta go. Later.

Wren could barely eat her next Kason Cake with her smile stretching her mouth so wide.

14

—————

Jordan sat in the car, unsure if he was actually going to get out. He looked over to the passenger seat and the pile of lilies, Wren's favorite flower, tied with a purple ribbon. They smelled incredible, and still weren't nearly as sweet as her when she wore the same scent.

Although he should have been up at the lake, figuring out a plan for his future, he hadn't been able to shake the feeling that he should come visit her first. Then again, he always wanted to do that. However, he rarely had an excuse to be in her vicinity.

If this had only been about him, his desire to see her, and his need to make sure she was okay after he'd obviously interrupted her evening with Kason, he would have turned around and left.

But he owed her an apology.

For last night. And for how he had ended things with her.

Now that they had mutual friends, they kept running into each other. He hated that things were awkward because of the choices he'd made. If he'd at least been man enough to tell her their relationship was over instead of letting her figure it out on her own, maybe today she would be able to stand being in the same room as him.

Jordan needed her to know that he'd been the one with his head shoved up his ass.

Both times.

He'd already resolved to do better and make things right with her. Then he'd come around that corner the night before and seen her making out with Kason Cox, the man who'd practically undressed Jordan with his stare while singing a ballad about forbidden desires. It had implanted wicked thoughts in his mind.

The hopes and dreams he'd had for his future with Wren and Johnny had seemed within reach again in a single moment. Except for the fact that he'd already ruined his chances with Wren. It would serve him right if she ended up in a committed, healthy ménage without him that made her happier than he'd ever seen her before.

Jordan had pretty much thought himself out of climbing from the car when someone approached and rapped on the window, scaring the shit out of him. It wasn't every day someone could sneak up on Jordan, a testament to how distracted his obsession with Wren had him.

"You gonna sit here all day and let those flowers wilt, or are you going to give them to Wren?" Quinn asked with a twisted grin.

"I'm calculating the odds of her appreciating them versus shoving them up my ass." Jordan winced because it was true.

"Pretty likely she'll opt for skewering you with them if

what Devra told me about last night is true. Did you really march in there and bust up Wren's first kiss with Kason?"

Jordan groaned. "I didn't know it was their first kiss, and I didn't mean to fuck it up either. I wasn't thinking at all, honestly."

"Dude. You'll be lucky if she stops with the flowers and doesn't put her boot up there, too. But you should definitely quit sitting here and make things right with her. I care about you both, and I hate to see you unhappy in general or with each other." Quinn leaned down closer and said quietly, "You have the power to wreck her. I've seen it myself. She wouldn't get so upset if she didn't still care about you. Go. Talk to her."

Jordan dropped his head back against the headrest then cursed. "You're right. I will. Thanks. And when I'm done, I'm coming over to talk about motorcycles with you. I've been thinking I'd like to buy one and could use some suggestions."

"That sounds awesome." Quinn grinned. "A lot easier problem to fix. Trevon and I would love to hook you up. We owe you one. A really big one."

"Nah. You took care of Wren like I asked. I say we're even." He grabbed the bouquet and got out of his car.

"Wren takes care of herself. I offered her a job because she's the best damn welder in the state, not to keep a close eye on her for you, though we love having her as part of our family, too," Quinn told Jordan. "Maybe that's where you need to start changing your thinking if you're going to come to peace."

Jordan blinked a few times, really listening to what Quinn was saying. His friend had something Jordan didn't —a thriving relationship involving three people. Maybe he should pay attention. "Okay, yeah. You're probably right. For the record, I know she doesn't *need* help from anyone. That doesn't mean I don't want her to have it anyway."

Quinn squeezed Jordan's shoulder. "Good luck."

"Thanks," Jordan said as he headed for Wren's house and Quinn went next door to his own.

Jordan cleared his throat and straightened his shirt before knocking on the door of the cute cottage Wren had moved into recently. Whether or not taking her under their wing had been the Hot Rides' sole intent of bringing her onboard, they looked out for their own. Jordan felt better knowing she was living up here with Quinn, Trevon, Ollie, Gavyn, and the entire Hot Rods gang nearby. They were good people and they'd watch out for her, even if she was more than capable of handling herself.

He waited forever for her to answer. She didn't.

So he knocked again.

Still no response. "Come on, Wren. I know you're here. Let me in. There's something I need to say to you, okay?"

Never one to hide, Wren rose to his challenge. She yanked open the door and glared at him. "What could you possibly have to say after last night?" She spread her legs, planting her feet wide apart as if she was wearing her work boots instead of colorful, striped fuzzy socks. Damn, she was gorgeous.

"I'm so sorry, Wren."

"For Cox-blocking me or for ghosting me five years ago after taking one last bang for the road?" She crossed her arms, refusing to accept his peace offering when he extended the flowers to her.

He couldn't help but be amused by her wit and candor despite the fact that she was throwing daggers at him.

"Both. I see you've only gotten sweeter over time. Unfortunately for you, I like when you bust my balls."

It reminded him of how strong she was. Ten times more than him.

Jordan took a step forward, pleased when she didn't retreat. Wren would always hold her ground. There was part of him that was mature enough to admit seeing her with Kason had reignited some of his possessive streak and a hell of a lot of his desire. That had never been the problem between them.

He didn't mind sharing, but did Kason know now that Wren had been Jordan's once, and would always be his in some way?

She scanned him up and down, her gaze landing on his. He let her see his suffering, his longing, and his confusion. Wren relented. She turned and waved him inside. So he went.

He decided he better start explaining before she changed her mind.

"I'm apologizing for hurting you. Then. Now. Whenever." He set the lilies on the small table nearby. Then he reached for her hand and was shocked when she allowed him to clasp it gently in his. "Even though I lost you, I still consider it one of the greatest honors of my life that you loved me once."

Some of the steel went out of her spine. Her shoulders slumped and she blinked a few times in rapid succession. "Don't say shit like that."

"Why not?"

"Because I might believe you." Wren sighed. "We both made mistakes, Jordan. Mine was letting you and Johnny pretend everything was fine between you when it wasn't. If I'd spoken up—"

"That wasn't your responsibility," Jordan insisted. "I should have done it."

"But when you struggled to, I should have stepped in and helped." She raised her voice bit by bit. "How could things between us ever have worked out if you were so unwilling to believe I could be an equal partner?"

"What?" Jordan held his hands out. "You were more than *equal*. You were the center of us."

"No. That's bullshit. You saw me as someone to shelter. Someone who wasn't capable of dealing with conflict. Someone weak and fragile." When he opened his mouth, she nearly shouted, "Don't deny it when the proof is irrefutable. Why else would you have left me when you did?"

"Because I wasn't good for you. Without Johnny..." He scrubbed his hand over his face. "I could never be enough for you on my own."

"I forgive you for being distraught and illogical. I forgive you for choosing a future without me. I even forgive you for abandoning me to figure out how to cope with my grief on my own. What I can't forgive is that you didn't think I was strong enough to love you, and that you made the decision for me. If you gave a shit about me, you never would have done that."

"I've fucked up a lot of things in my life. Of all of them, I regret hurting you the most." Jordan struggled to breathe.

"You're still not getting it, are you?" Wren pointed to the door. "You know what, you should have left. We never would have made it because you don't believe in me."

Maybe Quinn had been right. Jordan needed to give her more credit. How could he say he loved her if he wasn't willing to acknowledge how resilient and tough she was?

He hesitated before saying anything else, lest he make it worse instead of better. What he eventually settled on was, "I hope Kason treats you right and gives you what you need."

Wren narrowed her eyes at him. "What's that supposed to mean? Just say what you're thinking. I can see that you want to, so don't bother with code. I. Can. Handle. It."

Okay. Right.

"Has he ever said anything to you about being into guys? I googled him, but I didn't find any stories about him being bisexual or ever having a boyfriend or anything like that." Jordan wouldn't have held it against the man if he had. It was sort of the opposite, actually.

"No, but I haven't known him long. Why are you asking?" Wren tilted her head, trying to figure him out.

"I got a weird vibe from him last night. I probably imagined it." Jordan couldn't believe he was about to admit this, and to Wren of all people.

"You probably did, but tell me anyway." She nibbled her lower lip. Was she that afraid of being wounded again despite what she'd said before? Probably. He hated that he'd made her wary.

"During 'Secret Love,' he sang the song directly to me and I felt like—"

"No. You're wrong. He sang the song to *me*." Wren shook her head.

"The beginning?" Jordan couldn't believe she'd been anywhere near him. He would have noticed despite the crowd. He always noticed Wren.

"No, the end." She frowned.

"Yeah. When he crossed the stage? That was after something happened between us. I think. Maybe I'm delusional. It seemed like he understood what it's like when you can't have what you really want. It got to me. I mean, I knew exactly how he felt. I could have written those lyrics myself. It was exactly the emotion that consumed me when I loved Johnny but couldn't ever show it. It was agony. And I think Kason might have suffered the same thing. That's why I went backstage last night. I wanted to talk to him, to see if I was imagining it or if—possibly—he's like me. If he gets what I've been through, since no one else seems to understand."

Wren stepped closer then. She put her hands on his shoulders and squeezed. "I do. I was there, remember? And if you ever need someone to talk to about it, I'm still here, Jordan. You've always known where to find me. You chose not to. A decision I never agreed with, and don't to this day."

"Would you really have wanted me, and only me?" Jordan exposed himself in that moment, more completely than he ever had before. Being physically naked was nothing compared to baring his soul to her. "You were Johnny's first. I just tagged along for the ride."

"Fuck that." Wren shook him, then crushed him in a hug that was so powerful, he couldn't resist putting his arms around her too. This time to hold himself up instead of supporting her. "You two balanced each other out. I'm sorry I didn't do a better job of showing you how much I cared. I loved you, Jordan. For you, not because you and Johnny were a package deal."

Jordan knew he shouldn't do it, but he couldn't help himself. He ducked his head and nudged Wren's mouth with his, aligning their faces and letting her make the decision.

She leaned forward and took his lips, kissing him with five years' worth of pent-up emotions. Jordan consumed them, swallowing every bit of her grief, longing, desire, and regret.

He knew better than to try to take that away from her now, but at least they could share the burden. So he gave her everything he'd been holding back, too. Even if it was too late.

Jordan palmed Wren's ass and lifted her, groaning when she locked her legs around his waist. The motion ground her core against his steely shaft. He hadn't been with anyone in so long he might have been worried he didn't know how to make love anymore, except with Wren it all came back as if it had been yesterday that he'd buried himself inside her.

He carried her to the couch. Lying her down, he settled on top of her, unafraid that he would crush her as he blanketed her with his body. She had already shown she could bear the full weight of things much heavier than him.

Wren's hands snuck beneath his shirt and wandered up his back, caressing him, kneading him, and scoring him with her nails as she craned her neck upward to spear her tongue into his mouth.

Jordan couldn't keep his hips still when she goaded him by rocking against him.

He began to rub his cock on her through their clothing, wishing he'd been wearing something soft and thin like her sexy black moto jeggings instead of his traditional jeans.

The motion was as intuitive as the rhythm of their lips,

tongues, and teeth on each other. Wren's moans and sighs made him positive he was touching her in the right places. The softness of her small breasts against his chest was interrupted by the hard nubs of her nipples, which were clear through her thin tank top.

The fact that she hardly ever wore bras had always turned him on. Screw lingerie, her bare skin—there and easily accessible—was tempting. In fact, he slipped his hand between them, brushing his thumb over one peak before pinching it hard, like she'd always enjoyed.

Wren shuddered beneath him and clutched him tighter to her.

He stared into her eyes, wondering at how blue they were—like a summer sky—loving the heat and fierceness he saw in them. Wren spread her legs wider, dropping one to the floor so that she could brace herself against his humping.

Jordan was too into the moment to dare to pause even long enough to undo his pants and try to slip inside her. After so long on his own, this seemed nearly overwhelming in its intensity. Any more and he might die himself.

Wren must have felt the same way, because she began to grind on him as he echoed her motions. Before long, she stiffened, staring directly at him, then unraveled.

If it had been five hundred years since the last time he'd heard it, he'd never forget the guttural sound she made as she came, which she did right then and there in his arms. Nothing could have been more arousing to Jordan.

Her moans and grunts curled around his cock and gave him the tiny push he needed to join her.

He tore his lips from hers and sank his teeth into her

shoulder. His ass clenched over and over as he came, spilling his release into his underwear as if he were a horny teenager instead of the mature man he'd attempted to be when he came to apologize to her today.

Shit. What had he done?

How had they ended up like this again?

Who was he kidding? They *always* ended up like this. Even the night he'd tried to break up with her and had only ended up making love to her before wandering off without finding the strength to say the words he should have.

Wren didn't seem to have any regrets, though. She melted beneath him, every muscle in her body going limp as she looked up at the ceiling and laughed. "Damn, Jordan. That never gets old."

She hugged him, nuzzling her cheek against his. Here she was, being kind and sympathetic and accepting. What had he done but put her in a bad position the first moment it seemed like she was ready to move on? Damn it.

After a few more ragged breaths—during which he soaked in her affection, which he had been thirsty as fuck for—he tried to make things right. Again.

"Wren, I promise I didn't come here to screw things up for you with Kason." He brushed her hair off of her face. "Though it seems like I can't keep my hands off you, no matter what I intend."

"I can't say I hate that." Wren's grin morphed into a frown as she considered the repercussions of their impulsive release. "I am hoping for more with him, though it's early days. So I hope you understand that I'm going to tell him what just happened when he calls tonight."

"I'll be on the lookout in case he decides to plant one of those cowboy boots of his up my ass next time he sees me." Jordan grimaced. "He already thinks I'm a dickhead, so I'm sure this isn't going to help." He started to rise.

"Wait. You know what you said before, about wanting something you can't have?" Wren asked, halting him with a light touch on his cheek. "If exploring your bisexuality is what you really want, Jordan, then I'm sure there's a guy out there for you."

"There isn't. Not anymore." He shook his head. Johnny had been the one.

"It's not a betrayal to love—not fool around with, but truly love—as many people as possible in your lifetime, Jordan." Wren speared her fingers into his hair and tugged slightly until he met her gaze again. "Johnny wouldn't have wanted this for you. I'm almost certain that if you *had* told him about what you needed and he couldn't have given it to you, he would have been the first person out there helping you look for someone who could have."

That thought shocked Jordan, making all the blood rush to his head. He grew dizzy.

"He shared me with you, because he knew I cared for you both and that I needed more than he alone could give. I know he would have gladly found you someone else, because he wanted us all to be happy. And loved. And whole." Wren kissed him again, sweetly. "So do what Johnny would have. Find someone or however many someones it takes to give all the love inside you away."

"You're the smartest person I've ever known, Wren. And the most beautiful." He rested his forehead on hers and peered into her eyes for a few heartbeats before sitting up. "Kason Cox would be a fool not to come for you full force."

His gaze flicked away from hers as they both appeared to imagine what that might feel like if he came for Jordan instead. He knew they were on the same wavelength when she said, "You know, I won't be mad if you want to ask him out yourself."

Jordan laughed at that. "No, I'm not trying to poach the guy you're interested in."

Wren grew quiet. He realized the enchanted interlude they'd shared was officially over. Because reality was still there waiting for them and things were too complicated to navigate easily.

He got to his feet and searched for his keys until he spotted them on the floor near the door where he must have dropped them while they kissed. He took a step closer to them and then another.

"Hey, Jordan," Wren called drowsily from the couch. Her satisfied stretch did things to his pride that he hadn't felt in ages. Too bad it was the last time he'd ever experience it with her. She was hoping to move on with someone else and he wasn't going to ruin her chances because he was selfish. They'd already pushed the limits dangerously today.

"Yeah?"

"This time, will you pick me up some milk from the store?" She was calling him on his past bullshit while also telling him she felt it too. There was something missing between them, something that was still keeping them apart, and would always.

Without Johnny, they were disconnected. Broken. She'd be better off starting fresh.

Or...maybe he'd have to give Kason Cox a call and see if the guy would be willing to do a little experimenting next time he was in town.

Jordan's cock stirred in his pants at that thought. He had to go before he made things worse for Wren. So he snatched his keys off the floor and eyed the door as he said, "It might be expired by the time I get back."

Wren nodded. She was strong enough to handle the truth. He should have at least given her that courtesy the last time he'd left her.

So he did it then. "Goodbye, Wren."

"I hope you find what you're looking for."

"Same." With that, he walked out again.

15

———

Kason rushed off the stage at the end of his encore. He could honestly say it was the first time he could ever remember wishing he was doing something other than performing during a concert.

"Are you okay?" Van asked him as he practically sprinted to his dressing room. Kyra followed instead of going to her own, obviously also concerned.

"I'm fine, guys. I promise." He grinned as he turned to his two best friends. "I'm hurrying because I sort of have a date tonight."

Kyra whipped her head toward Van, who shrugged. Then she turned back to Kason. "Wait. The girl from last night? The tall, fancy-looking blonde?"

"Yep." He veered toward the shower, unwilling to delay his call any longer than necessary.

"Wren drove all the way out here to see you?" Van shouted over the noise of the spray as Kason stripped behind the door he partially closed out of respect for Kyra.

Damn. He should have suggested that. Or sent her a plane ticket.

He had to get better at this whole long-distance seduction thing. It was new and fun for him.

"Nope. But I told her I'd call her as soon as I get back to the bus." He stepped into the frigid water, hoping it would be enough to keep his erection at bay until he could get in touch with Wren and maybe convince her into talking dirty to him before bed. She seemed uninhibited and passionate. Her kiss the night before had proved she wasn't against taking things straight to sexytown.

Thank god, because he'd been dreaming of her since the first moment he'd walked into Hot Rides and spotted her behind the counter. He'd been hard for her since she'd revealed her inner strength and cut him down when he deserved it.

"You're this amped up over a conversation?" Kyra sounded like she was about to declare him a liar complete with fiery pants, if he'd been wearing any. Although it might have been hard to believe given his past proclivities for groupie sex, tonight it was true. He hoped he could spend more than ten minutes talking to the woman who'd completely captivated him.

Hours wouldn't be long enough, really.

Kason wanted to know everything about her, and—okay, to be totally honest—about her ex-boyfriends and their relationship, too. It fascinated him that the stoic, hardass man who'd come to a country rock concert in a fucking suit and tie would be willing to share his lover with another man.

And that he'd hoped to share even more than that with his lover's other boyfriend.

That poor bastard. Kason should have been pissed that Jordan had interrupted the night before, but he couldn't help feeling sorry for the guy. No wonder he'd caught Kason's eye during "Secret Love." The man had practically lived the song.

Kason aimed the shower head so that the icy streams poured directly onto his cock, which was not settling down, and wouldn't as long as he kept thinking about Wren and her harem of guys. Oh, maybe he could join their ranks.

Not. Helping.

He lathered his hair and washed himself as efficiently as possible. In less than five minutes he was toweling off. Kyra was hanging out with Van. They were speaking quietly together, making Kason wonder if maybe they might be edging closer to finally realizing what he'd known for months...

They were totally into each other.

He'd have to talk to Van about that later. Make sure his friend knew he didn't consider it any sort of unprofessional behavior if his bodyguard wanted to get naked with his drummer. As far as he was concerned, everyone deserved to be happy. The people he surrounded himself with should never be limited by their jobs when it came to who they could love.

Especially since he was. Kason didn't want anyone else to deal with that kind of drama and the negative impact it could have on a person's life.

Kyra averted her eyes as he got dressed, so he stepped to the side, strategically using a sofa to obscure his body from the waist down as he pulled on fresh clothes.

When he was decent, she came over to him, still dripping sweat from her massive workout. She was like a female Animal when she played. He held her at arm's length when she attempted to hug him, instead settling for patting his shoulder with a laugh. "I'm excited for you, Kason. Maybe you're actually growing up. Don't say anything stupid to scare her away, okay?"

"I'm going to try my best." He winced. "It's sort of in my nature to say dumb shit. I have no filter, you know?" He swallowed hard.

"I think that's a great quality and so will Wren. She seems like a no-nonsense kind of woman. I like her." Kyra smiled. "She held her own last night and left with her head high, even if she was in a panic."

His stomach dropped at that. "You think I scared her off?"

Van took Kason's side. "No way. Her ex might have, though."

"You two are blind idiots if you didn't see that she was trying something beyond her comfort zone by coming to the after party. She was willing to go out of her way for you, Kason. You should remember that and do the same for her." Kyra was talking to Kason, but somehow she was looking at Van, who was suddenly studying the floor extra-intently.

What the hell was happening around there? Kason vowed to find out later before two of his closest friends could hurt each other.

"I'm going to do my best." Kason thought about how Van and Kyra had picked him up at his lowest. He didn't have anything to hide from them—except that one massive secret love—so he said, "Thank you both for getting me to a place where talking to a woman like Wren is possible. Before, I wouldn't have been worth anything in a relationship that lasted longer than an orgasm or two. I'm hoping, maybe, things might be different now."

"I'm proud of you." The quiver in Kyra's tone weakened the resistance in Kason's elbows until he hugged her, perspiration and all.

Over her shoulder, Kason saw Van smiling at the two of them. He said, "I'm glad that you're trying something new. Just remember that if it doesn't work out this time, that doesn't mean it might not next time. You gotta keep trying."

Only because he was so close to Kyra did Kason hear her snort and say, "Take your own advice, asshole," under her breath.

Kason whispered in her ear, "Everything okay?"

She looked up at him and nodded, but her accompanying smile was weak. "Yeah. Go call your girl."

"She's not mine...yet." He winked, then waved before he turned to Van. "You have a back way out tonight?"

"Of course." The man went into business mode. There was no sense in bringing up Kyra then because Van wouldn't respond. He was all bodyguard and no friend as he shielded Kason. Together, they cut through the mob of fans outside the venue, milling around near Kason's bus.

When Van unlocked the door and ushered Kason inside, he said, "I'll wait here and make sure you're not disturbed."

"You don't have to stay outside." Kason laughed. "Wren's too far away for you to walk in on much except me and my hand in action."

Living on a tour bus meant that they'd both had that experience on accident with each other as well as their fellow band members from time to time. It also meant they'd learned to deal with a lack of privacy and greater than normal involvement in each other's lives, which didn't bother Kason in the least.

Could that mean he'd be better suited to hooking up with more than one person at a time than most people? Yeah, probably. The more he thought about it, and he honestly couldn't stop thinking about it now that the idea had come into his head, the more he realized that this could be what he'd really craved all along.

People who understood and embraced every part of himself because they yearned for the same thing.

"From here I can keep an eye on Kyra, the rest of the band, and the crew as they make the trek over later." Van shifted from foot to foot. Sure, they had additional personnel around, but Van was the best of the best and also had managerial duties over the rest of the security team.

Kason should have thought about how bailing impacted everyone else.

"Van, go. I'll lock up tight here and I promise I won't leave until you're back, okay?" Kason pointed toward the backstage area.

"You swear, you're not going to vanish for any sort of midnight runs without calling me first?" Van asked.

A year ago this would never have flown. Tonight was entirely different. "Look, I know there were times I needed you to keep me from doing stupid shit. This isn't one of them. I'm fine. I'll be here talking on the phone with a woman like the teenager I've apparently regressed to. Go keep an eye on Kyra before you lose your mind."

There, he'd said it.

Van didn't contradict him or pretend like he was equally concerned with guarding any other bodies either. "Thanks."

He stood and waited for Kason to secure the bus. Only then did he jog back to the arena's side-door in search of one curvy blonde instrumentalist. *Interesting.*

But not remarkable enough to delay Kason any further. He already had his phone out of his pocket and his finger hovering over Wren's name in his contacts before he'd reached his bedroom at the back of the bus.

16

By the time Wren's cell proclaimed it was eleven o'clock, she'd had enough time to convince herself that the conversation she'd been waiting the entire day to have would last three seconds. Max. She'd say hi, blurt out that she'd fooled around with Jordan, and Kason would hang up.

Game over.

She couldn't pace properly in her tiny home, so she went outside where she could at least rock herself in the porch swing as she counted the stars.

When her phone vibrated in her pocket, she nearly launched herself into the middle of Orion's Belt. Wren jumped up and jammed her hand in her pants to retrieve the device before it set her off.

Despite her earlier run in with Jordan, she was incredibly aroused. Because of the anticipation of talking to Kason or because she got off on living on the edge, she wasn't sure. It felt exhilarating and kind of fucked up to be caught in the middle of two men again.

Wren darted inside and shut the door. She wasn't

ready for the rest of the Hot Rides to know precisely how depraved she was if Jordan hadn't already spilled the beans. She'd been surprised that he'd gone over to Devra, Trevon, and Quinn's place after leaving her, but it wasn't her business to wonder about what he was up to.

Her phone buzzed again, startling her from her chaotic thoughts. She stabbed the icon to connect the call, then said, "Did you break a leg?"

Kason laughed. "Fortunately not. I have fallen off the stage once or twice but...uh...that's a story for another time. Or you could just look it up on the internet if you want to read about my fuck ups before we go any further."

Huh. Wren wanted to ask him more about that and why he'd hesitated, only...not now. Especially not when she had to disclose some sordid shit of her own. "I'll wait until you feel comfortable enough to tell me about it yourself, thanks."

He chuckled then said, "I've never met a woman like you before."

"I'm weird. I know." In fact, she'd been told she was unusual so often in her life it might have bothered her except... "The worst thing someone could ever call me is ordinary. Normal. I'm not and I'm mostly okay with that now, though I wasn't always."

"I respect that, and I'm sort of jealous." He sighed. "When you're in the public eye, you have to live up to other people's expectations of what you should be, even if that's not who you really are. It's my least favorite thing about my career."

"I know it's not the same exactly, but I went through that crap with my parents."

"They didn't dream of a beautiful rebel for a daughter? No offense, but I think they might not be the smartest people around. If I had a daughter, I'd want her to be just like you—able to take care of herself and passionate about the things that are important in her life."

Wren wasn't sure if it was the stuff he was saying or the way the rasp in his voice lent it more conviction, but she half fell in love with him right then. "Damn, Kason. You sound so good. Has anyone ever told you that before?"

He outright laughed, lifting her spirits too.

She hadn't meant to flirt before getting the hard stuff out of the way, it just came naturally with him. And now she didn't know how to bridge the gap from the warm, affectionate place they were at to the difficult discussion he didn't even know they had to have.

Fortunately, he was empathetic and kind. Sensitive. And he gave her the perfect opening.

"So, how'd your day go?" he asked, completely changing the topic. Sadly, not to one that was any less treacherous for either of them.

"Unexpectedly." Wren tapped her fingers on the phone furiously. She might have ruined her chances with Kason before they'd even gotten started.

"How so?"

"Well, first we got to text this morning and you weren't put off by my...complications." She took a deep breath and then laid it out honestly and directly. "Then Jordan came by to apologize. And he did a really good job of it."

"You forgave him for more than just last night?" Kason understood immediately.

"Yeah. And we fooled around some. Kissing and... stuff. Not *sex* sex, but we both enjoyed ourselves. I'd say I'm sorry, but I'm not exactly. I understand if you change your mind about getting to know me better because of it. I'll be disappointed but I'd get it."

Kason blew out a ragged breath. Was he pissed?

Wren could hardly breathe as she anticipated his reaction.

"Hey, don't stress, okay? You've known the guy for more than five years and had a meaningful relationship with him. I'm just some schmuck you've talked to a few times and kissed once. Do what you think is right, Wren. I won't hold it against you. If things work out between us and we get more serious we can draw some boundaries then, but we certainly didn't have any this morning."

Could Kason be any more perfect, really?

She was quick to reassure him. "It was a one-time thing, I swear. He made it clear he's not planning on coming back again. And even if he did, I think I gained some closure today. Without Johnny, we don't work right. Neither of us are gentle or especially tactful. I think we needed Johnny's emotional glue. He understood us both and sort of...interpreted. He helped each of us understand what the other needed and how to coexist peacefully."

"That makes a lot of sense, actually." Kason sounded interested instead of offended. Her hopes rose as he paid attention to what she was trying to explain about herself. "Tell me more. What happened exactly?"

"Are you asking because you're wondering what lines we crossed?" Wren double-checked.

"Uh, no. I'm asking because I want to picture it. Or is that too perverted for you?" Kason seemed genuinely worried that she might judge him after he'd been extremely compassionate. What kind of friends did he have if that was his reflex reaction?

Who was making him feel like he wasn't enough?

Not her, that was for damn sure.

"Not at all. If you really want to know, it was hot and

desperate. I think it shocked him as much as me. But that's how it's always been between us. If you don't already think I'm a slut for what I've told you—"

"Don't say shit like that, Wren. I think you follow your heart. Who needs to think a long time about something when it feels right?"

"Yes, exactly. The day I met Johnny and Jordan it wasn't right. It was *perfect*. I knew immediately. Within a few hours, we were making out. I ended up spending the entire weekend at their place on Lake Logan. We fucked and laughed and skinny-dipped and drank beers on a blanket under the moon. It was magical. We were never apart again, until..."

"Damn, Wren. I'm sorry," Kason whispered as if it upset him as much as her.

"Anyway..." She took a deep breath. "The night Jordan came to tell me about Johnny, we slept together. This was the first time I've been alone with him since. It just happens. I mean, it has. But I'll be sure it doesn't anymore if you decide you want more from me than to talk on the phone. Not that I think he and I will be spending any time together. Or that I'm assuming you're interested in dating me. Or...damn, I'm making this worse, right?"

"Calm down, Wren." He laughed quietly. "I'm not worried about your history or what went down between you and Jordan. I can't begin to understand what the two of you share. You told me about it right away. That's all I'm asking. If something happens, let me know. I don't own you. Hell, I'm pretty sure I'm not even your boyfriend. I'm just some guy who'd like to be more to you than I am today, who lives an unstable life and can only offer you phone calls and lonely nights in between visits. I wouldn't take me seriously either if I were you."

There it was again. That vein of insecurity. She wanted to punch whoever had made Kason think of himself as unworthy. If nothing else came of their acquaintance, Wren would settle for helping him see himself like she did. "I hate to break it to you, but I think you're being as dense as you said my parents were. You're an incredible guy. I'm so glad you came into Hot Rides that day. Thank you for being so patient with me while I figure things out."

"What if I call back every night so we can keep learning about each other and see if you might like me to become more than some singer you ran into a few times?"

"It's not you I'm unsure of, Kason. It's myself." Wren could only think of one way to make him understand completely and that was to give him exactly what he'd asked for. "Do you still want to hear details about what Jordan and I did today and how it made me feel?"

"Yes." He practically panted the response. "Would you be offended if my hands end up wandering while you tell me about it?"

She liked that he'd asked even though he already told her he got off on imagining her having sex, even if it was with another guy. It was the least she could do to let some of her pleasure rub off on him. Literally.

"No, I'd like that. I want to hear what it does to you when I tell you about how I am. If it turns you on, I think it'll make me feel less guilty."

"I already told you that's not necessary." His response was somewhat muffled.

"What are you doing now?" she asked.

"Getting undressed."

Wren had to swallow a whimper. She could imagine his toned and muscular, though not bulky, body. His performances had given him an incredible physique. It was highlighted by bright tattoos she wished she could trace with her tongue. "Mind if I do that too?"

"Not at all." He groaned.

Wren turned out the lights so she wouldn't give her neighbors an unintentional show. She climbed up the bookcase-ladder, then whipped her shirt over her head and wriggled out of her jeggings. When she settled into the comfy mattress and pulled the covers over herself, she hummed.

"Are you a pajamas kind of girl?" Kason asked.

"Nah. I love the way the sheets feel, cool and soft, on my skin at night."

"Me too," he admitted. "Plus I like having easy access in case I wake up in the middle of the night and decide to help myself get back to sleep."

"By making love to whatever woman is sharing your bed?" Wren snuffed out a flicker of jealousy. She had no right to that emotion, especially not when he was being so open-minded about her and Jordan.

"That's not a thing." Kason explained, "Most of the time I'm here on the tour bus. We all agreed early on it's best if we keep things simple. No sex on the bus. I guess I just carried that over to when I'm at my house in between tours or when we're recording. I live up on a mountain with a couple hundred acres of woods all around. There's nobody but me and my music."

"That sounds lonely."

"It can be. So help me forget about it by telling me what happened today."

Wren grinned. "You're not joking, are you? You're really into this."

"Do you want me to send a dick pic so you can have proof of how much?"

"No," she replied instinctively. Before amending her response. "Actually, yes, I do. I'm just embarrassed to admit it."

"Hang on." He disappeared for a moment, a rustling in the background taking the place of his seductive voice.

Then her phone buzzed against her ear, startling her. She looked at the screen and... "Oh. My."

Kason laughed. "Thanks, I think."

Not to be outdone, Wren composed a decently flattering picture of herself from her collarbones to her navel and fired it off to him before she could think better of it.

"Damn, Wren. I wasn't expecting you to do that. But I love that you did. I wish I was there to suck on your hard nipples. Is that what Jordan did?"

Jordan was the furthest thing from Wren's mind right then. Okay, not really, he was always there though he was far, far away at the moment. She hesitated. "Uh..."

"Because I'm stroking myself now, Wren, imagining how damn beautiful you'd look if he was doing that to you."

She moaned. "Sorry to disappoint you. We didn't even take our clothes off. I've gone further with you tonight than I did with him earlier."

Kason groaned at that. She could hear the slick glide of his palm over his flesh if she strained.

So she gave him what he'd asked for. "He brought me flowers. And told me he was sorry for screwing things up between you and me last night. For interrupting us..."

"Not going to lie. I wish he hadn't done that." Kason's voice was hoarse now. "I would have taken you to my dressing room and laid you back on the couch so I could have kissed my way up your legs until I ended up somewhere even more fun than your mouth."

Son of a bitch!

Wren put Kason on speakerphone, dropped the cell to her pillow, then put her hand over her mound, wishing she'd gotten to feel his talented tongue there. Her other hand flew to her chest, kneading her breasts and squeezing her nipples like he'd said he would like to do.

"I would have let you." She moaned softly as she began to finger herself, paying special attention to her clit. "It's been so long. Something about you calls to me. You're the first guy I've wanted in forever. Except Jordan."

"Tell me more. Hurry, Wren. I'm not going to last. I don't usually have dry spells, but I've never been with someone who affected me like you do. You're driving me out of my mind. I want you so bad." He got her with that one.

Jordan had always had the power to walk away from her when she wouldn't have been able to do the same. To hear that Kason would like to come closer, not leave, well...that was heady shit.

"He looked so lost. Something he said about wanting things he couldn't have, about your song 'Secret Love' and how hearing it live—seeing you perform it—touched him. It was genuine and sad and...I couldn't not comfort him."

Kason was breathing hard now. "That's...good, Wren. Keep going."

She sped up the motions of her hands as she retold the rest, remembering how incredible it had felt. And how much better it was now to share it with Kason. "We made out and before I knew it, his hands were on my ass. He picked me up and took me to the couch."

A grunt came from the other end of the phone. "I bet you looked amazing. On fire."

"I don't know. I didn't stop to think about it. I just needed to feel his skin. I put my hands under his shirt and touched him everywhere I could reach. I think I might have gotten carried away and maybe scratched him once or twice."

"Damn. I bet that felt so good. Your nails digging in and holding him tight to you." Kason cursed. "I'm getting close, Wren."

"Me too." She moaned. "That's how it was with Jordan too. No finesse. No drawing things out. We ground together. I could feel his hard cock rubbing over my pussy as we kissed."

"Fuck. Yes. I love it when you talk dirty. If I had been there, I wouldn't have let you two get away with that. I would have stripped you down and made you go slow. To enjoy what you can do to each other fully."

Where the hell had that come from? Wren wasn't sure, but it made her arch and tense. Fantasizing about being with them both at the same time was going to make story time come to an abrupt end if she wasn't careful.

"It was enough, combined with the weight of him on me and then watching him come when it got to be too much. As he lost it and shot in his pants, he bit my shoulder." Wren could hardly talk, hardly breathe now, and she knew she was going to climax again at the memory.

"Yes. I could see the mark he left. He claimed you." Kason groaned. "That's so fucking hot. Damn. I want to be someone's like that."

Wren was shocked that was the thing that tipped

Kason over the edge into orgasm. He shouted her name and groaned, long and hard.

She imagined his hand flying over his long, thick cock as he made a mess of his washboard abs. It was enough to have her joining him.

Wren moaned and slid her fingers deep as her muscles hugged them tight. "Kason! Kason! I wish you were here."

"Me too, Wren." He was still breathing hard when he said quietly, "I'm tired of sleeping alone."

"So am I," she whispered as her body kept quivering, clenching once more at the thought of curling up next to Kason.

They took a minute or two to catch their breath. Each content to bask in the afterglow of whatever the hell that was they'd done together.

"Damn. That was intense," he huffed.

"My run-in with Jordan or...you know...this?"

"Both." He groaned. "Damn, Wren. I didn't think I could come that hard only from talking to someone on the phone."

"Me either, but I liked it."

"Same here, and I bet it was even better in person. I'm envious. I've never had that kind of connection with someone else. I admire your devotion and how you gave yourself to those guys without reservation. That was brave. It makes me think more of you, not less, that you haven't been able to get past the kind of love you once had."

"I'm over it."

She could hear his wry smile in the puff of exhalation he made. "Don't start lying now, Wren. If you can be honest with me, you should give yourself the same courtesy."

She groaned, except this time not in pleasure.

"Have you been with anyone else since Jordan and Johnny?" he asked, though they both already knew the answer. "Even something simple like a date?"

"Not until I dressed up, came to the concert, and kissed you."

"Thank you for letting me in. I'll treasure that memory even more now." Kason tried to stifle a yawn. "I'm hoping to do that some more, too, you know. Maybe when I see you at the Hot Rods party."

"About that..." Wren winced.

"Let me guess, Jordan will be there?" He chuckled.

"Yeah. Sorry. He's friends with my boss, Quinn. Jordan helped them out earlier this year when his husband's wife was maliciously threatened with deportation. It's a long story, but Jordan really did come through for them. I think it meant something to Jordan to save them when he couldn't save us, you know?"

"Hold up." Kason seemed to rouse a bit. "Is my brain still stuck in perv mode or did you say...?"

"Oh. Yep." Wren grinned. "Quinn, Trevon, and Devra are a threesome too. Maybe tomorrow night I'll tell you about the Hot Rides. If you think we're fancy with our ménages over here, you haven't heard anything yet."

"You're serious? You're not the only one sharing two guys?"

"The Hot Rods would be the first to brag that they do a lot more than that. They're into group stuff. Quinn, Trevon, and Devra aren't as far as I know. But they're more equal than me, Jordan, and Johnny were."

"You mean the guys—"

"Yeah. Quinn and Trevon are lovers. Honestly, they're soul mates. They were meant to be together with Devra."

"Wow. Okay. I'm definitely going to need you to fill me in. You're opening my eyes to a lot of possibilities."

"Are they ones you're interested in for the sake of curiosity or because they appeal to you for yourself?" she wondered.

"Honestly, Wren, what I want doesn't really matter. Like I said, I don't have as much freedom as I wish sometimes. Not when the whole world is watching my every move." Kason cleared his throat as if reality stuck in his craw.

She frowned at her phone. Was he letting himself be imprisoned by his career? Fame, wealth, and the adulation of millions would be hard to sacrifice. She would do it in an instant for love. "I'm sorry, Kason."

"Don't be. I still want to hear all about you and your friends. I'll live vicariously through you. Tomorrow night. Same time?" he asked.

"Absolutely."

For a few minutes, neither of them said anything. Wren listened to the reassuring pattern of Kason's slow, deep breathing. It had been so long since she'd been able to be still and know her partner was equally sated and at peace.

It was a lovely sensation, one she'd missed.

"Still there?" he asked blearily.

"I'm sleepy, but I don't want to hang up." Wren burrowed into her pillow.

"What if I sing you a lullaby?" he asked.

"Would you? Really?" She tried not to perk up at that offer. She already knew it would be legendary.

Kason didn't bother to respond. Instead, he started crooning "Secret Love." Of course. Wren closed her eyes as the familiar melody washed over her. It was the first time she really let the lyrics sink in, or maybe dozing off allowed them to percolate through her subconscious.

And though she didn't rouse enough to question Kason about it then, his song inspired her dreams. Of him. Of them. Of her and Jordan. And what it might be like if she could convince the guys to love her—and each other.

It was the best night's sleep she'd had since before Johnny died.

Somewhere, he was smiling down at them.

17

It had been a terrible idea to come to Trevon's birthday party. Jordan couldn't say that was a shock. He had known it was dumb before he did it. Yet he hadn't been able to stop himself from showing up anyway.

He'd been invited because Quinn and Trevon had become his unlikely friends.

He'd come because they were excited to show him the progress they'd been making on his motorcycle and—of course—because he knew Wren would be there too.

With built-in chaperones surrounding them, maybe he could try to be civil this time and show her that they could move past what they'd been into something they could agree was healthy for the future.

Except once he was there, all he could do was watch her shooting the shit with the Hot Rods and helping Devra serve the food—which was laid out on folding tables covered in brightly colored paper tablecloths, in the field near the stream that ran behind Hot Rides—and pretend like he didn't see her glancing toward the driveway every five seconds.

Was she thinking of escaping because he was there or was she hoping to see someone else driving down it?

The next time Wren passed nearby, Jordan reached out and took a light hold of her elbow to steer her to a stop. He leaned in to murmur in her ear, "Am I making this weird for you? I can leave if..."

He never finished that thought because right then someone came over the crest of the hill, jogging from the direction of the Hot Rides parking lot, with another dude and a woman trailing a little way behind.

Wren stepped away from Jordan so quickly she might have fallen if she wasn't so damn athletic and lithe. She stared at the ground for a full three seconds before raising her gaze to the newcomer's.

Kason Cox.

Of course.

Jordan had been an idiot to assume he had anything to do with her anxiety. Wren had never been anything other than self-assured around Jordan. He didn't have the ability to impact her like Kason obviously did.

The guy slowed as his gaze flicked from Wren to Jordan then back. By the time he was within a few feet, his stride had become an amble. "Sorry I'm late. Traffic was terrible."

"That didn't keep him from pulling all kinds of stunts to get here before the party was over, though," a big, solid guy grumbled from behind Kason. Jordan remembered seeing the bodyguard the night of the concert, before he'd shown himself out. "If you're not careful, you're going to get yourself killed one of these days."

The curvy blonde with the bodyguard seemed to agree. "Damn, Kason. You almost lost us back there. No wonder

Van didn't want you to take one of your motorcycles. It would serve you right if he made you ride with him on the way home and let me transport your bike instead."

From the refreshment table closest to them, Ollie's head turned at that. "You ride?"

"Yeah." The woman crossed her arms. "Why wouldn't I?"

"That wasn't skepticism. That was me wondering if one of these guys would lend me his motorcycle so I could ask you out for a drive later. Or maybe you'll let me ride on the back of yours sometime?" He came closer, juggling his snacks so he could empty a hand and stick it out to her. "I'm Ollie."

The woman shot a look at Van that Jordan couldn't decipher, then beamed as she clasped Ollie's hand and shook. "Nice to meet you. I'm Kyra. Kason's drummer."

"You play the drums *and* ride motorcycles? I think I'm in love." Ollie grinned as he popped a cube of cheese into his mouth.

"Ollie falls in love with every woman he meets." Wren laughed as she took in her friend's antics.

"Nah, only the super-hot ones like you and Kyra." Ollie raised his brows at her.

Which was probably when she realized she was standing there between Jordan and Kason, looking guilty as fuck even though nothing inappropriate had been going on.

"Hey Kyra, want to see my hedgehog, Mr. Prickles?" Ollie asked.

She hesitated. "That's not some pervy euphemism is it?"

Wren laughed and vouched for her garagemate. "No.

Ollie's a good guy, and he really does have the cutest pet ever."

"Then, hell yes I do." Kyra held out her arm and Ollie put his through it. They were cracking up about something before they were even halfway up the hill.

Van was staring at them as they retreated.

"I'm fine if you want to go too," Kason said quietly to his friend. "No one's going to bug us here."

Van shook his head, though he wandered toward the snacks as if they were some sort of consolation prize. To be fair, the food was incredible.

"Hi," Wren said to Kason with a smile. "I'm glad you made it, though I don't like hearing you were reckless just to get here."

"You're worth the risk." Kason grinned at Wren.

She reached for Kason, smothering him in one of her famous hugs. She was a great hugger. She put her whole body into it, nuzzling Kason's collarbone as she rubbed his back.

Jordan had to turn around so he wouldn't get hard seeing her in another man's arms.

It hurt too much to do that.

Before they could get carried away, someone—Sally, Jordan thought—whistled loud enough to get the attention of every person in attendance plus the woodland creatures in a two-mile radius. Then she shouted, "Before we bring out the cake, Amber has something she wants to say, so pay attention!"

Gavyn, the owner of Hot Rides and Amber's husband, whipped his head around to find his wife. She was standing near the front of the gathering and gave everyone a jaunty finger wave. Gavyn joined her there.

With everyone's attention on them, she was clearly heard by everyone at the party.

"I know it's Trevon's birthday." Amber met her husband's bewildered stare. The smile she gave him was so dazzling that Gavyn seemed temporarily stunned, content to look at it and be near her. "But he said he wouldn't mind if I gave you a present since our friends and family are here with us today."

Gavyn canted his head and asked, "Me?"

"Oh my God," Wren whispered. Whether she thought about what she was doing or acted on instinct, she threw a hand out to each side, clasping Jordan's wrist in one of her hands and Kason's in the other. "Is she..."

Amber handed Gavyn the glossy black gift bag dangling from one of her fingers. "Go ahead, open it."

Gavyn made quick work of the tissue paper. And when he withdrew a onesie from inside it, the baby garment looked like doll's clothing in his huge hand. He stared at it, then looked at Amber, then stared at the onesie again as if he'd seen it wrong, inspiring most of the crowd gathered to crack up.

"A baby?" he asked Amber, with wide eyes, as if afraid to believe it could really be true. "We're having a baby?"

Jordan couldn't imagine what that feeling might be like, but the iron bracelet of Wren's fingers around his wrist told him plainly that she definitely could. He hadn't realized that was another dream he might have trampled on when he'd left her.

He'd made so many fucking mistakes.

Amber, completely unable to speak further, nodded and threw herself at her husband, who caught her and spun her around while laughing and crying. After he set her down carefully, he showed the onesie to the gathering.

A tricycle with flames coming out the back had been imprinted on the garment.

Nola and Ms. Brown—Amber's sister and mother—rushed the woman while Tom, Quinn, Trevon, and too many other people to keep track of swarmed Gavyn. There was a lot of back slapping and cheering plus excited conversation.

From where they were playing on the sidelines, one of the bigger kids that belonged to the Hot Rods and Powertools—he thought he'd heard Joe call him Nathan—shouted, "Uncle Gavyn, what's going on?"

The man blinked and grinned as he said, "Looks like you're going to have another friend to play with."

Ambrose, Nola and Kaige's daughter, asked, "Could you make sure it's a girl this time?"

Everyone cracked up at that, including Holden, who shook his head at his wife, Sabra. "I guess she's not impressed with our sons, huh?"

"That's okay, Swinger. I am." She kissed her husband's cheek as she watched their twins playing with a toy sailboat in the stream.

"I have no idea how I'm going to remember who's who around here," Kason said under his breath with a low whistle.

Jordan could relate. It had taken him a while to get to know everyone. Now that he had, he felt like he had a family again for the first time since his mother had passed away of a heart attack less than a year after his father had lost his battle with brain cancer.

After that, he'd kept to himself until he'd been assigned Johnny as a partner.

And when he'd lost his best friend, too, well... That had been all he could stand. Maybe that was part of why he'd walked away from Wren. He couldn't bear the thought of loving her more each day only for her to be taken away, so he'd cut his losses on his own terms.

Except he hadn't really, because here he was, standing right next to her thinking about how gorgeous she was and how sweet she smelled, like her signature lilies.

That's about when Wren realized she was clutching Kason...and Jordan. She blushed furiously and dropped both of their hands. "Sorry. I got carried away."

"I like it when you do that." Kason winked at her.

Jordan wondered if Kason could handle the intricacies of Wren's life. He'd come into this thing knowing about her past and how it was still something she carried within her, assuming she had really told Kason about what they'd done a few weeks ago.

If Kason wanted her, and it was clear to Jordan that he did by the way the man was staring at her like he wanted to gobble her up more than he wanted to devour a slice of birthday cake, then Kason had to accept all of her.

Including the part that loved Jordan, because after the way she'd reacted to him with compassion and kindness that afternoon in her cottage, Jordan was convinced that although he didn't deserve those gifts, she did.

Caught between them, Wren looked at Kason, then Jordan. She shook her head and said, "Excuse me a minute. I want to say congratulations."

Maybe she also needed a breather. Jordan hung back, which meant he was uncomfortably close to Kason. Honestly, that probably would work out fine. He had some things to say to the other man.

"Would you mind stepping inside the garage with me for a minute?" he asked Kason.

The guy turned toward where Van had stuck up a

conversation with Alanso. When Jordan focused on them, he realized they were speaking in rapid-fire Spanish in between cracking up about whatever they were discussing. It had taken no time for Kason and his friends to embed themselves in the Hot Rods and Hot Rides family.

Jordan tried not to be disgruntled about that.

"Hey, Van, I'll be right back," Kason called then turned toward the garage.

The bodyguard shot Jordan a look that dared him to try anything stupid. No need for that. Jordan just wanted to talk. To make sure Kason understood how special Wren was and that he'd take care of her, including nurturing her unique desires.

"I bet there's good fishing around here, huh?" Kason asked as he studied the stream glittering in the fall afternoon light.

"Yeah. Even better up at Lake Logan, about ten miles outside of town." At least they had something safe to talk about. He wasn't surprised they had more than their infatuation with Wren in common. If he'd met Kason under other circumstances, they might have been friends.

Good friends.

"Wren told me you have a cabin up there. Get out to it much?" Kason wondered as they neared Hot Rides.

"Staying there right now. I'm about halfway through a vacation from work." Jordan cleared his throat, not really wanting to rehash that. Every day he spent away from the office, he dreaded going back more. And still he hadn't figured out what else to do.

"I plan to see what's biting myself next weekend. I'm coming back for a test of the bike Hot Rides are building for me." Kason grinned. "Picturing Wren working on the damn thing is definitely going to make it my favorite in my collection."

Jordan snorted. "I don't have a collection or even a single motorcycle yet, but they're designing one for me too. Have to say it's a perk having Wren doing the welding. You know it will be solid."

"You ever see her work?" Kason asked. "I'm dying to watch her at it. Sparks, electricity, and molten metal. Seems perfect for her."

They stepped into the building via a side door that led into the stock room. Shelving units lined the walls and made narrow corridors of black metal. Jordan turned and leaned up against one as the door shut with a clang behind them. "It is. She's tough and capable and likes to toy with dangerous things."

"Look, it's obvious that you still love her." Kason put his hand on Jordan's shoulder. While Kason's touch should have made him recoil, he leaned into the contact instead. "I'm not trying to take her away from you or disrespect the history you two share. I'm interested in her, though. Seriously. And I hope you're okay with me pursuing her given that you chose to let her go."

"I didn't choose shit," Jordan snapped, trying not to be offended. Except he was. "I didn't ask for my best friend to get killed. It should have been me that day. Only it wasn't. After that, how could I have acted like everything was fine knowing what I took from her?"

"Sounds to me like you did a hell of a lot more damage when you walked away and left her to grieve on her own." Kason didn't say it unkindly, but his words still stung. No, they stabbed Jordan right in the heart.

In pain, he lashed out. "What the hell are you doing giving me shit about leaving the door open for you? Can't you see how into you Wren is? Are you toying with her or are you stupid?" Jordan snarled. "I don't want her to get hurt."

"You're such a hypocrite." Kason's grip turned decidedly less friendly. He rattled Jordan, banging his shoulder against the rack behind him. "You're the one who crushed an amazing woman because you were struggling with your love for another man."

"Did Wren tell you that?" Jordan's hand flashed out and crumpled Kason's collar in his fist. They were locked together.

"She didn't have to. It was obvious the night of the concert. I could see it written on your face when I starting singing 'Secret Love.' Is that why things fell apart once he'd died? Because you knew that if you stayed with her and her alone, you'd never experience loving a man like you so desperately wanted?"

"Don't talk about things you can't understand."

"How do you know I can't?" Kason asked, his tone so strangled that Jordan immediately realized he hadn't imagined the way Kason had looked at him in return the night Kason sang "Secret Love" in his direction.

"You saying we have more in common than fishing, motorcycles, and being attracted to Wren?" Jordan's training kicked in. The undercover agent in him went on high alert.

Kason wasn't straight. He was bisexual and wrestling with it, too. *Fuck.* That was irresistible to Jordan. No one should ever feel like the love they had to give was unwanted.

Instead of using his grip on Kason's collar to hold him still while he clocked the guy, he used it to drag him closer instead. He growled, "Tell me if I'm reading this wrong."

Kason blinked, but didn't say a word.

So Jordan crushed his mouth over the other guy's. Not because he was angry or trying to subjugate him, but because he had waited years for the chance to share this with someone.

Who better than another guy who'd grappled with this part of himself, attempting futilely to suppress it?

Well, maybe someone his ex-girlfriend wasn't into would have been ideal. If every single one of his brain cells hadn't been overwhelmed with the feel of Kason—so different than the women he'd been with—and the possibility that his deepest desires might finally be fulfilled, Jordan probably would have thought about Wren and the impact fooling around with Kason could have on her for more than a millisecond.

He pressed his chest to Kason's, walking forward as he nudged the other guy back.

And when Kason's shoulders hit the shelving unit on the opposite side of the aisle, he leaned in, pinning the man with his hands at Kason's wrists, and his knee, which parted Kason's legs. The position allowed their pelvises to collide, even if they were slightly off center.

Kason's erection prodded Jordan's hip, making him sure the other guy was as into this as he was. So he rocked against the singer, letting him sense Jordan's own arousal as clearly.

"You feel what you do to me?" he growled against Kason's lips.

Kason nodded, threatening to unseal their mouths. So Jordan bit his lower lip, then sucked on it to ease the sting. He had no idea where this person had come from, similar to the in-charge man he became when he slept with women, but on steroids.

Once he'd unleashed this side of him, he couldn't rein it in again.

He figured he wouldn't have any shot of that until he'd come. Hard. With Kason.

"You want to do more than feel my dick through your clothes?" he asked.

When Kason stared straight into his eyes and moaned, Jordan acted. He took Kason's hand and shoved it between them.

Kason's fingers clenched over Jordan's shaft, then rubbed it, measuring his length.

"Take it out," Jordan ordered.

Kason did as instructed. He had Jordan's pants undone and his cock freed faster than Jordan could have done it himself. The singer licked his lips and groaned the moment his palm connected with Jordan's flesh.

"Did I tell you to touch me?" he asked, shaking Kason to get his attention.

Kason froze, his eyes widening. Immediately, Jordan felt like a monster. "It's fine if you do. It felt incredible. Why don't you do it some more?"

Kason swallowed hard and reached for Jordan again. This time he was more thorough in his explorations. He glided his fingers down Jordan's shaft to his balls, rolling them around in his palm before traveling upward once more.

Jordan speared his hands into Kason's longer hair and used his grip to position Kason where he could continue to feast on the man's lush mouth while Kason stroked him. If he hadn't already been as hard as he'd ever been in his life, those tentative, though skilled, caresses would have brought him to full attention.

Kason worked Jordan like he probably did himself,

with a combination of short and fast strokes followed by a few long glides that would do him in if they weren't careful.

Although that might not be such a bad thing. They didn't have a lot of time.

Someone could walk in at any moment. And if they did, Jordan wanted it to be after they'd sampled a few taboo pleasures together. He put a hairsbreadth of distance between their faces so that he could urge, "We have to hurry. Do you want to suck it?"

Kason didn't bother responding. Instead, he dropped to his knees and took Jordan into his mouth with a single long plunge that made Jordan's knees weak. He braced himself on Kason's shoulders, using the leverage to pull Kason closer and impale his dick deeper in that sweet mouth.

Which was now licking and sucking him like only another man could understand how to do so well. Kason concentrated on the sensitive spot right below the crown of Jordan's dick, bobbing over it while sucking before sliding deep. A little too deep.

Before Kason could gag, Jordan put his fist at the base of his cock, cupping his balls and creating a stop. Kason's lips rested on the sides of Jordan's fingers, proving he'd take as much as he was allowed.

The man was everything Jordan had ever wished for, had ever fantasized about in the darkest parts of the night.

He hoped that when he drained his balls down Kason's throat, the guy would understand how brilliantly he'd performed. When Kason hummed around Jordan's shaft and his hand began to massage Jordan's balls, Jordan knew he was about to lose control.

"If you don't want to drink my come, you'd better stop

now," he told Kason despite the effort it took to grind the words out between his clenched teeth when he wanted to shout from the rooftop how fucking good Kason was making him feel.

Instead of hesitating, Kason redoubled his efforts. He twisted his head over Jordan's shaft like he'd given a million blowjobs in his life. Jordan would have believed he had tons of practice if he hasn't seen the mirrored agony in Kason's eyes when they'd argued about abstaining from sex with men.

Hopefully, after all the time Kason had waited, Jordan didn't disappoint. He held Kason's head in his hands and fucked the man's mouth, spurred on by the moans and grunts Kason made. He attempted to suck every inch of Jordan's cock as Jordan plunged in and out of the guy's face.

It was coarse, raw, frantic, and so damn thrilling that Jordan couldn't resist another moment.

He threw his head back, clenched his teeth, and gripped Kason's shoulders for balance as an unrelenting tidal wave of ecstasy broke over him.

Jordan poured himself into Kason's sucking mouth, which eagerly drained his balls and leeched the last of Jordan's fury from him. All he wanted to do was make Kason feel as wonderful as he did now, high on endorphins and the fulfillment of a decade-long desire.

"Come here so I can return the favor." Jordan put his hands under Kason's arms and began to lift him.

Which was when a blinding flash of light momentarily illuminated the warehouse.

The thick metal door slammed shut right after, and Jordan could barely make out Alanso's garbled voice.

"They're fine. Just...*busy*." His nervous chuckle cut through the absolute silence between Kason and Jordan.

Jordan knew Wren. If it was her on the other side of that door, they only had seconds before she plowed through it, kicking it down if need be.

He tried to shield Kason from the mess he'd gotten them tangled up in, but he had only halfway stepped in front of the other guy—his cock still out and slick with salvia and come—before Wren crashed their private party. It scared him how much his dick perked up at the thought of her witnessing him with Kason.

Would she be pissed or turned on if he went down on her boyfriend right then?

They were about to find out.

18

Wren probably should have realized that catastrophe was the only possible outcome of her, Kason, and Jordan colliding at Trevon's birthday party. But if she wanted Kason to be part of her life, like Jordan already was, they were going to have to learn how to get along or at least tolerate each other.

That didn't mean she was excited by Jordan's presence the very first time she was going to see Kason in person since Jordan had interrupted their make-out session after the concert. Especially since she'd then fooled around with Jordan after that.

Things were tangled enough as it was. She didn't want Kason to think there'd been more going on than she'd admitted to. Because there hadn't been.

If seeing Jordan there today, while she was anticipating Kason's arrival with every cell in her body, only ramped up the intensity of her desire, well...that was fine. Because soon she'd have someone to slake her lust with.

Kason probably wouldn't mind reaping those extra benefits.

Now that she'd congratulated her friends on their amazing news, she didn't think anyone would notice or mind if she and Kason stole away for some quality alone time. After spending every night the past two weeks talking for hours and falling more and more in like with him, she was ready for some hands-on activities.

She turned in a slow circle, but didn't see either Jordan or Kason. *Uh oh.*

"Hey, Alanso," she called to her friend, who'd been standing closest to the guys last time she'd seen them. "Did you see where Kason went?"

"Unless your singer and Jordan were going to check out a project in the garage, I think they went to have a man-to-man discussion." He winced. "Hopefully with their words and not with their fists, yeah?"

Wren was thinking the exact same thing. Apparently so was Van. He was beside her in a flash. "I'll help you find them."

"Great, thank you." She smiled up at him as they both took off across the grass.

Alanso shrugged and jogged until he was a few steps ahead of them. "I probably should have said something sooner, but I figured they're grown-ups. If they want to discuss which of them likes Wren more and what they're going to do to each other if someone hurts her, that's not really my business."

Van chuckled at that, though he didn't stop his trek up the slope.

"I'm the only one who's going to be kicking asses around here if you guys don't quit acting like I can't take care of myself." Wren glared at the back of both men as they neared the garage.

"Just because you can, doesn't mean they—or I—want you to have to. It's chivalry, not chauvinism, Wren." Alanso made everything sound romantic when he purposefully thickened his Cuban accent to get off the hook with her.

And it kind of worked.

When they were about ten feet away, he said, "I'm going to take a peek. If they're just talking, there's no reason for either of you two to get involved."

"Fair enough," Van said, letting Alanso go first.

The bald, tattooed Hot Rod barely opened the door more than a crack before he slammed it closed again as fast as if there were actual flames on the other side instead of the ones painted on the exterior.

"Are they in there?" Van asked.

"Um, yup. They are." Alanso nodded but wouldn't meet Wren's questioning gaze.

She stepped forward, but he flung his arms out across the door. "I don't think you should go in there yet."

"Why? Are they beating each other up or something?" Wren tried to reach around Alanso. "Come on, let me talk to them. I promise I won't do anything dumb."

"No, no. They're fine. Just...*busy.*"

"Busy doing what?" She stood up straighter and lunged toward the door, but Alanso caught her around the waist.

That didn't stop Van, though. He wasn't about to let his boss get into trouble on his watch. He knocked Alanso aside, opened the door, then shut it again, too. Harder than Alanso had. "Oh. I didn't realize... Holy shit."

Van immediately plastered himself against the metal taking his turn keeping Wren away.

"Wait." Wren looked between Alanso, who looked guilty, and Van, whose cheeks were flushing by the instant. She went dead still. "They're getting it on? Are you fucking serious?"

Her first instinct was to run—not away, but closer.

"You sure you want to see that, hon?" Alanso asked gently.

"Hell yes, I do." She yanked her arm from Alanso's grip and dodged Van.

Alanso stopped her again. He'd been Kason once. Of course he would understand what they were going through. "Because you're pissed or because you're horny?"

Wren stared straight into his eyes so he couldn't mistake her sincerity when she said, "Both. But I'm mad because they didn't include me, not because they did it at all."

"Let her go," Mustang Sally, who had come up behind them with her husband Eli, ordered her other husband. Alanso instantaneously did as she commanded. "She has a right to be involved. And if that's not what Jordan or Kason wants, they owe her the courtesy of telling her to her face."

Wren realized they'd struck a nerve. Sally had an experience not so different than this once, not long before she and her two husbands had figured things out between them. It had nearly torn her, Eli, and Alanso apart. Eli glowered, probably kicking himself or wishing he could keep Jordan and Kason from making the same mistakes he and Alanso had with Sally.

Both Alanso and Van stepped aside.

"Thank you," she said to her friend before going inside.

When her eyes adjusted, she saw two things

simultaneously. Kason was wiping his flushed mouth with the back of his hand and Jordan was attempting to put his still-swollen cock back into his pants. He cursed as he wrestled with the zipper.

"Wren, shit. I'm so sorry." Kason scrunched his eyes closed. "I didn't mean for that to happen."

"No, it was my fault. I made the first move. We were arguing and then we weren't..." Jordan stepped in front of Kason, protecting him, like he always did for her.

The blend of emotions that swamped her nearly brought her to her knees. "Don't apologize for who you are and what you like. That's what you've always told me, Jordan. Did you mean it?"

"I did."

"Well, it applies to you, too." She looked at Kason then. "I see now why you got off on hearing about me and Jordan and our past."

"I didn't understand it myself, entirely, until..." Kason licked his lips.

Wren stepped closer and then closer still. She opened her arms and put one around Jordan, then scooped Kason into her embrace as well. "It's okay, guys. Really. I'm happy for you. And I can't act like I don't understand. I told you, Kason, when I'm near Jordan...it just happens. It's a powerful, primal reaction. I get it."

Wren discovered it was possible to be happy for someone else even when you were crying inside. She kissed Kason's cheek, then squeezed Jordan. "I'll leave you alone now. Treat each other right, okay? I care so much for you both."

Before she'd made it half a step away, both Jordan and Kason objected.

"Don't go," Kason begged.

"Wait!" Jordan shouted.

"Why?" She held her hands out to the sides, palms facing up.

Kason answered first. "Because I came here to see *you* today. What happened doesn't erase everything we've shared the past few weeks. Does it?"

As she asked herself the same thing, Jordan lifted his gaze from the floor. The intensity of his desire, especially considering he'd obviously come a few minutes ago, rocked her backward. "I'm hoping you'll help me take care of Kason."

"I'm fine," Kason said, although he grimaced when he said it. "I just want a chance to talk this through."

"Are you telling me that he hasn't come yet?" Wren asked Jordan, ignoring Kason's objections.

Jordan at least had the decency to seem embarrassed by that fact. "I was getting around to it..."

"Well, you'd better." She couldn't say what came over her then except a bone-deep assuredness that this was the right approach to take. No more fucking around. No more secrets. No more long, slow ride toward their destination. No more detours.

This was going to happen and it was going to happen now.

"What?" Jordan and Kason asked simultaneously.

"I said you'd better take care of him. I'm not moving from this spot until I watch you blow him as well as he did you. You're a man of honor, aren't you? Do the right thing and give the man what he's earned." Wren propped her hands on her hips.

"And what about you?" Jordan wondered.

"I'm plenty capable of fending for myself, remember?"

She crossed her arms, daring either one of the men staring incredulously at her to argue.

Kason seemed like he might object but Jordan didn't give him the chance, because he nodded at Wren and—for once in their damn lives—did as she asked as if he realized this was a test he needed to pass.

He dropped to his knees on the concrete floor and ripped open Kason's pants.

The dick pics he'd texted her hadn't done him justice. He was lengthy and thick and so damn hard it had to hurt.

"What are you waiting for?" she asked Jordan.

He shrugged. "Trying to figure out if this is real life or another dream."

"Maybe it's both." She stepped closer, putting her hands on his head. She massaged his scalp until his eyelids grew heavy. Meanwhile, she leaned in closer and smiled up at Kason. "Hi."

"Hey." His grin was crooked. "You were right, you know. I didn't mean for that to happen, but he's hard to resist."

"So are you." Wren leaned in over Jordan and kissed Kason. He relaxed as they made out, even while Jordan hovered an inch or less from Kason's cock.

She didn't feel like breaking their exchange, so instead she used the hand on the back of Jordan's skull, nudging him toward Kason's crotch. He got the hint and went for it.

Whatever he did was effective, because Kason stiffened and gasped.

Then he kissed her twice as hard. His tongue pressed between her lips, so she let him in, sucking on him in a mirror image of what Jordan must be doing to his dick. Kason shuddered. Wren was glad he was already so aroused. Van and who knew who else were right on the other side of that door and could waltz in there any moment.

Her entire focus became making sure Kason experienced as much pleasure as possible before their time ran out. He put one arm around her and tugged her close. If Jordan minded being squished between her and Kason, he didn't complain.

The wet, slurping noises he made as he devoured Kason's hard-on made Wren squirm. She shoved one hand into her pants and rubbed her clit as she continued to make out with Kason.

She and Kason had talked about scenarios like this— threesomes—late at night, but never in a million years had she expected it to come to pass. Especially not with Jordan. And extra-especially not within minutes of Kason showing up at Hot Rides again.

How the hell were they ever going to manage to talk about what was happening without doing it over and over until they exhausted every last orgasm they'd stored up—and she had a feeling that was about five years' worth of them?

Kason's motions became erratic. His teeth pressed against her lips. The resulting sting might have made her pause under other circumstances. Knowing he was about to pour himself down Jordan's throat made the pain welcome. It held her in check. Otherwise she'd be shattering before him and that wasn't what she wanted.

Wren needed to share this moment with him. With them.

It didn't take more than another ten seconds before Kason was trying to warn them both. His moans escalated until they culminated in a long, guttural groan. Jordan put one hand behind his own back, squeezing Wren's calf.

She joined Kason in rapture.

Wren came so hard, she wished there was a cock buried in her to squeeze and ripple around. Next time, she promised herself.

Kason clung to her as she did the same to him. His hips jerked as he shot deep into Jordan's eager mouth.

It was the best orgasm of Wren's life. Something she immediately felt ashamed of. Then, somehow, she knew that Johnny wouldn't mind. He would adamantly approve of anything that brought his two best friends and companions the most joy.

Which was exactly how she felt about Kason and Jordan. Whatever they'd been doing before she arrived, she was fine with it. From the shit-eating grin spreading across Kason's face and the bewildered laughter coming from Jordan, whatever it was that had passed between them had been life-changing.

For all three of them.

"I don't give a fuck what your job title is, you're not going in there," Ollie was shouting, presumably at Van.

"You heard that! If something happens to Kason, I'm taking it out of your hide," Van growled.

"If something happens to your boss, it's on him and the dumb shit he's pulling. He deserves to get balls twisted off by Wren if he's betrayed her, and I'll be next in line despite your Hulk-ass trying to stop me."

Kyra yelled Van's name, then Ollie's. She started arguing over top of their snarling at each other. "Stop it. Both of you. You're not helping."

Wren looked up and noticed Kason had gone white. "Are you okay?"

Jordan was on his feet in an instant, helping Kason get

it together. He licked his lips as he put Kason's dick back into his jeans and zipped him up carefully.

"I'd better go before someone gets hurt," Kason said without looking at her or Jordan. "This...this shouldn't have happened."

Wren and Jordan exchanged a worried glance, but not before Kason bolted for the door.

When he was a few feet away, he turned and broke her heart all over again. "This was phenomenal. The best of my life. We can't do it again. There's too much at stake."

Wren bent over, clutching her knees as she tried to suck a breath in through the razor blades slicing her chest open when Kason slipped out the door. Jordan looked down at her then to where Kason had disappeared as if trying to decide who to chase.

"Go after him. Make sure he's okay," she begged Jordan.

"There's no use. He's running, like I was before." Jordan crouched in front of her, then lifted her chin so he could stare into her eyes. "Those days are over, Wren."

"What are you saying?"

"I'm ready to fight for us. For this. Like I should have done all along." He kissed her sweetly, sharing the taste of Kason, which still lingered on his lips. "If he isn't right for us, I'll find the man who is. Because I'm sure now. We were meant for this. You and me and...somebody else."

As satisfying as it would have been to leave him there empty-handed as payback, Wren couldn't bring herself to do it when everything inside her was screaming that he was right.

This was what they'd been missing.

"Will you take me back?" he asked, his voice shredded.

"I never let you go." Wren collapsed into his arms and let him cradle her as she wept.

Not because she was devastated or miserable, but because she was finally sure again that she could be so very happy.

For the first time in five years, Wren had hope.

19

Jordan spent the day after Trevon's birthday party in the office at Hot Rides, fielding phone calls and scheduling appointments in between staring at Wren while she did her thing. He had nothing better to do than watch her weld and hang out with Gavyn, Quinn, Trevon, Devra, and Ollie when they took breaks from working or studying or going bananas about being a dad soon, whatever they were each up to. Plus, talking to the customers about their motorcycles and showing them his own work-in-progress was pretty sweet, too.

Though he hadn't so much as glimpsed a fishing pole, it had been the best day of Jordan's "vacation" so far.

These fuckers were up here every day doing something they loved, working hard but having fun they were building an empire they all shared in. Meanwhile, he'd been barely surviving, taking orders he didn't agree with, and enduring the drudgery of his job—one that no longer aligned with his values.

It was eye opening.

He *had* to make a change.

Once the Hot Rides called it quits for the evening, they shared dinner in the middle of the lawn at the picnic tables huddled around a stone pit where Jordan had helped Ollie build a roaring fire. It wouldn't be long before the evenings got too chilly for even that, but it seemed like everyone gathered together was reluctant to give up the tradition they'd started that summer. Jordan was shocked when he glanced at his watch and saw they'd been out there for hours.

He hadn't laughed or eaten so much in as long as he remembered. He promised himself that he'd pitch in more tomorrow, maybe bring some burgers to grill or ask Devra to help him learn to make a couple side dishes.

He peeked at Wren and found her watching him, a soft smile on her face. Her hand was resting on his knee and she squeezed it reassuringly.

It was only then that Jordan realized he'd been punishing himself. It might as well have been him who'd died that day for all he'd lived in the past five years. No more.

"Ready to go inside?" he asked her.

She winked. "If you are."

Around the table, people were yawning and the crackling flames had become glowing embers. Ollie offered to tend to them, so Jordan and Wren said goodnight and went into her cabin. He'd stayed the night following the party but hadn't taken the time to really admire the efficient space. It didn't have a lot of bells and whistles, but it had everything they needed, including the comfy couch where they'd first rekindled their physical relationship a few weeks ago. It was where they landed now, content to sit and talk or say nothing at all for a while.

After everything that had gone down with Kason the day before, they'd been too exhausted, mentally and physically, to do more than collapse into bed and snuggle until they—very quickly—dropped off to sleep.

Tonight could be different.

Jordan put his arm around Wren. Naturally, she rested her head on his shoulder, in the spot that had always been hers. It was so familiar and comforting that he didn't move even long after he'd lost feeling in his fingertips.

Despite his joy in her company, he could sense the underlying note of Wren's sadness.

"You miss him, don't you?" Jordan took a deep breath and prepared himself for her to say she'd changed her mind. He wouldn't hold it against her if she did.

"Johnny or Kason?" she asked.

"Both." He squeezed her tighter, thinking of what she'd been forced to sacrifice because of him.

"Yeah. Johnny always, though it's more of a dull ache than a stabbing pain these days. And Kason... He's been calling me every night around this time since the day after the concert." Wren sighed. "I enjoyed talking with him. He has this way of really listening that a lot of people don't."

"I'll try to be better at it." Jordan frowned.

"You've improved already. Hell, you're doing a great job right now." She kissed his cheek. "Time for bed?"

"Your call. I know you have to get up early again tomorrow." He tucked her hair behind her ear then stood and followed Wren as she ascended the bookcase to the loft.

He'd be lying if he said he didn't stare at her ass the whole way.

By the time he'd joined her in the surprisingly cozy nest, she'd already stripped off her sleeveless shirt and the soft sweatpants he'd swear she'd had since they were together before. They were well-loved, well-worn, and had a couple holes in interesting places.

Naked, she stunned him with her beauty. Always had.

"You're so gorgeous," he murmured appreciatively as he ditched the Hot Rides T-shirt he'd bought from the shop and the jeans he'd worn the day before. He'd have to leave sometime soon, even if temporarily, to bring a few more things over to Wren's place.

But not tonight.

There was no way he would be separated from her now.

"You are too, you know." Wren's lips parted and her eyes dilated as she raked her gaze over his body from his head to his toes, pausing as she focused on his hardening cock.

He crawled toward her on the bed to keep from hitting his head on the exposed beams of the ceiling not far above him, then hooked an arm around her waist, bringing her down beside him. "I mean it, Wren. You were always pretty, but now you've matured. You're more shapely—"

He cupped her hip, loving how it filled his hand.

"Damn it. I told Devra this would happen. It's her fault, cooking delicious food every damn day," she grumbled.

Jordan laughed as he kissed her, knowing she wasn't the sort to be self-conscious. "That's not what I mean, and you know it. Though I'm not complaining about your curves. You're not a girl anymore. You're all woman."

"Oh yeah? Does that mean you'll let me be on top?"

she asked as she threw her arms around his neck and dragged him to his side.

Jordan tumbled with her, both of them laughing as they rolled over and under each other across the mattress. He landed above her, and took her mouth in a searing kiss. The flavor of her lips, still tinged with the caramel ice cream they'd shared for dessert, intoxicated him. That's the only reason he could think of to explain why he didn't realize her phone was buzzing on the nightstand for several seconds after the clatter began.

Wren froze beneath him.

"What's wrong?" he asked.

"I bet that's Kason." Her gaze flew to her phone as it buzzed again.

Jordan slid off of her, trying not to groan as they lost contact. "So answer it."

She hesitated, turning onto her side as she looked over her shoulder at him and then back to the phone in front of her.

"Go ahead. Get it." He smacked her ass.

Wren nodded, then dove for her cell. She connected the call.

"Did you break a leg?" she asked with a huge grin.

Damn, she must really have it bad for Kason. Jordan hadn't realized their attraction went that far beyond the physical already.

"I'm glad you called. I wasn't sure..." Wren blew out a breath big enough to flutter the strands of platinum hair that settled around her face.

She hesitated while Kason said something and then responded, "Actually, Jordan is here. Do you mind if I put you on speaker phone?"

He must have agreed, because she did.

"Hey," Kason said.

It was impossible to read him from that single word. If Johnny were there, he would have been able to. He had been so much better at that kind of stuff than Jordan was. He'd always seemed to know how someone was feeling and how to resolve their anxieties.

Though he'd seemed to have no trouble chatting with Wren, now that he was on speaker, Kason didn't say anything else.

"Are you traumatized by what happened yesterday or do you not like talking to me on the phone as much as you enjoy chatting with Wren?" Jordan wondered aloud.

"I'm...confused," Kason admitted. "Everything happened so fast and then I left and came back to this life where I have to pretend that's not who I am. I guess I started to doubt it had even really happened."

"Oh, it happened. I didn't imagine your mouth on my dick. It was heaven. *You* were incredible." Jordan rubbed his cock at the memory.

Wren noticed and kicked up a brow at his motions. He clasped her hand and tugged it to his lap, encouraging her to take over for him. She did, idly stroking him as she talked to Kason.

"I didn't realize you were bisexual," she said. "I mean, not that you needed to disclose that or anything, I just thought after everything we'd talked about—how I was with Jordan and Johnny, and how Jordan wanted more from Johnny—it might have come up."

She'd told him that? Jeez. Thanks, Wren. Though maybe that's why Kason had been willing to experiment the day before. In that case, Jordan did owe her one.

"Truth is, I don't know what I am." Kason swallowed

hard enough they could hear it. "I've never done that before. I got caught up in the moment."

Wren rolled her eyes, making Jordan laugh, though he did it silently so Kason wouldn't get the wrong idea. They weren't making fun of him. They were boggled by his impressive levels of self-denial. Jordan knew what it was like to keep your feelings and passions bottled up. He was glad Kason hadn't done that in the storeroom.

"I'm pretty sure what happened yesterday was more than a fluke. It wasn't like oops, I slipped and look, now your dick is in my mouth." Jordan shook his head, remembering how Kason had practically launched himself at Jordan's erection.

"I'm not gay," Kason said. "Look, I'm just some poor kid from Mississippi. We're chocolate-and-vanilla kind of people. There weren't any fancy flavors there. No in-betweens. I love women. I love fucking women. This is... taboo or something. Attractive because it's like drugs or gambling or other shit you shouldn't do but enjoy anyway until the repercussions smack you in the face."

"I'm going to give you the benefit of the doubt here. You don't really believe that shit, do you? Hopefully you've learned a thing or two since you left your hometown. We all have." Wren stared at the phone as if Kason could see her reaction. "There's no shame in being bisexual, Kason."

"There is, according to some people. That's not what fans expect of me when they come to a show or buy my songs online. If people knew what I am—yeah, bisexual I guess, I never thought of myself like that but it feels right —it would destroy my image and my career." Something in the way he said it made Jordan sure that someone else had put that nonsense in Kason's head.

Wren had never been one to live in denial. She faced

difficult things head on. Always had. She didn't disappoint him now.

"And for that matter," Wren continued, "however you identify—straight, gay, bi, whatever—that doesn't mean you're like Jordan and me, who enjoy being in a relationship with more than one partner at a time. That's poly."

"Oh, I definitely loved that part of what we did yesterday. *Fucking loved it.*" Kason sighed. "More than anything, I'm sure of that. And not only the sex stuff. There was something...intoxicating...about imagining what it might feel like to belong to you both instead of just sleeping with you. I think *that's* what made me come so damn hard."

"Well, there you go." Wren smiled softly. "There are perks, you know? Just think, you have a better chance of finding a life partner. More people to pick from."

Jordan cleared his throat; he wasn't about to let there be any miscommunications. "And so you know, Wren is mine. My life partner, I mean. I told her last night that I was an idiot for leaving her and I don't intend to keep fucking up where she's concerned. Somehow I'm lucky enough that she hasn't kicked me out yet."

"That's...fantastic. I know how much she loves you." Kason seemed genuinely happy for them.

"That doesn't mean I'm planning on keeping her to myself." Jordan kissed her forehead, then said, "She's plenty of woman for two men. And...well, I do want to explore both my bisexuality and my poly sides, too. This is who I am, even if it took me forever to figure it out. I hope you're smarter than me. Don't waste time agonizing over something you can't change when you could be spending it happy."

Wren took his hand in hers and squeezed. She also rippled the fingers of her other hand over his cock, which was solid now and huge in her grip.

"If you're not interested in us, that's okay. No pressure." Wren scrunched her eyes closed when she said, "We'll be here for you no matter what as you figure things out."

Jordan was less generous. "As your friends, she means. I'm not going to wait around forever to start looking for someone who meshes with us. Like I said, I wasted enough time already."

Wren smacked his shoulder with the back of her hand. He shrugged. It was the truth.

"I wish you were here tonight, Kason." Wren told him. "Or that you didn't have to go last night. If you could have come here and talked through things, maybe we'd be having a different conversation right now."

"Or maybe our mouths would be busy doing stuff besides blabbering," Jordan said.

"That would have been good." Kason's voice seemed raspier as he considered the possibilities.

Wren looked directly into Jordan's eyes when she made a very indecent, very sexy proposal. "Do you want us to show you what we'd be doing if you were with us right now? If so, why don't we switch to videochat? I know how much you get off on watching."

"You two have done this before?" Jordan asked, his cock jerking at the thought of Kason and Wren having videophone sex as they pleasured themselves. No wonder she'd been so glad to see the guy at Trevon's party. And he'd messed up their reunion like he'd ruined their first kiss. Damn. He promised himself he'd make it up to Wren tonight.

"Maybe once or twice," Kason said with an infectious laugh. "Okay, yeah. I'm in. I'll call you right back."

He hung up. Less than half a second later, Wren's phone was making a different noise to indicate an incoming videochat, which she connected.

"Oh fuck, you're naked. You were talking to me and you didn't even have clothes on?" Kason's eyes widened. And that was before Wren tilted her phone so that Kason could see where her hand was, still fondling Jordan's dick.

"He's a handful, isn't he?" Wren asked Kason.

"More like a mouthful, I'd say," the guy answered, staring at where they intersected.

Jordan's cock began to leak precome at the thought of what they were about to do. He hadn't quite realized he was such an exhibitionist until yesterday, when Wren had watched them. This solidified it. He officially liked to put on a show. So he decided to make it a good one.

"Kason, why don't you strip too?" he asked, wanting to see how much they impacted him.

The other man did, getting rid of his clothes while Jordan and Wren shared another kiss, this one far less gentle or patient.

"Damn, that's so sexy," he groaned as he climbed into bed and wrapped his hand around his own shaft. He aimed his phone to make sure they could see exactly how hard he was while witnessing their shared affection. "Jordan, will you suck on her tits for me? I wanted to so bad and I didn't get the chance."

"Sure." Jordan grinned, happy to oblige. He spent some quality time filling his mouth with Wren's soft flesh, tugging on her nipples with his teeth the way she liked best. She arched and moaned, her legs coming around his waist to lock him close to her.

"Don't worry," he whispered to her. "I'm not going anywhere. Not tonight and not ever."

"Fuck." Kason groaned as they kissed and rubbed their bodies together, enjoying the energy that consumed them when they touched skin-on-skin.

"I can't wait to be inside you again," Jordan rasped. "It's been so long. I need my dick in you."

"You guys didn't..." Kason asked on a pant.

"No," Wren promised him. "You'll be here with us when we fuck for the first time since we got back together. Do you like that?"

"Yes!" he shouted.

"Will you try to come with us?" Wren wondered.

"Yes!" Kason cried out again.

Jordan aimed his cock at Wren's pussy and advanced. He'd barely made contact with her hot, slick flesh when a loud bang startled him.

"What the fuck is that?" he asked, his gaze shifting to the phone screen.

Several more thuds blasted from the speaker followed by someone shouting, "Kason, open up! I know you're in there. We need to talk."

The other man's face went blank and his cheeks drained of color. His cock went from ready to explode to wilting in a matter of seconds.

"Who the fuck is that?" Jordan asked.

Kason muffled the phone, taking it off of speaker. He whispered, "It's Rick, my manager. I'm going to mute you for a minute. Be right back."

He threw his sheet over the phone so everything on their screen went black. Jordan instantly rebelled against being Kason's dirty little secret, left in the dark. He'd already been through that phase in his life.

Wren must have realized what he was thinking. She curled up tighter against him and hugged him.

Meanwhile, Kason must have opened his door.

"Who were you talking to in there?" Rick sounded clearer now, as if he'd poked his head in Kason's room at the back of the bus.

Kason laughed, though it wasn't genuine. "I was watching porn. Got a problem with that?"

His voice held an edge Jordan hadn't heard from him before. Was his manager the one giving him a hard time? Jordan promised himself he'd put his agent skills to good use checking the man out in the morning.

"Considering we were supposed to talk about the summer concert series contract before you left town, yeah, I'd prefer if we could get that out of the way before you jack off and pass out," Rick said. "Get dressed and meet me out at the table in the front of the bus. You're holding everyone up. It's an eight-hour drive to the next city."

"Shit. Sorry. I totally forgot. I'll be right there." Kason sounded defeated. Completely unlike himself.

The door slammed, and then Kason appeared in front of them. He whispered, "Gotta go. Sorry."

Since he couldn't hear them, Wren blew him a kiss. But the picture cut off as he hung up on them. Jordan wasn't sure the other guy had even seen her sweet gesture.

He was horny, and frustrated, and irritated at the same time.

Kason had the potential to hurt Wren, which Jordan didn't like at all. Maybe he was letting his desires put her in danger again.

"Should we keep going?" Jordan was torn. He wanted to make slow, sweet love to Wren. But it felt weird now that it was just the two of them again. Like they were cheating on Kason, who'd helped to get them both so fired up.

"Would you hate me if I said I wanted to wait?" Wren put her hand over her face. "I mean, I don't *want* to, but I feel like it might be the right thing to do."

"Can you tell me more about why you feel that way?" Maybe it would help him understand why he did too.

"I don't want whoever we end up with to look at us as a couple and themselves as the third wheel, you know?" Wren sighed. "Especially if we can make things work with Kason, like I hope. It's important for him to feel equal. He's already so tormented by this. I'm afraid of making things worse. He needs to feel accepted and loved by us."

Jordan nodded. That made a lot of sense, actually. As much as his cock objected, he resigned himself to another platonic night in Wren's bed. "I'm happy to simply be here with you. Let me hold you at least?"

"Yeah." She snuggled up to his side.

It took a while before either of them settled enough to be sleepy, but when she did, Wren dozed off in the shelter of Jordan's arms. It was one of the best nights of his life, even if he didn't get to relieve the pressure building between them.

20

Kason felt like a kid called to the principal's office. He made the trek from his admittedly luxurious bedroom at the back of the tour bus, past the bathroom and down the hall that was lined with six bunks, three on each side, where Kyra, the rest of the band, and Van slept. He emerged into the common space that held a long leather sectional, two recliners on swivels that could face out the front windows or into the living room, a kitchenette, and a glossy fancy-wood table that seated four.

That's where Rick Rosner had situated himself. Although it was nearing midnight, the asshole was still in his full suit and tie complete with a gaudy gold watch that Kason's hard work had paid for. Not that the guy didn't deserve his cut. He was a ruthless negotiator and had always pushed Kason to the next level.

Only now that he was at the top of his game did Rick start to grate.

The sooner they got this shit taken care of, the sooner they could leave Los Angeles and good ol' Rick behind for a while. The next leg of the tour would carry them toward the heart of the country, and Hot Rides territory—well, within a few hundred miles anyway.

Something about the look Rick shot Kason put him on edge.

Kyra and Van were splayed out on the couch while Kyra kicked Van's ass at one of the video games she enjoyed so much. It irked Van to no end since he was actually a trained security specialist and she out-played him in nearly every first-person shooter they brought on the bus.

The other guys were either in their bunks with the curtains drawn or out in the parking lot stretching their legs—or scratching a few itches with groupies—before another long drive. Kason didn't blame them.

He slid into a seat at the table, sitting on his hands so Rick wouldn't have any indication that he was nervous. And he was, given what he'd just been doing and the warning Rick had given Kason a couple years ago.

Kason sat across the table from his manager and acted like everything was cool. "Where do I need to sign?"

"You don't want to hear about the proposal?" Rick didn't seem surprised.

"No. You know what I wanted and I assume you did your job like you always do to get it." Kason shrugged one shoulder. "Am I wrong?"

"You're not." Rick sat up straighter and flashed a sharkish grin. "I got what we discussed, plus an extra twenty percent."

"Nice. Thanks." Kason hoped they wrapped this up quick enough for him to call Wren and Jordan back. What were they doing right then?

He couldn't think about that or things would get even more uncomfortable than they were already.

From a leather briefcase, Rick withdrew a contract and put it in front of Kason before laying a gleaming gold pen on top with the tip resting on a long black line. "Sign here."

Kason did.

And that's when Rick sprung his trap.

"You're lucky that's fucking locked in. Are you trying to make my job impossible?" Rick glared as he snatched the contract, slipped it in his briefcase, and snapped the thing closed.

Out of the corner of Kason's eye, he saw Van's posture change slightly.

Then Kyra gave a whoop and fist pump. "Got you!" She didn't realize Van had stopped playing and was working, paying close attention to what was about to go down at the table. It was nice to know that if Kason needed backup, he'd...probably...have it. Van hadn't said a single word to him about what had happened at Hot Rides yesterday. Kyra either.

There'd been a lot of tense silences around the stage today. And it was about to get worse.

"I think the quality of my performances has been pretty damn great this time out, considering I'm sober. And the music I've been writing in the past month or so... Well, I'm actually proud of it again," Kason said quietly. "What do you have to complain about?"

"This." Rick took another stack of papers from the case and slapped them on the table. "Why is Allied Online writing stories about you?"

Kason blinked. He tried to think of a way to explain the photograph lying there. A full-width picture of him singing "Secret Love" to Jordan—him crouched down, Jordan in their front row, their eyes locked—followed by a snarky headline that Rick was too happy to read, loudly, in a smarmy tone. "'Kason Cox gets in touch with his cocky side, making gay men swoon across the internet.'"

The gossip magazine had then done what looked like a surprisingly insightful piece about his interaction that night along with a mention of rumors of Kason's close relationship with his childhood best friend, who had recently come out. Well, not so recently. More like a few years ago. Right after he'd professed his crush and tried to kiss Kason, who'd bolted—both because he didn't reciprocate those feelings, and because he thought he might like to try kissing his friend anyway. Right before everything had started circling the drain in Kason's personal life.

Kyra and Van had both set aside their game controllers and were trying not to look at him as Rick ripped him a new one.

"It's not only your life you have to consider, Kason." Spittle dotted the papers on the table as Rick got riled up. "You need to think about the people who make a living running this operation. Your band mates. The security team. Hell, even me. I bank on your popularity and if you fuck with that, you fuck with me."

Kason couldn't stand to be wrong and this time he was.

Van started to rise from the couch, but Kason held out a hand in his friend's direction. Kason had gotten them into this and he would take care of it. Van had a right to be pissed, as did Kyra, who Van was now holding back.

Rick was right. Kason was risking the livelihoods of

dozens of people who'd only ever fought for his success. He couldn't repay them this way.

"I've made you into a star from nothing. Don't you dare fuck it up after I've invested so much of my own career into yours. If you need to get high again, I'd rather that. At least that's becoming of a country-rock god." Rick stood then, swiping the papers off the table and into his briefcase. He snatched it up and stormed out of the bus, slamming the door behind him.

Kason slumped at the table. As if it wasn't bad enough that his friends had witnessed him losing his mind over Jordan the day before. Now this.

He had to face them, and apologize for letting them— and everyone else—down.

Kason cleared his throat, rage simmering beneath his shame and embarrassment. He pointed first at Van and then at Kyra. "Which one of you blabbed to Rick about yesterday?"

Van stepped in front of Kyra, protecting her as always. Even if it had been her who ratted him out, Van would take the fall and Kyra wouldn't notice. They were just as fucked up as he was.

She shoved Van aside and met Kason's gaze. "Neither of us would betray you like that, revealing your private business. We didn't say a word."

Kason looked from one to the other, carefully scrutinizing their expressions. He believed her and added being a dick to his list of sins.

But now that it was there, out in the open between them, it seemed they had more to say about it.

"When were you going to tell us?" Van asked quietly.

"I wasn't." Kason crossed his arms. He hadn't planned on acting on his unwise urges, for exactly these reasons.

Look at the chaos it was causing. Rick had told him it would, warned him, three years ago when he'd caught Kason about to make out with his old friend, who'd surprised him at a show near their hometown, despite the fact that he'd be taking advantage of the man's emotions.

Until Jordan, and Wren, he'd never been tempted to make the same mistake again.

"Obviously." The other guy frowned. "I'll remember from now on that I'm strictly your employee."

"Fuck that, Van. You know that's bullshit."

"No, I don't. First it was sneaking around for the gambling and the drinking. The drugs. And now this." Van shook his head. "I'm not some redneck bigot. As long as your partners treat you well and don't jeopardize your safety, I don't care who you sleep with. So why all the secrets? I don't know how much more I can put up with. What's next?"

"Nothing." Kason pivoted, staring straight ahead, where he needed to focus. "I'm going to be a robot. I'll sing and dance and do what I need to so you guys can ride the gravy train until I'm old and ugly and my voice goes to hell and no one gives a fuck about me anymore and the money runs out. Who'll be left by my side then? Will you?"

Van stumbled backward, nearly crashing into the couch. He didn't say anything for a solid ten seconds. Then he said, "Not if you keep treating me like the help. Fuck you. Fuck this. I'm out."

Kason choked on the pathetic shout that clawed to escape his throat and call Van back.

Everything Rick had promised would happen was coming true. Kason's dick and his poor choices were already ripping everything he'd worked his whole life for to shreds. And he was nearly willing to give it up to dash into his bedroom and call Jordan and Wren back right then.

He needed to hear their voices. See them smiling. And hope that everything would be okay.

If this was only about him, he just might.

He picked up his phone. Unlocked it. Relocked it. Unlocked it. Relocked it.

Then he threw the fucking thing against the wall and watched it shatter into a billion pieces, like his heart and soul.

Kyra's shriek jolted him from the pit of darkness about to swallow him. He'd forgotten she was there. She raced to his side and put her hands on his biceps. "Kason, please. Calm down. We'll figure this out. It's going to be okay."

"Were you listening to anything that Rick said?" He didn't mean to yell at her and hated the flash of fear that nearly made her recoil from him.

"He's a slimy bastard who's only looking out for himself." Kyra leaned in, getting right in his face. "I promise you I have a lot more to say about that. But if you can wait a few minutes, I think I should get Van back here first. We have the whole night to talk about this."

"There's nothing more to say." Kason put his head in his hands, mortified because of how he'd acted and the things he'd done to bring this on in the first place. "Find him. Please."

Kyra peered at Kason, her eyes glittering, then out the front of the bus, where there was no sign of Van. She bit her lip. Her voice shredded as she said, "I can't decide who needs me more, you or him."

Kason looked up at her and told the biggest lie of his life. "I want to be alone. Go."

Kyra threw her arms around him, hugging him tight. "It's going to be okay, Kason. I get it, and Van will too once he has time to cool off. *This* is why you tried those other things, to fill the void. You'll figure this out, with Jordan or someone else."

Oh yeah, he hadn't even told them the juicy part about how he wanted both Jordan *and* Wren, at the same time even.

How could they ever accept his sordid desires? Like Rick had said, being bisexual would be enough to sink him. Poly too? Forget about it. Jordan and Wren might have the freedom to love whoever they wanted, but he—fettered by golden handcuffs—didn't have that luxury.

He stared at his hands and said again, "Go."

"I'll be back as quickly as I can be. Do you want me to send in anyone else to keep you company and...safe...until I get back?"

"Thank you, but I'll be okay." He had to be or the same fate awaited his team. He wasn't going to let them down. "I swear."

"Okay. See you soon then. We've got your back, Kason." She kissed his cheek and smoothed his ruffled hair.

"I don't deserve you guys."

"Nope, but we love you anyway," she said with a sad smile as she jogged down the stairs and out of the bus. He didn't hold it against her when she locked the door with the external keypad on the front that he'd never bothered to learn the code to so that he couldn't get out and do more harm to himself and the people who relied on him.

He'd earned her skepticism.

Kason was glad he'd smashed his phone because even now, after all that had happened and how close to disaster he'd come because of desires he couldn't control, he still wanted to call Jordan and Wren. To talk through his crisis or so they could make him forget his problems. Either would be fine with him.

But like Van, Kyra, and Rick had taken the alcohol, drugs, and access to gambling sites out of his reach, now Wren and Jordan were beyond his grasp also.

He hoped at least that they were having a hell of a time together.

Without him.

21

Van decided he'd had enough. It was his job to look out for Kason and he was going to do what was necessary to make sure his friend didn't go off the deep end...again. He'd spent the past week staggering through life like a zombie. Most of the time he wasn't performing, he spent sleeping or pretending to, shut in the opulent bedroom of the tour bus.

This wasn't a sustainable life for Kason—or anyone, really.

Van looked at Kyra, who was scrolling through social media on her phone next to him, and figured he had more in common with Kason than he wanted to admit. The woman had friend-zoned him since that one time they'd kissed and she'd called it a "mistake". It had been the best damn mistake of his life, and living each day so close to her and yet emotionally distant was killing him.

He'd figure out what to do about that right after he took care of Kason.

"Hey, Kyra. Do you still have Ollie's number? That guy

from Hot Rides?" Van asked, trying not to clench his jaw so hard he'd bust a tooth.

"Yeah. He's sweet. We've been texting sometimes. He sends me pictures of Mr. Prickles." She laughed.

"I bet he does." Van forced himself to concentrate on the task at hand and not be sidetracked by his jealousy.

"Want to see?" Kyra flipped her phone around and showed him some shots in between some regular, if a little flirty, texts.

Okay, fine. The hedgehog was kind of cute. "Nice. So, would you mind talking to him about Kason?"

"You want me to be nosey and get the dirt on Jordan and Wren and what's up?" Kyra perked up. "Because I'm totally in if you do."

"Maybe." Van scrubbed his hand over his face, hoping they were doing the right thing. "At the very least see if Gavyn might be willing to talk to him. Or that other guy, what was his name? Roman? Someone who knows about the stuff Kason is struggling with better than us."

"Yeah, Roman is Quinn's brother. He's married to a man. Ollie told me that he's a recovering addict. He actually met Gavyn when they were both in a treatment facility."

"We need help. *Kason* needs help," Van told her. "Without any outlets, he's going to lose it sooner or later."

Kyra nodded. "I'm scared for him too. I'll do it."

Her fingers flew over her phone as she typed out a message to Ollie, then clicked send. She looked up at Van and flashed him a wobbly smile. "You're a good guy, you know that?"

"But not good enough for you?" *Shit!* Why had he said that out loud?

All of Kyra's warmth and openness vanished in an

instant. At the same time, her phone binged. "It's Ollie. I'm going to go outside to call him."

Great, just Van's luck. She would end up falling for the quirky, free-spirited salvage man, who was pretty much the complete opposite of Van's tight-assed, military background, head of security, play-by-the-book self.

Whatever. At least Kason would be safe. Ensuring that was both his job and his duty as the guy's friend. Van leaned over the back of the bus's couch and spread the blinds apart a bit so he could watch over Kyra while she was outside alone.

Sure enough, she was wearing a smile that was very unlike the glare she'd shot him as she stomped out of the bus a minute ago.

Fuck my life.

22

____

"Are you guys sure this is a good idea?" Kason hesitated before climbing into Van's monstrosity of a truck.

"Of course." Kyra held out her hand. "Come on. You've been talking with the Hot Rods and Hot Rides for a couple weeks. It'll be good to hang out with them for a bit. Plus your motorcycle is ready. Aren't you excited to see it?"

"Hell yes." A flicker of his old self seemed to bubble up, but if he was being honest...and he really wanted to finally be truthful with both his friends and himself... "But you know Wren and Jordan will be there. If everyone is getting together to help Devra with her restaurant remodel today, there's no way they won't support her."

"I'm going to say this now. We're coming with you today as your friends. Anything and everything we see or hear is off the record," Van promised. "Do whatever it is that will make things better for you. Not Kason Cox, the brand. But you, personally."

"You need to talk to Wren and Jordan and work things out between you, even if it's to apologize for walking away like you did. Ollie told me Wren's been worried sick." Kyra cleared her throat. "It's not healthy for anyone to leave things unresolved."

Kason caught the incredulous stare Van winged at her when she said that. He should lock them in the truck and make them fucking hash things out while they were at it. They were making some sort of sense though. He couldn't keep going like this for long. Gavyn and Roman had told him pretty much the same thing. If he didn't face his problems, he'd end up relying on crutches like he had before.

"Okay, fine." He boosted himself into the truck. Van was driving and Kyra was sitting between them on the wide bench seat. For the entire three-hour drive to Middletown, he wondered what it would be like if he was riding with Jordan and Wren instead.

Despite what Rick had said the night everything blew up, Kason couldn't shake the feeling that cutting himself off from them had been an even bigger mistake than letting his whole team down. His fingers drummed furiously on the door as they rolled into town.

If he'd had any hopes of finding a quiet moment to apologize to Wren and Jordan, they were shattered when they pulled up to the modest commercial building Trevon and his wife had bought. The place was swarming with people. Unlike the team supporting one of Kason shows, they were there because they loved Devra, Quinn, and Trevon, not because the trio was paying them. Must be nice.

"Whoa." Kyra took in the bustle and said, "How do they have so many friends? I only know like ten people. Mostly you guys, and you're kind of assholes."

"I guess we gave up more than we realized for our

lifestyle. How about for today we pretend to be normal, huh?" Kason took a deep breath then slid out of the truck. It wasn't going to get any easier the longer he sat there.

Fortunately, the first familiar face he spotted was Gavyn's. The man came over to them with a huge smile. He shook Kason's hand and used the connection to drag him in for a manly half-hug, half-back slap. "I'm glad you made it. How are you doing?"

"Still here," he said simply.

Gavyn nodded. "It will get better over time. I promise. I last saw Wren and Jordan inside. She's welding some stainless steel shit in the kitchen and he's painting the dining area, if you want to prepare yourself before you see them."

Kason took a deep breath and tried to stand taller.

"Good. Now, come on over here. I want to introduce you to our friends from out of town. They're part of a construction crew called Powertools, and they're helping out with the renovations."

"More like doing all the work while you mechanics are sitting around gossiping," said one guy, who was installing a motorized awning, though his grin made it clear he wasn't especially serious.

"That's Mike. He's their foreman, and this is Joe." Gavyn pointed to the man holding the other end of the heavy contraption. "Dave is the big guy sitting down making the floor tile cuts. He's got a bum leg. And those three over there are James, Devon, and Neil. They're a threesome too."

"Damn, it's like there's something in the water around here," Van said from over Kason's shoulder.

Kason tried not to be jealous of the bonds he could practically see tying everyone together. Everyone but him.

He was an island. "You guys, I'm not sure this is so smart. Maybe I should go…"

Except right then Quinn stepped outside and saw them. "Kason! Van! Kyra! Hey!"

It settled him to see another familiar face, and realize that maybe he might not be as alone as he'd suspected, so they went over to meet the Hot Rides manager.

He waved them around back to where a canvas tarp covered what had to be Kason's dramatically improved purple-and-orange bike. They'd agreed to bring it over to Devra's future restaurant once Kason had confirmed he was on his way.

"Count me down," Quinn said, gathering the fabric in his fists and grinning. "I hope you love it. Otherwise, I think Ollie might try to buy it off you. He's been eyeing it lately."

Kyra started by shouting, "Three!"

Van joined in for, "Two!"

And together all three of them yelled, "One!"

Then Quinn whipped the tarp off and Kason's breath caught in his chest. The Ducati gleamed in the sunshine, and he forgot his worries. "Holy shit. It's gorgeous."

He rushed to the motorcycle and swung his leg over it. He'd never needed to go for a ride and blow off steam more than he did right then. Kyra whipped out her phone and started snapping pictures of him on the crown jewel of his collection. Kason ran his finger down the seam between the chassis and the fuel tank, fingering the weld there.

"When we wrap up here, maybe we'll all go for a cruise together," Quinn suggested. "Between the Hot Rods and us, we could have our own parade."

"No joke. It looked like a classic car show as we came

down the street." Van glanced over his shoulder. "You guys know what the hell you're doing."

"Thanks." Quinn beamed. "Now get off that so I can cover it up and protect it from the dust again. If we mess up Sally's paintjob, she'll be pissed."

Kason was in the process of caressing the handlebars goodbye-for-now when the side door opened and Wren stepped out in her fireproof jumper and facemask.

He didn't need to see any bit of her to know who it was. The way she carried herself was enough to shower him with sparks as intense as the ones she created when she was welding.

Wren flipped up her mask, squinting into the sunshine as she took in the sight of him astride the motorcycle. "Damn. It looks even better with you on it. I mean... Hey."

She gave a weak wave before fanning her face with her gloves.

It was the perfect thing to say, as always. Kason laughed and felt at home despite what could have been an awkward reunion. He climbed off the motorcycle and went to her, giving her a hug that didn't cross any boundaries between friend and lover. "Hi."

And where Wren was, Jordan wasn't far behind. He strolled outside and stopped dead when he saw Kason with his arms around her. Was he pissed? Kason couldn't tell.

Quinn nodded to Kyra and Van. "Ollie's inside trying to figure out how to put some furniture together. Want to see if he needs a hand?"

"Yeah, let's do that," Van said with a grimace even as Kyra perked up. They disappeared inside the future restaurant, leaving Kason, Wren, and Jordan in relative peace.

He knew it wouldn't last so he got right to the point. "I'm sorry I bailed on you guys."

Jordan frowned as he stepped closer. "I don't care about that. I just want to know if you're okay. We were concerned. What the hell happened?"

"It's complicated." Kason dropped his arms from Wren and stood apart so he could face them both. "I have to be careful of public opinion. Not for myself, or not only, but because there are so many people who depend on me. My manager, Rick—"

"Was that the asshole yelling at you that night when we were on the phone?" Jordan asked.

Kason nodded. "Yeah. Well, he saw an article online speculating about my sexuality. I poked around some more after he showed it to me and it was even on one of those gossip sites with a poll. Almost half of the people responded that if I was gay they wouldn't listen to my music anymore. My fan base...isn't necessarily the most enlightened, you know?"

"Dumbasses who care enough to give feedback like that tend to be angry and hateful. I wouldn't say they're representative. Besides, you already told us you're not gay." Wren tipped her head, looking like she wanted to smack some intolerant skulls together.

"I know. But Wren, if people can't even come to terms with something familiar and should-be ordinary, they're not going to get the subtleties and nuances of whatever nontraditional life I would like to build if I could." He shrugged. "I hate it, but that doesn't make it any less true."

Jordan stepped forward and put his hand on Kason's

shoulder. He squeezed it as he said, "I understand. It's hard. We support you, no matter what."

Wren beamed at him, and for the first time, Kason felt a sliver of jealousy. Jordan got to live the life he wanted and have the woman of his dreams be proud of him. That was something Kason was never going to experience. Not as long as he was hiding, taking the coward's way out. And he didn't see that changing anytime soon.

Wren swallowed hard, then looked between them both. "You know this was the only thing in my life I really wanted to stick together and it fell apart on me. Twice. Too bad I can't learn how to weld people. It'd be a hell of a lot easier than this."

Jordan gathered her into his arms and kissed her forehead. "We're going to make things work. I promise. It's taken us a while, but we're getting there. Why don't we go inside and finish what we started here today? Take out some of our frustration with strenuous physical labor. You up for that, Kason?"

"Hell yes. If it involves smashing things, that's even better. I'd like to do whatever I can to help Devra out and spend some more time with you all, if you don't mind me being around." He couldn't meet their stares.

"We want you here. We always want you here," Wren told him matter-of-factly.

"Okay then." He smiled.

Jordan opened the door and held it for him and Wren. When he walked inside, Devra squealed and rushed over to him. "You're here! Thank you so much for coming. I've been thinking a lot about you and hoping everything was okay."

Kason found himself surrounded by plenty of people he'd met before and several new ones too. They tolerated his presence, and even made him feel welcome, though they had to know what had happened at Trevon's party and probably also with the addiction issues he'd been discussing with Roman and Gavyn.

When an older yet still damn impressive man walked over with a woman who looked like a more mature version of Amber and Nola, Kason was on his best behavior. Wren had told him about Tom and Ms. Brown and how they were the foundation of this entire special clan.

They'd been at Trevon's party, but Kason hadn't had the chance to officially be introduced to them before things had blown up in his face.

He held out his hand, but Ms. Brown bypassed it and swooped in for a hug. She patted his back and whispered in his ear, "Everything's going to be okay, Kason. You're doing your best. Keep trying."

He had to pretend that something from the construction debris got in his eyes then as he blinked away the moisture in them. Damn, these people packed a punch.

Everywhere he looked, there were couples, or more, smiling, joking, and sweating as they built something together for the benefit of one of their own. They inspired him, and made him consider dreams more outlandish than being a star. Maybe there was something worth giving his fame up for.

This.

For several hours, he immersed himself in whatever tasks Devra or Mike assigned to him. Even Kyra and Van —somewhat reluctantly—seemed to be having a blast teaming up with Ollie to make a three-man assembly line for about a hundred chairs and twenty tables. Tom and

Ms. Brown were keeping the mix of Powertools and Hot Rides kids entertained by letting them draw a "mural" on the alley wall with chalk.

It was incredible what one day and a bunch of people who rooted for each other could do.

By the time they were invited to the pavilion at Hot Rods for an end-of-the-day barbeque, Kason's perspective had shifted drastically.

Van leaned his hip on the picnic table next to Kason as he sucked down a bottle of water. "I have to say, you have pretty good taste. These are quality people. I can see why you'd want to be a part of their family."

Kyra wandered over with Ollie in tow. She said, "Are we talking about how Kason needs to make up with Wren and Jordan, yet?"

He widened his eyes dramatically at her in a universal sign for "Shhhhhhhhhhhh!"

Ollie chuckled. "If you think I haven't heard Wren and Jordan whining about how much they've missed you pretty much every day for the past week, you're crazy. Would you please put them out of their misery?"

Okay so...keeping anything private around here was going to be impossible. It was a tradeoff Kason was willing to make. Because suddenly he wanted to fight. Even if he didn't yet know how he could win.

"When I went through that rough patch the past couple of years, you two were always there trying to get me out of it. But now...you're saying...you think *this* indulgence is good for me? Smart?" He couldn't believe they were being so cool about the possibility of him hooking up with not one but two people, one of whom was a man. It was their jobs on the line, too. "Really?"

"I mean, it's only sex with a couple you care deeply about." Kyra shrugged. "What could be wrong with that?"

Ollie perked up at that. "You mean you'd theoretically be into a threesome?"

Van chugged the rest of his water.

"If I found two guys I wanted and they were into it, too? Hell yeah." Kyra flung her arm out. "Look at these people. They're the happiest bunch of motherfuckers I've ever seen. They must be doing something right."

"I agree." Van nodded solemnly.

"You do?" Kason rubbed his ear in case he was hearing things funny. "Mr. By-the-Book?"

"Sometimes you need to do a little re-writing." Van looked at his watch. "Not to be the party pooper here, but we've got to hit the road soon if we're going to rejoin the bus before they move on to the next city tonight. You've only got a few minutes. Why don't you spend them trying to make things right with the people you really came here to see today?"

Kason listened, really listened, to what his best friends were telling him.

He nodded. Then jogged over to the tire swing where Jordan was pushing Wren gently back and forth.

"Hey," he said lamely as he approached. "I'm going to have to hit the road soon, but I thought...maybe...if it's not too late, could I start calling you two after my shows again?"

Wren hopped off the swing and crushed him in a hug. "Yes. Please. That would be... Yes."

She surreptitiously swiped her knuckle over the corner of her eyes.

Jordan put an arm around her and nodded. "You might as well join in. We've been spending hours every night learning who we are these days and how we might fit together."

"In the biblical sense?" Kason couldn't wait to watch them fucking in his very own private live sex show.

"Uh..." Wren's porcelain skin blushed bright red. "Actually, no."

Jordan winced. "We haven't had sex. Haven't done more than kiss since you hung up on us."

"*What?*" Kason said it loud enough that a handful of people turned to look and Buster McHightops, Bryce's dog, barked excitedly. "Sorry. But...are you joking?"

"Nope." Wren groaned. "Though I'm not sure how much longer we can hold out. It seemed like a good idea at the time and we really have gotten to know each other so much better than before. We thought it would be best if we didn't seem like a couple for someone else to tack onto. That's not what we want. We want an even partner. Someone who's joining us for the ride, not coming in after the fact."

Him.

They'd been waiting for him. *Holy shit.*

"If there weren't a bunch of kids around, I'd drag you behind that shed and rectify this situation right this second." He stepped closer to them, then admitted, grudgingly, "Look, I don't have all the answers. I don't know how to fix everything between us. I still have the same issues as before. The only thing I'm sure of is that I missed you two a hell of a lot and I don't want to pretend like nothing happened between us. I couldn't stand it if this was goodbye forever."

"That's a good place to start." Wren kissed his cheek.

He took her hand and one of Jordan's as he began to

walk toward Van's truck, where his friends were waiting for him to wrap things up and get on the road.

When they were a few feet away, Jordan imparted a last bit of wisdom.

"I think that's how I fucked up before," he said quietly. "I couldn't see a solution, so I didn't attempt to work on the problem. Why don't we take it little by little and see what we can unravel together, okay? If it becomes too much or it's too hard, then we can always decide to give up later. We shouldn't quit before we start."

Van and Kyra exchanged a glance at that. Kason thought the same would apply to them. If it was easy to see about his friends, he was probably missing the obvious himself. So he went for it.

"We have three more shows and then there's a gap in the schedule to give everyone a break so they can go home, see their family, whatever..." Kason looked over to Van and Kyra, who smiled at him encouragingly.

Wren clasped Jordan's hand and squeezed. Kason realized, maybe for the first time, that this was important to them too. They were finding their way and giving him a chance. He didn't want to blow it. "Would you guys like to come check out my place? The one I told you about, Wren, where I write new music? It's actually not that far from here."

"How *not far*?" Jordan asked, as if he had very keen Spidey senses. The man was a special agent, after all.

"Let's just say I agree with you about the fishing on Lake Logan. I've enjoyed it myself many times." Kason couldn't help but grin at their widened eyes. They were cute when they were surprised. "That's how I heard about Hot Rides in the first place."

"You said the week after next?" Jordan confirmed, shaking his head.

"Yeah. Could you guys maybe find some time to spend with me?" He sounded like he was begging, but fuck it, he was.

"That's my last week of leave, so yeah. I'm good." Jordan nodded, then looked at Wren.

"Let me talk to Quinn. Things are busier every day and with Gavyn preparing to be a father, I think we're going to have to hire some more people. It's still a long way away, but Amber has her own business to run, so Gavyn's planning to be a stay-at-home dad for a while and let Quinn take on more responsibility for the shop. He's been interviewing a couple of guys so we can have more coverage. Anyway...what I'm trying to say is, I think we can figure something out."

"Great." Kason grinned. "I'll see you then."

He waved, then headed toward his waiting bike, parked beside Van's truck, thrilled to be riding it home even if it was only because of the illusion of freedom it gave him.

When he was nearly out of earshot, Wren shouted to him, "Hey, Kason! You remember my phone number, right?"

He gave her a thumbs-up. "Talk to you tonight."

"Drive safe!" Jordan shouted right before Kason put his helmet on.

23

Wren whistled as she passed through the elaborate wrought iron and stone gate then proceeded to drive up the long, manicured blacktop driveway that sliced through the forest. Kason's "cabin" didn't have much in common with the place Johnny and Jordan had shared on the opposite shore of Lake Logan.

From the passenger side of her Jeep, which the Hot Rods kept begging her to trick out, Jordan agreed, "Damn. If he owns everything from there to the top of the mountain, this place is worth millions."

"I'm starting to feel like maybe we don't belong." Wren tapped her fingers on the steering wheel. It'd been a while since she was around people with money and the memories spurred her anxiety. Thing was Kason had never made her feel like she wasn't enough.

Sort of the opposite, really.

Did he have no idea of his self-worth, and not only because of how many digits were in his bank account? "Jordan, I think we have a lot of work to do."

"Yeah. He's nearly as hardheaded as I used to be and not thinking straight."

"Maybe tonight, if we have time to ourselves without interruptions, we can get through to him." She glanced at her partner as she rounded another bend in the never-ending driveway.

"I'm hoping that's the case." Jordan reached over and squeezed her knee. "Are you planning to talk your way around his walls or fuck right through them? I'm okay with either tactic, you know."

"I feel like we might need to do something a little more drastic than chat. We've been doing that for nearly a month already. And...if I'm being honest...it's what I need, too. We've waited long enough, Jordan. If it's not for him, of course that's fine. But either way, I want to be with you tonight."

Jordan cleared his throat and shifted in the seat, not-so-subtly rearranging his package. "Same. I'm dying to make love to you, Wren. If he wants in on that, I'll be thrilled. If he wants to see what it's like between us, I'd take that as a consolation prize and put on the performance of a lifetime. If we go home alone, at least we've got each other. Right?"

"Yes. You'll always have me." She took one hand off the wheel to lace her fingers with his. "I'm so glad you're doing this with me tonight. Otherwise, I probably already would have lost my nerve."

"Nah, not you." Jordan rubbed his thumb in an arc on the inside of her knee that did nothing to make her less riled up. "You're the bravest person I know."

"I'm scared of getting my heart broken. It nearly killed me last time." She stared straight out the windshield as she admitted it.

"I'm sorry," he said for the millionth time. "But I swear to you, you'll never have to go through that alone again."

She might have continued their heart-to-heart, except they finally reached the summit of the mountain and the blacktop gave way to something more elaborate and yet rustic-looking. Hewn stones were laid in a herringbone pattern for the final stretch of driveway and a wide-open lot that would allow dozens of vehicles to park beside the most gorgeous wood-and-stone structure she'd ever seen.

It was big enough that it could have been some sort of exclusive lodge. And anything that wasn't natural material was glass. Enormous windows spanned entire walls, allowing the gorgeous surroundings to become part of the home's décor.

The jewel tones of the fall foliage made the trees surrounding the mountainside mansion a living painting. She was sure from the angle of the building and the slope of the mountain that from the rear, there was an incredible panoramic view of Lake Logan.

She couldn't wait to see it.

Almost as much as she was anticipating seeing Kason.

"What the hell does he want with us?" she whispered, her mouth suddenly dry.

"You're more precious than a thousand mansions to me, Wren." Jordan lifted her hand now that she'd parked, and kissed her knuckles before getting out and rounding the vehicle to open her door. "He's the same guy we've gotten to know. He doesn't want people who treat him differently. He wants us, I'm sure of it. Let's go prove it to him if he's not as positive yet."

Wren grinned at that. "I like that plan."

"Good." Jordan leaned in as if he couldn't help but kiss

her then, both to steady their nerves and to hold him over for the main course.

"Well, hello there," Kason called from the massive wrap around porch.

They both jumped.

"Don't stop on my account." Kason grinned from where he stood at the railing in jeans and a soft cotton T-shirt, his feet bare. "It's not like I've never seen you two make out before."

Jordan groaned then kissed Wren again, ten times more passionately. She wasn't complaining, but she at least wanted to make it inside before they got naked. The chill of the changing seasons hung in the air.

They held hands as they turned and climbed the wide stone stairs toward Kason, who opened his arms to them. "Welcome to my humble abode."

"Humble? I'm going to buy you a dictionary for Christmas," Jordan grumbled. "You can put it in your library, since I'm sure this place has one."

Instead of laughing, Kason looked sheepish. "I bought this house because my financial advisor told me I needed to diversify my portfolio with some real estate, and to be honest, once I saw the listing, I fell in love. It's a hell of a splurge, but..."

"You don't have to justify your choices, about houses or anything else, to anyone." Wren went into his arms and hugged him tight. "It's gorgeous, Kason. Thank you for inviting us."

"Would you mind if I saved the tour for later?" He hugged Jordan too before facing them both. "Dinner is almost finished and I don't want to burn—"

Just then a piercing shriek cut through the evening.

Kason's emerald eyes widened. He sprinted inside yelling, "Shit! Shit! Shit!"

They followed, but he didn't go as far as the kitchen. He slapped his hand on a security system right inside the door and started talking to the box on the wall. "Hey, Van. Turn that off would you? Do *not* let the fire trucks come. It's just me trying to cook."

The alarms were silenced in moments.

"I told you, you should have hired Devra to do it for you." Van was cracking up on the other end of the line. "You sure you don't need me to call for takeout or stay around here tonight?"

"Next time I'll listen. And yes. Go hang out with Ollie like you planned." Kason looked over at Jordan and Wren and winked. "You can bitch and moan about how gorgeous Kyra is and how neither of you have the balls to ask her out."

Van quit laughing pretty quick after that. "One date makes you an expert, huh? Hell, Kyra and I practically did it for you."

"True." Kason softened his blow. "Thank you. I'm going to spend the rest of the night enjoying my company. I'm resetting the alarm now. Your guys are down in their post at the gate. We'll be fine. Take the night off, Van."

"Not planning on letting them leave, huh?" Van tried to get some of his own back.

"Jordan and I weren't intending on going home tonight anyway," Wren spoke up.

From the choking and coughing on the other end of the line, Van hadn't realized they had arrived yet.

"Oh, hey, Wren," he said in a tight voice. "I have to do...something. Bye."

Jordan laughed, the deep, resonating sort she hadn't heard in years.

Kason winced. "Sorry. I was trying to make everything perfect."

Wren leaned in and kissed him lightly. "It is. We're here with you. That's all I hoped for."

Jordan nodded. "She's right. The only thing that matters is that we're together."

"Well then, I hope you're hungry for some dinner made with a lot of good intentions and little skill." Kason waved them to follow him as he headed through a soaring great room complete with a stone fireplace, more of those glorious windows flanking it, and exposed beams that were like the great grand-daddies of the ones in her cottage.

She'd been right, the sunset made the lake below glow with pastel pinks and oranges, taking her breath away. But it couldn't captivate her attention for long because she was distracted by witnessing Jordan stare at Kason's ass as their host escorted them to the open kitchen. A dining table suitable for at least a dozen sat on the other side of a bar made from a slab of a tree nearly wider than her entire tiny home.

Kason took the rolls he'd been baking from the stove and waved a hand towel over them to dissipate some of the smoke. They looked like bricks of charcoal.

"Bread is probably bad for us anyway," Wren said with a grin as he tossed them in the garbage can.

"Go sit at the table." Kason pointed. "I'm going to serve you both. I...uh...don't get to do stuff like this often. Humor me."

Jordan led the way, pulling out the chair for her at the head of the table, where a place was set. He took the one beside her and left Kason the spot on her other side. The thought of perching between them for an entire meal made her shift in her seat.

It wasn't long before Kason carried over a wooden tray with three salad bowls and matching plates of pasta with a cream sauce and shrimp on top. There was already a pitcher of iced tea and a saucer of sliced lemons on the table. It wasn't a five-star meal, but it had obviously been cooked with...love.

"This looks fantastic, Kason." Wren picked up her fork and prepared to dig in, suddenly ravenous.

The three of them ate in silence for a while, enjoying what turned out to be a really tasty dinner. Jordan finished first and kicked back in his chair, his hands folded on his six-pack. "Damn. If that's your idea of half-assed, I'd like to see you when you think you're great at something."

"You have." Kason looked up then. "Music is what I'm meant for."

Wren couldn't argue with that. "I loved seeing you perform at the concert. I've always thought your songs were soulful, but that night...you're right. You were a superstar."

Jordan nodded. "And when you sang 'Secret Love', I swear I almost lost it right there in the front row."

"I noticed." Kason winced. "And so did my manager. They had a photo of that moment in the article he called me out over."

"Fuck, really?"

Kason set down his fork and wiped his hands on his linen napkin. "Yeah. And you know what? I saved it to my phone and looked at it about a thousand times since then. Want to see?"

He was already hauling his phone out of his back pocket.

Wren held her breath.

When he tapped the screen a few times then turned the device around, she gasped. Jordan cursed. It was plain. Their eyes were locked and the expression on Jordan's face was overwhelmed with emotion—longing, loneliness, grief, unspent passion. Everything the song was about.

Kason was reflecting it right back as he poured his heart out into the song and into the crowd.

"Damn." Wren wiped her mouth.

"I can see why your manager was pissed." Jordan frowned. "This could ruin your reputation as a stud, and I know that's important to your image."

"I've been thinking a lot about that and I'm starting to wonder if I really care. In the beginning, my music was only for me. A way to escape the shithole my life was growing up. I've done that. Even if I never make another album or sell out another stadium." Kason stared at the elaborate house around them for a few moments. Then he said, "It's time to admit there are other things on my bucket list."

"Like what?" Wren asked.

"Like getting to ride the motorcycles I collect, and traveling to more places outside the country, and having a family someday, and...falling in love." He looked her in the eyes before turning to Jordan and doing the same. "But I think I might already be on the way to checking that one off. Twice."

He laid his hands on the table, palms up. Wren put hers on top of one and Jordan did the same with the other. To make sure they were clear, she said, "I am, too. After

Johnny, I swore to myself I'd never do that again. Never put myself in a position where I could get burned so badly, but...here we are."

Jordan cleared his throat. "You know, Kason, we have more in common than you realize. I'm at a crossroads, too. Yesterday, I wrote a resignation letter. Now I have to decide if I'm going to hand it in when my leave is up on Monday. I don't want to go backward, to keep being miserable, but I'm scared shitless to make the call. If I'm not Special Agent Mikalski, then who the fuck am I?"

Wren leaned halfway across the table. "Seriously? What the hell happened? You used to love being an agent. Has that changed?"

"I guess a lot has. The agency doesn't stand for what it used to. It's a toxic environment right now, and although I know that means I should stay and fight, I'm getting sidelined more and more. I'm already in the office instead of the field, and pretty soon they're going to find a way to force me out. It's better if I leave on my own terms, I think."

"What else would you want to do if you had the choice?" Kason asked as he held Jordan's hand tight, grounding him. If they clung together they would be so much less likely to break apart.

"I've been thinking about setting up a security consulting firm." He shrugged. "I talked to Van about it some and I've been emailing with this guy, Andersen, a private investigator who's helped out the Hot Rods in the past. They think it's a solid idea. I also had a conversation with Tom—"

Kason interrupted, "He's Eli's dad, right? The guy who adopted the Hot Rods?"

Wren nodded, and Jordan said, "Yeah. He's married to

Nola and Amber's mom, Ms. Brown, now. He lost his first wife to cancer when Eli was young, then continued her work at the youth shelter. I think I'd like to start an outreach program for kids wondering where they fit in the neat boxes of straight or gay, to raise awareness about bisexuality or pansexuality or polyamory—the gray areas that get lost sometimes—or the fact that labels don't really matter. I want as many people still trying to figure how they're built to know it's okay to accept themselves for however they're wired and to love whoever they want. Maybe if I'd had some positive reinforcement about stuff like that, I wouldn't have fucked up so badly before."

There was dead silence for a minute as Wren tried desperately not to bawl. Jordan seemed to tense, waiting for criticism that sure as hell would never come from her, and Kason appeared to be thinking hard. She wondered if he was wishing he'd met future-Jordan or someone like him when he'd been in his formative years. It seemed like he really could have used a role model.

"Could I help you with that?" she said when she could finally squeeze the words out of her tight throat. "It sounds perfect. I'd love to work at the center with you."

"I was hoping you'd say that. With you, I can do anything." Jordan looked at Kason then, as if seeking his approval when Wren knew he already had it.

"I don't have the luxury of time, but I'd be honored if you'd let me fund the program." Kason had to pause before he continued, "I want every person who might be like us to feel the way I do right now—in awe of their lovers and bursting with a joy like they've never imagined before. A happiness they could never find by looking in the wrong places their whole lives."

Jordan shot to his feet, his chair shoving back from the

table. "I have to...I'm going to take the dishes to the kitchen."

He gathered the plates, then put his back to them as he carried them to the kitchen sink, though not before Wren saw the shimmer in his eyes that solidified her resolve to bring them together before they left the sanctuary of Kason's home and the bubble they were in tonight.

While Jordan was out of earshot, Wren squeezed Kason's hand to get his attention and murmured, "What are your plans for the rest of the evening?"

"Are you asking if I want to sleep with you?" He swallowed hard.

Wren nodded. "Me *and* Jordan. Yeah. I think you know by now that's what I want. But I'm not sure if you're ready tonight, or if you'll ever be. It's okay if you aren't."

"If this was only about me, we'd have done it a long time ago." He pinched the bridge of his nose. "What if we sleep together and then I can't follow through with forever? I don't want to hurt either of you like that just because I'm dying to give myself to you now."

"I understand your concerns, but I think you're listening to someone who's biased. Your manager is looking out for himself. Not you." She held up one finger when he would have interrupted. "And even if we're not guaranteed tomorrow, we have tonight. I've learned you have to make the most of the time you're given. I'm telling you this is what I want, and what Jordan wants. Respect our decisions. The only thing you have to think about is what *you* want and act on that."

It took him less than two seconds to decide.

"I've never done this before. With three people, I

mean. How should we start?" Kason's eagerness to satisfy was plain to see.

"Kiss me," Wren said urgently.

"Like when Jordan sits down or..."

"Kiss me," she repeated, putting her hands on his shoulders and drawing him near. "*Now*."

What he couldn't see was that Jordan was already on his way back. If he walked in to a clear signal about Kason's feelings and his intentions, he'd do the rest. That's how Jordan operated. All they had to do was trust him, and he would make things so good for them, Kason wasn't going to believe it. Not until he'd experienced it for himself.

Which he was about to do.

24

Jordan rinsed the dishes and put them in one of the side-by-side gleaming stainless dishwashers. He focused on taking long, deep breaths while his hands performed the mindless task. Had that really just happened?

He felt like he'd cracked open a part of him he'd never shared with anyone before, not even Wren—either lately or back in the day. Despite what Kason feared, they were making progress. All of them. And he was dying for more.

Would Kason be ready to take the next step with them tonight?

He hoped so, but he wouldn't push. He'd wait for Kason to expose himself to the possibilities the future held, as Jordan had finally been ready to do tonight.

After washing and drying his hands, he folded the hand towel that had more in common with his fluffy bath towels than the thin dollar-store rags hanging off the door handle of the stove in his own apartment, and tried not to be intimidated by everything Kason had. It clearly wasn't enough to keep him content.

Jordan could give him that—through pleasure, companionship, and physical and emotional intimacy. Wren could, too. They had things to share that were valuable if not costly.

As he turned and headed back to the man and woman he'd like to call his lovers by morning, he saw that Wren had already gotten a head start on things.

Jordan nearly tripped over his own feet as he realized she and Kason were making out right there at the tip of the monolithic dining room table. They didn't spring apart or even stop as he approached. Thank God. They weren't ashamed of what they were doing or embarrassed to let him witness the mutual passion they shared.

He stood between their chairs and put a hand on the back of each of their heads, craving the connection. He couldn't wait a minute longer to be naked with them and absorbing even more of their positive energy.

Kason looked up at him and grinned. "Hey."

"Take us somewhere with a big, soft bed." Jordan waited until he had both Kason and Wren's full attention before he added, "I don't want our first time together to be on the dining room floor."

Fortunately, neither of them disagreed with his assessment of where the night was heading.

"Come with me." Kason stood and held out his hands. They each took one.

"I plan to," Wren said with a naughty smile that made Jordan's heart stutter.

Kason laughed, the sound as melodic as one of his songs, then practically dragged them through the great room to the back door. A sprawling deck waited on the other side, giving them access to a view of Lake Logan in the moonlight that would have enthralled Jordan at any other time.

"It's too cold out there. And not any comfier than the floor over there." Jordan balked, pulling them to a stop.

"Trust me," Kason said. "This way."

He held the door for them, then resumed leading them along the wide wooden planks to a spot where a suspension bridge branched off and extended into the woods. They'd only gone about fifty feet when Jordan realized that the endless line of trees wasn't exactly as it seemed.

One of them, the one with the thickest truck, was surrounded by two octagonal platforms encased in glass, forming a transparent, two-story tree house. *Woah.*

"The first floor is my recording studio. Up top is where I usually sleep." He looked at them somewhat sheepishly and said, "I get lonely in the big house by myself, so I mostly leave it for guests or Van, Kyra, and the rest of the band, who stay here when we're recording or preparing a new show. This is where I come to recharge. This is my happy place."

"What a fucking place, Kason." Wren sounded as awed as Jordan was.

"And we're about to fill it with a lot more incredible memories for you," Jordan promised.

They went inside and up an open-backed staircase that curved around the outside of the tree trunk, which was at the heart of the space. Jordan let his fingertips trail over the rough bark as they ascended together into Kason's bedroom.

It got even better as they rose. Flaming foliage surrounded them, stars burned in the sky overhead. Off to one side, a waterfall churned and cascaded down the mountain toward the placid lake in the background.

Wren and Jordan were struck speechless as they took it in.

Kason came up behind them and put one arm around each of their waists. "It was this—okay, and the indoor pool—that sold me on the house."

"You'll have to show us that tomorrow," Wren said. "Because I'm not leaving here until then at least."

She turned to face Kason and the rest of the room, where a gigantic bed with an open canopy occupied the majority of the floor. Gauzy blue fabric draped over the wooden frame lent it a romantic feel without blocking the view of the universe hanging above them. A clever half-wall made a convenient spot for a kitchenette and obscured what was probably a toilet and sink. Best of all, a jetted tub had been sunk into the floor so that it resembled one of the natural pools that formed at one of the plateaus in the waterfall beyond. Out on the porch, a hammock swung in the breeze.

If this were Jordan's home, he'd never leave.

"You have to invite the Powertools crew over here sometime," he murmured, afraid to break the spell set by the nature around them. "They would love to see this."

"Maybe their resort needs tree houses next," Wren nodded. "It would be the perfect destination for the honeymooners they've been attracting lately. Because I swear this might be the most turned on I've ever been in my life."

"I don't think that's because of the tree house, Wren." Kason leaned in and kissed her again, making Jordan remember exactly why they were here with him. "I've never felt like this before when I sleep here."

"You know that Kayla's resort is for naturists?" Wren asked with a mischievous smile.

"Forgive me if I'm not thinking clearly at the moment," Kason said. "But what's that mean?"

"It's a clothing-optional retreat," Jordan filled him in.

"And I'm feeling inspired to follow their teachings right now." Wren reached down and lifted the hem of the little black dress she'd worn. Not because she needed it to feel appropriately dressed for their date or because the traditionally feminine clothes made her sexier, but because they were a reflection of her truest self that she only shared with the men she trusted and cared for.

With them.

Kason followed her example and reached for his shirt, so Jordan did, too.

Wren was naked by the time they had stripped to the waist. They didn't bother with their jeans. Not yet anyway, when everything they wanted was right there in front of them. They looked at each other and grinned before advancing on Wren simultaneously.

"Oh damn." She sat on the bed, then scooted back, luring them closer. Wren kept going until she was in the center of the bed, then braced herself on her elbows, stared directly at them, and spread her long, long legs.

Jordan didn't need any more invitation than that. Apparently, neither did Kason.

They crawled toward her, their shoulders pressed together. And when they reached her, they slid between her legs. Each of them took one of her thighs in one of their hands, lifting and spreading her to make room for them both near her core.

Kason's eyes were slitted as he breathed deep of the scent of Wren's arousal. "Mind if I have dessert first?"

Jordan took Kason's chin in his hand and kissed the fuck out of the man for being so adventurous and so damn hot at the same time. Then he separated them enough to breathe, "Eat her pussy. Gently at first. She's sensitive until after the first orgasm."

Wren moaned and arched her back. "Quit talking and fucking do something better with your mouths, would you please?"

With a growl that made Jordan's dick hard enough to risk poking a hole in the mattress, Kason sealed his mouth to Wren and began kissing her cunt as thoroughly as he'd so recently made out with Jordan's mouth.

A cross between a shriek and a roar of triumph escaped Wren's parted lips. Her head dropped back, her platinum hair streaming behind her. She put her hand between her legs to hold Kason's head where she liked it best while she rode his mouth. She'd never been a timid lover, but now she was even more uninhibited and honest about her desires.

"Take turns," she croaked between moans, staring into Jordan's eyes. "Want you both."

Kason lifted his face. His chin glistened with Wren's arousal.

So Jordan leaned in and licked him clean, pausing only to kiss him again briefly before burying his own face between Wren's thighs. He did his best to please her, not because it was some sort of sordid competition but because he wanted to make this the best night of her life.

Just in case it was the last one they had like this for a while...or ever.

Jordan flicked his tongue over Wren's clit, drawing her closer to the edge of orgasm. And when he felt her hovering there, he tapped Kason. They kissed again, making Wren curse and thrust her hips in their general direction. "That's so fucking hot."

"She's going to come soon," Jordan told Kason. "I want you to take her there. Wait until you see how beautiful she is then."

"Hurry," Wren commanded, though Jordan knew it was also a plea.

"Fuck yes." Kason took up where Jordan had left off, this time sucking on Wren's clit. The man might not be experienced with other men, but he sure as shit knew his way around a woman's body. When he slipped his middle finger into Wren's tight pussy, she screamed, then exploded.

Kason never once let up. He drew out her pleasure for what felt like minutes.

And when she collapsed, he crawled up beside her and took her into his arms. They exchanged a sweet, lingering kiss that made sure Jordan lost the last of his self-control. He stood on the bed, wobbling some as he practically ripped his jeans off. Kason wriggled on the bed until his were gone too.

Then Jordan sank back down, sitting on his heels between Wren's legs. His cock was standing straight out, ready to fuck. More than ready. The past month had tested his limits, and he was there.

He looked between Wren—who nodded—and Kason, who said, "Go ahead. Show me what it's like between you two."

Meanwhile, Kason's hand came up to cup Wren's petite breast and strum his thumb over her hard nipple. They tipped their heads toward each other, and when their lips touched, Jordan advanced.

His cock nudged Wren's opening before he realized he wasn't wearing a condom.

She lifted her head from Kason and stared at Jordan, "What? Don't tell me you're changing your mind?"

Jordan's heart ached. She thought he could walk away from her again? Not at that moment or ever again. "No, I'm not. I just need to get one of the condoms from the pocket of my jeans."

"I can't wait that long," Wren said. "Fuck me."

"I'll never leave you unprotected." Not in this or anything, really.

"I told you I watch out for myself. I'm on the pill and I haven't had sex with anyone since you. Five years ago." Wren closed her eyes as if embarrassed by something that made his heart soar.

"Look at me," he demanded. Both she and Kason did as he told them. "I haven't been with anyone else either. I swear it. I'm STI free."

Kason shrugged and said, "So am I. My insurance company forces me to get extensive physicals every few months."

"So what the hell are you waiting for, Jordan? Get in me." Wren used her leg to hook around his waist and draw him closer. His cock penetrated the ring of muscles at her entrance, making them both groan.

"Distract her for a second," he told Kason, aware this might not be especially comfortable for her. She'd always been tight and they were both out of practice.

Kason did as he was told, his own cock jabbing into Wren's hip as he kissed his way down her throat then to her breast, where he sucked and nipped.

Wren's leg kept the pressure on Jordan's waist, so he gave her what she was begging for. He worked his cock into her bit by bit until his balls were resting against her flesh.

When he began to move within her silky sheath, her hand roamed down Kason's sculpted body to his cock and fisted him. The guy began to rock his hips, fucking into her fingers as they made out. Jordan loved watching them together.

He sped up, knowing this first round wasn't going to last very long. He needed to take the edge off. Five years was a long fucking time to stay away from Wren and sex that blew his mind.

Jordan thought he could hold out a few minutes more, except Wren couldn't. She froze. Her eyes flew open and locked on his even as her free hand crumpled the sheets and clung for dear life.

Kason noticed too and talked her through it. "Yes, Wren. Come for him. Hug his cock and show him how much you missed him. Make him come in you so that when I'm buried in your pussy next I'll know how turned on you both are by sharing this with me. It's going to make me so fucking hard to feel how wet you are."

Wren didn't stand a chance against that. Neither did Jordan.

She climaxed, her body spasming and massaging his cock until jet after jet of his release flooded her. Kason was going to get what he'd asked for. "Fuck, yes. Wren. I love you."

He hadn't meant to say that. Not here or now. Not in front of Kason, because the last thing he'd wanted to do was pressure the guy into feeling like he had to say—or feel—the same thing. But there it was, out in the open between them.

It seemed to only make her orgasm more intensely,

squeezing his cock from her body in the process. A trail of white fluid iced her well-used body, making both Kason and Jordan groan. Immediately, she held out the hand not stroking Kason. It's how they'd done things in the past. She could work him over and keep him stiff or get him hard again, while Kason was riding her.

He gladly went into her arms, collapsing on her side, opposite from Kason.

She tipped her head toward him, kissed his forehead, then promised, "I love you too, Jordan. I always have."

Then she looked back at Kason. "Your turn."

"Already? Are you sure?" He hesitated, looking at her and Jordan cuddling with lust and maybe a little envy.

Wren knew how to make it right, though. She always did. "Absolutely. I need you, Kason."

She gave the other man something he could easily and truthfully echo. "I need you, too."

Jordan found his voice in time to say, "If you fuck her slowly at first, she'll be ready again when you are. It doesn't take her long to recover. We used to be able to do this all night back when I was young and shit."

"I'm too turned on. I can't draw it out," Kason said.

Wren smiled up at him. "Enjoy it, for however long it lasts."

Sex? Their relationship? Whatever the hell this was they were doing together? Yeah...she was right.

Kason must have thought so too. He used Jordan's release as lube and buried his cock in her with a single long stroke that made his eyes roll back. Jordan reached out and put a hand on Kason's hip to steady him as he lost himself in the rapture that came from fucking Wren.

Kason had barely begun to pump into her when their

combined cries made Jordan's cock perk up. Wren wrapping her soft hand around it didn't help either. He stiffened in her hold. Too soon. Damn it.

Kason dropped low over Wren, blanketing her with his strong yet lean body. He possessed the grace of a predatory animal as he pistoned within her. If Jordan stared at Kason's clenching ass while he did it, well, that wasn't something he could help.

Wren and Kason paused their endless chain of kisses when she tried to tell them something that was garbled by the collision of their lips.

"Kason, slow down. Hang on a second." She put her hand on his chest.

He immediately did as she asked, blinking out of a haze of desire. "You okay?"

"I am, but Jordan's not. He's hard again already." She took her hand off Jordan and held it out to Kason, who licked the smear of precome and mingled fluids from her palm.

Wren looked at them both, then said, "Change of plans. We're going to come together."

"We are?" Jordan asked.

She nodded. "Kason, do you have any lube?"

He grunted. "Yeah. I sleep here alone, remember? Sometimes me and my hand have to make do."

Desperate to see if Wren was thinking what he was thinking, Jordan asked, "Where is it?"

He grabbed the tube out of the bedside drawer Kason indicated and started slicking up his shaft even before Wren rolled onto her side, flipping Kason over with her. By the time Kason had taken hold of her knee and lifted it, spreading her for his continued strokes, Jordan was already spooning her from behind. His cock rode the furrow of her ass, transferring the slippery gel to her skin.

"You want me here?" he asked her, his voice gravelly.

She shouted, "Yes! Fuck me, Jordan. Fuck my ass."

Kason stiffened. He stared into Jordan's eyes as if he was wondering what it would feel like if he was ready to ask for the same decadent pleasure. Maybe someday they'd find out. But not that day, because there was no way the three of them were going to survive the orgasm they were about to trigger in each other like a chain reaction.

"Should I wait?" Kason asked Jordan, though the muscle pulsing in his jaw said he wasn't sure if he could.

"No, she needs you to make it good for her, while she makes it good for me. At least at first." He hoped he was making sense. Jordan didn't have a lot of brain cells still firing. He worked a finger and then two into Wren, trying to prepare her for what was to come.

Her breath caught. Then she smiled at Kason and said, "Kiss me some more. I want to look into your eyes and see the moment you can feel his cock against yours through me, as I hold you both inside me. Together."

"Fuck!" Jordan had forgotten how her honesty affected him.

He'd planned to take things gently, carefully, and gradually. None of those things happened. He withdrew his fingers and pressed his cock against her ass until the tip of it spread her open. He kept the steady pressure on her until she swallowed him, taking him fully inside. And when he did feel his shaft rubbing against Kason's through the tissue hardly separating them, he pressed himself as close as he could get.

He leaned in, adding his mouth to theirs in a three-way kiss that merged their lips as seamlessly as the rest of their bodies.

Then he began to thrust, fucking Wren as Kason did the same. He pulled off enough to ramp up his motions, knowing something this intense couldn't be sustained. Kason fucked into Wren from the front as she ground on him, trying to rub her pussy against his pelvis.

Happy to help, Jordan reached around and slid his hand down her softly rounded stomach to her mound. He used the pad of his middle finger to rub circles around her clit as Kason filled her with long, fluid strokes that looked like they felt good, even to Jordan.

He wanted both of these people to know that what they were sharing was special. But he didn't have any more words, so he tried to show them with his body.

Jordan hunched over Wren and sank his teeth into her shoulder like both of them enjoyed. He forced his eyes open and stared into Kason's bright green ones as he did it, hoping that the man knew if he had two mouths he'd be biting Kason too.

That was for next time, when he was sure Kason wasn't going to get spooked by the intensity of what they were sharing. It was powerful stuff.

Wren felt it too, because she quaked between them. "I'm ready again."

"Me too," Jordan said, unashamed of how quickly she'd brought him back to the brink.

"Are you with us?" Wren asked Kason. Jordan wasn't sure if she meant it as it sounded, as if she was asking about a hell of a lot more than an orgasm.

For now that would have to do, because it was going to happen any moment.

"Yes!" Kason cried. He put his hand on Wren's hip to

brace himself, then fucked furiously. Only then did Jordan realize how much he'd been holding in reserve. The rubbing of his cock over Jordan's and the contraction of Wren's muscles in response was all it took for him to shatter.

"I'm coming, Wren. I'm going to fill you up." He kept watching Kason, who jerked at that.

Kason groaned, the tendons in his neck standing out as he finally fell. He yelled first Wren's name and then Jordan's before his abs rippled and his graceful arcs turned into short jabs.

Wren must have felt the heat of them both pouring into her. She screamed and clawed at them, trying to pull them as close as possible. With one hand behind her, on Jordan's ass, and the other on Kason's back, she clutched them to her as she came and came and came.

Jordan jerked, his cock twitching as it tried to keep going when it had already been spent. The pleasure lasted, though. It washed over him in waves that they all rode together.

When the storm had passed, they didn't move. None of them, as if they couldn't bear to be separated. They snuggled together without saying a word until long after Jordan's dick softened and slipped free of Wren's body.

He'd dozed off once or twice before he got up and cleaned himself then returned to do the same for Wren and Kason. Neither of them objected to his care.

He hoped it stayed that way.

Because he wanted a million more nights like this one.

The three of them crawled under the covers and interwove themselves into a knot of limbs and bodies that was comfortable as fuck and reassured Jordan. His arms and his heart were full.

As if by tacit agreement, they didn't talk. They didn't discuss what they knew had been a life-changing experience, maybe because they were each afraid of ruining it.

There would be time enough for that in the morning.

25

Kason had thought yesterday would go down as the best day of his life. It had certainly culminated with the best sex of his life. But today was even better. They'd woken naturally when the sun rose and filled his tree house apartment with light that somehow didn't feel as bright or as warm as the affection from the two people sharing his bed.

They'd snuggled and enjoyed a lazy start to the day before heading back to the main house to refuel. They hadn't done much else except enjoy each other's company, yet he'd never felt so...at peace as he did right then, strumming his acoustic guitar and jotting down snippets of lyrics for a new song. He wasn't ready to sing them out loud yet, but they were filled with optimism, infatuation, and a love he didn't want to keep secret anymore.

Wren and Jordan inspired him, even when they were simply having a calm weekend at a mountain retreat. Wren was stretched out on the couch, flipping through one of the hardback biographies of Kason that had been sitting on the coffee table. Jordan had one hand resting possessively on her shoulder and the other was playing idly with her hair. He was looking out at the lake, deep in thought. Kason wondered if he was remembering the night before, looking forward to the future, or thinking of Johnny and their cabin on the other side of the water.

Something in his chest did a flip flop.

After the night before and envisioning what his life could be like if they kept taking this long, slow ride together toward something permanent, Kason was ready to prove to Jordan that this wasn't only about each of them loving Wren and being good friends while they were at it.

His fingers fumbled the next chord on his guitar and he set it aside. He'd lost his concentration in the best of ways. "You two want to check out the pool now?"

Wren perked up and Jordan blinked out of his daze. She turned to him and grinned. "I'm assuming bathing suits aren't required?"

"It's an indoor pool, completely private. What you wear is up to you." Skinny-dipping was one of his favorite activities. It had only been recently replaced at the top of the list by sex with the two people he was coming to think of as his best friends in addition to his lovers.

"In that case..." Wren stood and stretched before ditching her clothes. He loved how bold she was, how confident and unafraid of others' opinions. He wished he could be more like her.

Jordan smacked her ass, then joined her, folding his clothes neatly and stacking them on the couch. Kason struggled to form coherent thoughts, never mind to coordinate his limbs long enough to stand and do the same. "Damn, you two are so fucking sexy by yourselves and even more so together."

"We do fit together pretty well, don't we?" Wren smiled as she pulled Jordan down to her for a languid kiss.

That did it. Kason bolted to his feet and stripped, hopping on one foot to tug his jeans off as fast as possible. They turned to him and grinned as he rushed to join them. Kason kissed Wren first, loving the lingering taste of Jordan on her lips, then turned to the other man and stared straight into his eyes as he sealed their mouths too.

Today would change the rest of his life. And hopefully theirs also.

"Kason?" Jordan asked, his voice husky.

"Yeah?"

"If you don't show us this pool soon, it's going to have to wait until much, much later."

He wanted to go exactly where Jordan was headed, but he'd always fantasized about making love to someone in the exotic paradise located down one floor from the room they were in. He'd never felt strongly enough about one of the people he'd slept with to bring them there, though. Or to his mountain retreat at all.

They were the first. And the only, as far as he was concerned. So he didn't want to blow his shot. Besides, he had a feeling they were going to love it since they'd been in perfect harmony with his own adoration of the glass tree house.

He took their hands and guided them along the shortest path to the pool, completely comfortable being naked around them. He'd never had any hang-ups about his body, but he didn't often enjoy being exposed to others. With Wren and Jordan, he knew what he'd already shown was far more important than his skin.

When he opened the door and ushered them into the pool room, Wren gasped.

Kason didn't blame her. The lush tropical paradise was unexpected in the middle of the autumnal woods. The elevated temperature in the room due to the heated water and the humid conditions were perfect for growing monstrous plants. Flowers bloomed in every direction. He had no idea what the names of them were, but they were lush and colorful, spiky, and foreign.

They reminded him of things he'd seen during tours in Hawaii or on a vacation he'd taken to Fiji, once. He picked one of the white blooms with a deep yellow center and tucked it into Wren's hair.

Jordan didn't begrudge Kason his show of affection. He smiled as he wandered around the bend to where the stamped concrete floor sloped downward and became sandy. "Holy shit, Wren. Check this out. There's a fucking beach and everything."

Her eyes lit up and glittered like sapphires. Kason loved soaking in her excitement. He loved this place even more than he already had, seeing how much she and Jordan enjoyed it.

She ran over to the beach and scrunched her toes in the sand, laughing. "I've never been to the ocean."

Kason swore he'd rectify that situation for her someday. He had the resources to take them anywhere they wanted to go. So how sad was it that he didn't care where they were, so long as they were together? In fact, he'd be happy to stay there with them for the rest of his life.

It was right about then that he realized how serious things had gotten.

He wasn't thinking about this as a weekend fling or even a fuck buddy situation anymore.

Kason wanted a commitment. That started with himself. He promised to be true to his desires so that he could offer himself to them. He hoped they would accept.

They were about to find out.

Jordan waded into the water, his powerful thighs and tight ass framed by the glowing aqua pool lights, shining from beneath the surface. He looked over his shoulder, giving Kason a glimpse of his defined chest and abs. Kason's cock grew harder by the second, imagining what it was going to be like when Jordan put those muscles to good use, teaching Kason how to love him properly.

Wren came up beside him and murmured, "Just go with it. You're going to be amazing together. I can't wait to see what it's like when the two of you finally give in and go for it."

"I don't think you're going to have to wait much longer." He took his cock in hand and stroked it a few times before sprinting down the beach and diving into the pool.

Wren matched him stroke for stroke as they swam out to where Jordan was waiting.

When Kason reached him, he didn't stop. He kept his kicking steady as he cut through the water, heading for a waterfall that looked like the edge of the pool. Without saying anything, Jordan and Wren followed him.

He paused and looked over his shoulder at them before finding the ledge there and stepping up through the curtain of water. He'd only made it a few feet inside before Wren and Jordan materialized through the glassy sheet.

"What the fuck else are you hiding in here?" Wren whispered in awe.

Jordan, however, was silent as he took in the hidden "cave" and the comforts it afforded. The shallow section of the pool was only about a foot deep with a smooth floor that looked like natural stone. A platform jutted about six inches out of the water and kept the plush day bed on top of it dry. An assortment of teal, yellow, and magenta pillows blended with the tropical theme and added to the ridiculous extravagance of the spot. The colored lights from beneath the water reflected off the ceiling of the cave, lending it a mystical vibe. Kason loved to nap there and recharge during what downtime he had from the road and other obligations.

Today he hoped it would be used for something more lively, though no less satisfying. He strode through the pool, water splashing in front of his shins, until he reached the bed and climbed on top. Like Wren had done the day before, he positioned himself in the center and stared at them both, inviting them to take everything he had to give.

He was ready.

"Fuck yes," Jordan growled as he grabbed Wren's hand and approached.

But before they could so much as kiss him, a shrill chirp shattered the moment, especially when it sounded again and again. Kason's eyes slammed closed. "Not now. Damn it, not now."

"What's that?" Jordan asked, going on high alert, his special agent showing as he prepared for an intruder.

"A call. Only a few people have this number. It's either Van or someone else on the security team. Or...more likely...my manager." Kason cursed and put a pillow over his crotch as if Rick would be able to see his hard-on through the phone. "Do you mind if I take care of this quick? Rick was waiting for the final version of an endorsement deal. I promised him I'd be available to sign today before the execs change their mind. It's electronic document shit, should take two seconds. I'll get rid of him as fast as I can."

"Go ahead. Do whatever you need to. I'd rather you not be distracted if we keep heading down this path." Jordan brushed his thumb over Kason's swollen lower lip, making Kason's cock get harder despite another damn ring of the phone.

"I'll be right back." Kason got out of the bed and walked behind it, out of the pool. He rounded a stone pillar and opened the hidden door inside it. Good thing the phone was waterproof because droplets still rained off him as he reached for it. The sharp ringtone irritated him as it sliced through the peaceful weekend he'd been enjoying.

Before he'd even brought the phone to his ear, Rick was barking at him. "Kason. I need your ass back at the tour bus for a few hours. I'm on my way there now."

"What? Why?" Kason had no intentions of going anywhere.

Rick blew out an exasperated sigh. "I'm your manager. Could you trust me for once? I'm doing what's best for you, and for us all. We don't have time to waste. The head of marketing wants a few test shots of you wearing their jackets before they sign."

"Can't it wait until Tuesday, when I'm back on tour?" He winced as he tried not to meet Jordan and Wren's hungry gazes.

"No. It has to be tonight. Get up here. I've got a

photographer and a stylist on the way too. Take a few pictures and you can take off again."

"I don't know, Rick. Isn't there anyone around Middletown? Hell, pay the photographer a huge bonus out of my half and have him come to me."

"Kason. We're talking about twenty million dollars here. What's the damn problem?"

It was right about that time that Jordan and Wren began to roughhouse in the background to amuse themselves and work out some of the energy that had been building between them. Wren half-lifted, half-shoved Jordan onto the bed, where he bounced and reached for her, tugging her down beside him.

"I've got company," Kason admitted, grinning at their antics. He couldn't wait to cannonball between them and take up where they'd left off. Fuck Rick and fuck more money he didn't need.

Wren played dirty. She reached around and twisted Jordan's nipple. He roared and flipped her over, smothering her body with his.

"That doesn't sound like Van." Rick got quiet. "What's going on, Kason?"

"None of your business."

"*You're* my business," he corrected with acid in his tone. "You know I checked out those motorcycle and car freaks you've been hanging out with. They're not good for your image. You'd better get back here as soon as possible."

"You know what?" Kason decided he needed to have a discussion with Rick, face to face. The guy had to understand their boundaries and what Kason hoped the future might look like. If his manager wasn't onboard, maybe he wasn't a good fit for Kason anymore. "You're right. I'm coming."

"That's better." Rick sounded so smug Kason clamped his hands around the phone as if he was strangling it. He hung up before Rick could piss him off further.

He took a long, deep breath. Then another before turning to face the couple now making out in his secret sanctuary. When he approached, Wren looked up then pushed Jordan away. "Everything okay?"

"I'm sorry, guys." Kason hoped they knew he truly was. "I'll have to do this in person after all. I'll make it as fast as I can. Hang out here. Enjoy the pool or anything else you want in the house. My motorcycle collection is down the hall from here. Take any of them for a ride if you like. Make yourselves at home. As far as I'm concerned...you are."

Wren smiled as she boosted herself up onto straight-locked arms even as he leaned in so she could kiss him. Then she flashed him a wolfish smile. "We'll wait for you. So hurry back."

"Drive safe," Jordan added before clapping Kason on the back. It was as if he understood that if they kissed, Kason wouldn't be able to leave no matter how important it was that he did.

"I'll do both," he promised before he stormed from the pool room. He'd gotten dressed and was jogging down the stairs to the garage in ten minutes flat. When he looked at the hundred or so motorcycles inside, there was no doubt which one he wanted to ride.

He took the Ducati the Hot Rides team had customized especially for him. At least he'd have Wren's work with him as he rode.

Pissed and—okay, fine—scared too, Kason headed north.

If he exceeded the speed limit by a healthy margin, so fucking what? He had to have some outlet and besides, the sooner he fulfilled his obligations and made it clear he was done for the rest of the break, the sooner he could get back to Wren and Jordan.

He felt like shit. Torn between responsibility and the need to unwind and to explore parts of himself he'd been denying for far too long.

When it started to rain, he figured it suited his mood.

Kason slowed and let the cool water dissipate some of his sour attitude. Unfortunately it also reminded him of the pool and how he'd walked out on the two people who mattered most to him when they'd been about to give him something he'd been craving for...pretty much forever.

Maybe he was too lost in thought.

Maybe he was still going too fast for the conditions.

Maybe his luck was shit.

Either way, when an enormous buck bolted out of the woods right in front of him, he didn't have a lot of time to think. All he could do was react. He swerved, narrowly missing smashing into several hundred pounds of muscle and bone at fifty or sixty miles an hour.

That was the good news. The bad news was that the rear tire lost its grip on the slick pavement and he started to spin. Time really did slow when you were having a near-death experience, he realized. It was almost like an out-of-body experience, watching himself as he prepared for impact, laid the motorcycle down, then tumbled free of the heavy metal as he skidded down the road, praying that every bit of protective gear he was wearing held up.

Kason couldn't tell if it was shock keeping him from

experiencing too much pain, or if he was doing okay, until he hit a bump in the road and began to tumble. Oh yeah, that hurt.

Especially when his boot got stuck on who-knew-what and his leg turned in a direction it was definitely not intended to go. He heard the snap of his bone a moment before white-hot lightning shot up his leg.

As he came to a stop, the deer looked at him as if he couldn't believe that had happened either before it bounded into the woods on the other side of the road. Headlights approached, terrifying Kason even more. He tried to scramble off to the shoulder, but it was tough when he couldn't put any weight on his left leg.

Fortunately, his poor wrecked motorcycle made a pretty decent speed bump. The approaching vehicle had to slow for it. And when the driver spotted Kason, they veered onto the side of the road and put on their hazards.

"Oh my God, dude! Are you okay?" A guy about twenty years old rushed over to help Kason make it the rest of the way to the grass.

"I think so. Mostly," he said, surprised by how hard it was to push air out of his lungs.

The passerby might have had an easier time believing Kason if he hadn't collapsed in the dirt. The world spun around him. "Could you...call help? Just in case."

Every word took as much effort as it had to walk away from Jordan and Wren.

"Yeah. Yeah. I'm on it." The guy had his cell in his hand already, dialing 911.

"Thanks," Kason said. Then nothing else would come out. He tried to suck in a shaky breath then another, but it wasn't enough.

"You sure you're okay?" the guy asked, crouching down as the dispatcher began asking a lot of questions.

Kason nodded, but even that was too much. Agony radiated from his leg now and his vision started to get fuzzy around the edges. The last thought he had was: *At least I got to make love to them once.*

Then he was out cold.

26

Wren clung to Jordan's hand so hard she was probably in danger of ripping it off.

"Sorry," she muttered, and tried to let go.

He wouldn't let her. "It's okay, Wren. We're almost there. Then we can see for ourselves that he's mostly in one piece."

"I think I might be sick." She groaned and wrapped her free hand around her middle.

"Need me to pull over?" Van asked. "We're almost there. GPS says three minutes."

"Don't stop," she begged, and Jordan tucked her against his side and rubbed circles on her back with his open palm.

They'd raced to the middle of nowhere, halfway between Middletown and whatever city Kason had been planning to meet Rick and the tour bus in. Van's systems told him the tour bus was parked in the hospital lot, so Rick must have come as soon as he'd heard too.

Fortunately Van had thought to collect them from

Kason's pool, given them time to find their clothes despite his obvious panic, then driven them straight to the hospital with him.

Wren's frantic phone call to Devra meant most of their friends were probably not far behind them either. Van had reached out to Rick for status updates, but for some reason Kason's manager wasn't responding.

What did that mean? Had the accident been worse than they'd first thought?

Could Kason be dead? Was Rick avoiding talking to them on phone? She knew from experience people preferred to deliver that sort of news in person.

Her stomach roiled. No! She refused to believe fate could be so cruel as to take away not one but two of her soul mates before she'd gotten a chance to tell either one that she was in love with them. There, she'd admitted it, even if only to herself.

Kason was so confident on stage and with her that his sweet sincerity and uncertainty around Jordan completely undid her. She would make sure she told him so next time she had the opportunity. Hopefully it wouldn't shock him too bad, because she planned to fight for the potential she saw between the three of them.

As she should have done in the past. She knew too well what was at stake if she failed.

Though not right now. Not while he was hurt and... "Please, let him be okay."

"Wren, this probably isn't the time, but... I want you to know that seeing you this way has made up my mind." Jordan's jaw was set.

"About what?" She looked up at him, grateful for the distraction.

"I'm quitting my job. I'm never going to put you in this

position again. Accidents happen, sure, but there's no reason for me to keep risking my life for something I don't even support any more. I'll hand in my resignation letter first thing Monday." He rested his forehead on hers. "I could never bear to scare you like this. It's going to be okay, Wren. Whatever happens when we go in there, we'll get through it together."

She took the first full breath she'd managed in over an hour. "Thank you."

They might have discussed it some more except they turned into a parking lot and whizzed past Kason's fancy bus out on the perimeter.

Van skidded to a stop under the emergency room portico, tires chirping as he slammed his car into park. They filed from the car at the same time and ran for the hospital.

They were met at the door by someone who recognized Van and immediately began to give him a status update. Probably another member of Kason's security team, or maybe the bus driver. He walked as he talked, leading them to Kason.

Wren couldn't hear a single word the man said as her worries buzzed around her brain. She needed to see him, to hug him, to make sure for herself that he would be okay.

Jordan still held her hand. When she stuttered in the doorway to Kason's room, it nearly yanked Jordan's arm out of the socket. He turned to face her and she wondered if he could tell she was completely losing her mind seeing Kason in a hospital bed. It took a moment before she realized he wasn't hooked to any of the machines on the periphery of the space, and that he looked aggravated, not weak or broken.

His left leg was propped up on a stack of pillows, encased in a cast from the knee down.

"Come on, Wren. He's all right. See for yourself." Jordan nudged her along. Then she couldn't stop herself. She crossed the distance between her and Kason and crushed him in a hug that probably didn't feel as good to him as it did to her, given his tumble across the blacktop.

Then she pulled back and scanned him from his head to his toes, which stuck out of the black cast. Other than a few scrapes on his forearms and a patch of abrasion and a bruise on one cheek, he seemed okay.

Before she could stop herself she asked, "Did you break a leg?"

Kason's gaze whipped up and met hers. He smiled slow and wide, then laughed before wincing. "Yeah. I guess this time I did. My tibia, to be exact."

Wren kissed the shit out of him, only stopping when someone cleared their throat. Loudly.

She peeked over her shoulder, but it hadn't been Jordan who'd made the noise in the hopes of taking his turn.

Wren followed his hostile stare to the object of his ire. A man in a suit with slicked-back hair was watching them intently from the corner. Immediately, she knew who it was.

"This is my manager, Rick." Kason rolled his eyes as if he too wished they could have their reunion in private. It didn't seem like the guy was going to take the hint, though. "Rick, this is Wren and Jordan."

"So I see." Rick crossed his arms. "Kason has had a rough day. He could probably use time alone to recover. He's got shows to perform this week, and reconfiguring everything to accommodate his broken leg is going to be a pain in the ass."

Kason winced at that. "We'll make it work. Maybe I can get one of those fancy scooter things and the Hot Rides and Hot Rods guys can spiff it up for me."

"Absolutely not," Rick barked at the same time Wren said, "That's a great idea. And of course they would."

Rick glowered. His disposition didn't improve any when a ruckus echoed along the hallway. It sounded like half of Middletown was out there, overwhelming Van, who'd waited outside so Wren and Jordan could have an almost-private moment to themselves.

"Did I hear someone say Hot Rides?" Quinn poked his head around the edge of the doorway. "Was it because you made a hell of a lot more work for me and the rest of the team fixing up your poor bike?"

Kason winced. "It's going to need some love and attention."

"We've got you covered," Trevon said from beside Quinn. Devra was there too, her lip wobbling as she took in not only Kason, but Wren and Jordan fussing over him.

Ollie showed up next, creating a gap so Kyra could slip past him into the room. Had she been spending her time off with the Hot Rides to give Kason some alone time with Wren and Jordan at the cabin? As soon as she thought about it, Wren knew Kyra had. Kason had told them the rest of the band usually stayed up at the mountain retreat with him unless they took trips to decompress or visited family. Kyra and Van seemed to be Kason's family. They would have been there if it wasn't for whatever had been going on earlier. The network of friends and support Wren had now was so different from how things had been when it was only her, Jordan, and Johnny against the world. It kept growing bigger, too.

This time, if something terrible did happen, there would be people to help her through it.

Something inside her settled. Life was unpredictable, but she was stronger now and prepared to deal with whatever might come their way. As long as Jordan and Kason felt the same, she knew nothing could break the bonds forming between them.

"For once your hard head came in handy," Kyra said with a rueful smile as she took in Kason's bum leg.

Kason snorted, "Yup. Don't worry, we're already planning how the show can go on this week. We're not going to miss any dates."

Kyra jerked back so hard she crashed into Van, who was suddenly there to steady her. "You think I give a shit about that? You know what? You guys are so dense, I'm over it." She scowled first at Kason, then Van, and even Ollie. Then she looked up at Wren. "I hope you have better luck getting through to him than me."

Kyra shook her head and wove through Ollie and Van, heading straight for Devra, who was standing with Sally. "How the hell do you put up with *two* of them? Ugh!"

Van shook his head. "She cares about *you*, Kason. We all do."

Wren watched as his gaze traveled from her and Jordan, to Rick, to Van, Ollie, Quinn, Trevon, Devra, and the rest of the Hot Rods and Hot Rides packing the hallway beyond them.

Ms. Brown was standing beside Tom. She blew him a kiss.

Kason put his hands over his face then and rubbed them up and down. When he pulled them away, his eyes were brighter and he had to clear his throat before responding. "Thank you, everyone, for coming to check on me. I'm fine, or at least I will be in no time. It could have been so much worse."

He scanned across them, then swallowed. "I'm so lucky."

Wren knew it was difficult for him to see that people he worked with cared about more than what he could do for him, but it was impossible to deny that others—not part of his band—had come simply because they were concerned. Not about his money, or even his music, but for the man behind those things. Quinn's brother, Roman, and Gavyn especially. The guys had been asking her about Kason enough that she'd figured out he must have reached out to them to talk about...something...related to addiction.

Whether or not things became permanent between her, Kason, and Jordan—and god, she hoped it did—Kason had already been claimed as one of theirs. He was becoming part of their family-by-choice, same as she and Jordan had.

Nothing could have made her more satisfied, or prouder.

"Yes, you are." Rick spoke up then, shattering the moment as he scrolled through his phone. "I just got a text from the CEO of the outerwear company. They understand there's been a delay and are fine with waiting a few more hours for us to send them the proofs. You ready to get back to work?"

"What?" Wren put her hand on Kason's and tugged it toward her as if she could shelter him from Rick and the demands of his career, which she was starting to realize weighed awfully heavily on him.

"No. He's not," Jordan added, edging closer.

Even Van shot Kason an incredulous look. "You're not really going to go through with that, are you?"

The flicker of resentment in Kason's gaze might have been unnoticeable if Wren hadn't been standing right next to him. Still, he shrugged. "Everyone's here now. I guess we might as well take a couple shots as long as we can take them from my good side."

He gestured toward the cheek that wasn't worse for wear.

"Perfect. I'll let the nurse know we're not going to do those extra tests they ordered. You're fine. Buck up." Rick smacked Kason's shoulder, then shoved through the crowd. If he noticed the unkind looks he got from one of the friendliest group of people Wren had ever met, he didn't seem to give a shit.

He had brass balls, Wren would give him that.

If that's what it took to be successful in his field, she was glad she was a simple welder and not a star-wrangler.

"Why don't we help you to your bus so you can at least relax before they put you through your paces?" Jordan asked.

It was a fitting turn of phrase. Rick certainly thought of Kason as some sort of prized thoroughbred. And she didn't doubt for a second that the man would be the first to shoot Kason between the eyes if he'd outlived his usefulness. Hopefully Kason knew that wasn't how she or Jordan or anyone else there would treat him, but she was afraid years in the spotlight might have distorted his vision of the world around him and what made him worthy of love and admiration.

Unfortunately, she wasn't sure how to unblind him

except to keep showing him over and over how much she cared.

"I'd appreciate that. Thanks." Kason let his head drop back against his pillow and stared up at the hospital room ceiling for a few seconds before he held out one hand to Jordan and another toward Van. Wren quickly grabbed the crutches that were leaning up against the wall nearby and prepared to offer them to Kason once he was steady on his good leg.

As he usually did, Wren was starting to realize, Kason disarmed everyone with a flashy smile that didn't reach as deep as the more genuine ones he'd shared with her and Jordan this past weekend. He nodded at Gavyn and Roman, neither of whom seemed amused. "Good thing I know how to use these. Maybe those intoxicated headers off the stage were good for something after all. Don't worry, I didn't let them give me any pain pills."

Ah ha. So she'd been right!

Wren flicked her gaze to Jordan, who was frowning. Probably as he was putting the pieces together too. She wasn't sure how to hold them together, but suddenly Wren felt like they were as unstable as Kason.

If they could make it to the bus and have a chance to regroup and unpack everything that had happened today, maybe they would have a chance to finish the weekend as she'd thought they would a few hours ago.

Though the mountain fortress had done a good job of keeping reality at bay, even it hadn't fully succeeded. Suddenly, an urgency and desperation hit her. It was similar to the one she'd experienced during every hour of the time between when those officers had told her Johnny was gone forever and the second Jordan had walked through her door.

It felt momentous. Like she could lose Kason, too, if they weren't very careful.

She looked at Jordan and tried to steel herself.

The only problem was that, as she'd found out before, she could only do so much of the fighting for them. It took more than one person's effort to overcome the obstacles standing in the way of a healthy relationship.

She was in.

Jordan took her hand and she knew, finally, he was with her too, and would be to the end.

But Kason? He put his head down. Slowly, he swung out of the room and along the hall toward his responsibilities, ignoring his own desires, whatever they might be.

Tom and Ms. Brown exchanged a worried glance that didn't make Wren feel any better. Tom looked up and said quietly, "You need to get through to him. Both of you. Go now before he hurts himself any worse."

Jordan and Wren nodded, then flanked Kason as he made his way toward the bus. Wren knew the older couple wasn't talking about his physical health.

She hoped she could make him see what they did. Otherwise, there was no hope for a future with him in their lives except as that haunting voice on the radio.

27

"Kason! Kason!" a pack of fans screamed as they raced down the sidewalk.

Jordan tensed. He wasn't sure how to handle a situation like this. He suppressed his training on how to take down actual bad guys. Though he could neutralize civilians hoping to fill their autograph books without breaking a sweat, he didn't want to step on Van's toes. Plus, he had no idea what Kason would want them to do.

"Sorry, guys. I didn't realize word was out already," Kason apologized to both Jordan and Wren. Rick, who'd been trailing them, stood back a few feet to avoid being mobbed. "Give me a second and we'll be inside where we can talk."

Van moved to intercept the half dozen or so people, who were carrying flowers, balloons, a teddy bear, and a sign that said *Get Well Soon!*

Though Jordan was vibrating with lingering adrenaline and worry for both Kason and Wren—who was biting her nails to the quick while sticking close by his side, very unlike her—he respected that Kason took the time to treat his admirers well. He never took anything for granted when it came to his career.

As for things with him and Wren, well, Jordan was giving Kason the benefit of the doubt. How could he agree to work tonight when they needed to regroup? Maybe he didn't realize how triggered Wren was right now. She needed them to reassure her everything would be okay, even if they weren't sure it would be.

They were only getting started. Things were still fragile.

Today had shown him that they could easily be broken apart if they weren't careful. If Kason changed his mind now about everything he'd said and done at the cabin, in the face of his real life, Wren would be devastated. And so would he.

More than that, Kason might not survive. Watching him limp to the bus, Jordan had been more worried about his spirit than his leg. They needed time alone to fix the damage.

The fans approached Kason and gave him their gifts. He accepted them graciously, then turned to go when one of the crowd spoke up.

"Hey, we saw that guy in an article online." The young man pointed at Jordan. Then he asked, "Is it true that he's your boyfriend?"

Jordan looked at Wren and smiled. It sent warmth and light through him to hear himself referred to that way for the first time in his life. The expression died on his face when Kason denied it swiftly and a little too loud to be casual. "No! But that woman he's with, Wren, is my girlfriend. Don't tell anyone, but you heard it here first. She's beautiful, isn't she?"

The guy fist bumped Kason and said, "Hell yeah. I knew that site was trash. Hope we didn't bother you too much. Glad you're okay."

Kason might be fine, but Jordan wasn't sure he was going to make it.

He hadn't felt such a yawning emptiness trying to swallow him since he'd watched Johnny's eyes go blank as his spirit left his body. It felt like his had tried to go with it. And this was no different.

He would rather have crashed a thousand motorcycles than experience the brutal disappointment and shame that swamped him at Kason's denial of everything they were and had been working toward. How could this man sponsor a program that meant so much to Jordan while lying about his own desires?

He couldn't.

On the inside, Jordan was shriveling into nothing.

On the outside, he smiled wanly and absorbed the blow. He masked his wounds even when Wren went as stiff as one of her welding projects beneath his arm. After all, he'd been Kason once. Afraid to admit to himself—never mind his partners or the rest of the world—that he was falling for another man.

As the fans trickled off, Kason and Jordan started off toward the bus again.

Wren did not.

Oh shit. Jordan looked back at her then ahead to Kason, caught between them, wondering who needed him more. Selfishly, he also thought for a millisecond about who would take better care of him, then felt guilty about putting himself first.

It had been an emotional rollercoaster of a day. None of them were thinking clearly.

"I can't do this." Wren's voice cracked.

"What?" He put his hand out toward her, still feet away. Was she about to bail?

Maybe for the first time, he truly comprehended how badly he'd fucked up when he'd walked away from her. Not that he hadn't understood theoretically before, but because if she left now, he wasn't going to be able to handle it. The thought alone nearly made him sick. He'd already lost the part of him that was an agent. Forging a lasting relationship with Wren, and hopefully Kason, was his purpose. It had given him something to focus on that was positive and meaningful.

Without that...he had nothing. Was nothing.

Kason realized something was off and turned around about the time Wren took a step back and then another. "Wren? What's wrong?"

"I have to go," she told Jordan, as tears welled in her beautiful eyes. He nodded, understanding even if he didn't like it.

"Wait? What?" Kason raised his voice and started hobbling toward them.

Van cursed, and encouraged them to take their exchange inside before anyone else—especially tabloid reporters, Jordan figured—noticed them.

No one listened to him.

When Wren retreated farther, Kason dropped the gifts he'd been given, the balloon floating away as he attempted to pursue her. Wren was fast and nimble. If she bolted, Kason wouldn't have a chance, so Jordan tried to intervene.

"Wren, it's okay. I'm sure he didn't mean anything by it. It's new and he hasn't had a chance to process it himself. It isn't any of those strangers' business what happens between us. It doesn't matter what anyone else thinks. You and I know the truth."

Liar. His own mind was railing at him for uttering such bullshit, but he was willing to accept it if it kept them together so they could do better next time. He should have known that wouldn't fly with Wren.

"That's no excuse." She shook her head, launching tears down her cheeks.

Then he did get pissed. No one made Wren cry on his watch.

Kason started to catch on. "You're upset because I didn't spill the juicy details of my love life?"

"Don't." Wren stabbed her finger in Kason's general direction. "You didn't hesitate to brag about how we were involved, but you denied Jordan. That's not how this works. In fact, it won't work at all. Because I'm sure as hell not a weapon to be used against him—to gut him like you just did. No." Wren waved her hands in front of her. She choked on a sob, breaking Jordan's heart and kindling his rage.

"Come inside, so we can talk. Please?" Kason begged, exhaustion and pain clear in his strangled request.

"There's no point." Wren shook her head, causing another round of tears to leak from her eyes. "If you can't accept Jordan—or should I say the parts of yourself that love him and want him—then there's no way we can be in a relationship together. I refuse to be with someone who forces Jordan to hide. Where he has to be someone's 'Secret Love' or wonder if he's even really cared for on the most basic levels."

Jordan should have spoken up, but it was impossible to defend Kason when Wren was right. He wanted to keep them together, but he wasn't strong enough to do it alone.

"I've done that before and I already know how it would have ended." Wren turned to Jordan then and said, "You know that, right? Whether or not Johnny died, we were doomed."

He nodded.

"I'm not going to make that mistake again. It will only hurt worse if we pretend like we've found everything we need because I have what I want." Wren started to cry in earnest then. When Jordan and Kason reached for her, she stumbled away from them both. "I'm not selfish enough to accept that arrangement."

"You're leaving me?" Kason lunged for her then, nearly tipping over on his crutches when she remained out of reach. "Don't go. I need you."

She looked up then, took a deep if shaky breath and dashed the tears from her face. "I love you, Kason. It's not enough, though. I'll always care for you and support you. I'm not going to vanish from your life. But I can't pretend we have any hope for true happiness. If almost dying didn't make you see what's most important, nothing will. Jordan and I deserve better than that."

Kason didn't argue. All it would have taken was one *sorry* or a promise to do better. He said nothing. The last shred of Jordan's hope evaporated.

"This is over." Wren spun on her heel. Her shoulders heaved as she broke down.

Jordan had never seen her inconsolable before.

His horrified stare whipped between her and Kason, who was sagging on his crutches, defeated. He looked up barely long enough to croak, "She's right. Go, Jordan. Take care of her. She deserves you."

Rick stood off to the side, a smug smirk twisting his lips as they imploded.

Jordan had never wanted to punch someone so bad in his entire life. He snapped at the guy. "You win, asshole. I hope you can live with yourself once you realize what you've done. Someday, you're going to love someone. Then you'll see that the best things in life can't be bought."

Van put a hand on Jordan's upper arm, keeping him from making a mistake by taking out his frustration and agony on the bastard's pretty face. He leaned in and said, "Wren needs you. Don't end up spending the night in a holding cell and leaving her alone. I'll take care of Kason. You go after her."

Jordan nodded. He glanced back at Kason, who was standing alone, defeated, in the middle of the hospital parking lot with his giant, flashy bus in the background behind him. Maybe fame and everything that came with it really were more important to him. If so, that wasn't the kind of man Jordan could give his heart to.

Wren was smarter than him. She'd nailed this. It was time to go. He said simply, "Goodbye."

Then he chased after Wren, who was already nearing their friends as they piled into their cars to head back to Middletown.

When he caught up to her, he put his hand on Wren's shoulder and spun her around before squashing her in a bear hug. "I'm so sorry."

She laid her head on his shoulder and looped her arms around her waist. As he held her and rocked her softly, she shook in his embrace. "No, I am. You deserve so much better than that. I'm so stupid. I believed that this was the time. That he was the right man for us both. That this is the way things were supposed to have worked out that made all the rest of what we've gone through worthwhile. I was wrong. So wrong."

Jordan heard what she didn't say. There was no sense in putting any more of her tears, angst, or faith into the situation only to be shattered when things fell apart down the line.

Still he couldn't keep himself from checking over his shoulder one last time. Kason was still where they'd left him, being lectured by Rick. Nothing was going to change.

"Devra, will you guys give us a ride home?" he asked, trying to stay strong for Wren's sake.

"Of course, but I'm sorry we have to." She came over and hugged them both, as did Trevon and Quinn. They understood how bad Wren and Jordan were hurting since they'd nearly been torn apart once, not too long ago.

It was ironic that Jordan had been the one to help them, but he was powerless to do the same in his own case.

28

"What the hell are you doing?" Eli, the owner of Hot Rods, marched over to Kason, making Van edge closer. Kason didn't plan to so much as lift a finger, or a crutch, if the other guy tried to take a swing at him. He deserved that and more for the agony he'd seen on both Jordan and Wren's faces.

He hadn't been prepared.

With everything that had happened, he'd been caught off guard. Denial was a reflex reaction. His old habits had ruined everything.

"Giving up." Kason thought about sitting down right there in the parking lot. "I can't make everyone happy."

"That's not your job," Eli told him. "All you have to do is make yourself happy. Are you doing that?"

"I should be. I'm at the top of my game, have more money than I know what to do with, fame, and people listen to my music across the globe. It's all I've ever wanted."

"Are. You. Happy." Eli stared at him like Kason was

stupid while his husband and his wife flanked him, shooting Kason matching half-pitying, half-furious glares.

"Nope, which probably makes me ungrateful as well. Guess I'm screwing everything up."

"Yes, you are." Eli didn't cut him any slack. As the King of their gang, he'd gotten used to doling out tough love when necessary. That didn't mean he thought he was perfect. "Listen, I've done it too. So believe me when I tell you that you're making a huge mistake. I've seen the three of you together. You remind me of us. Get Wren and Jordan back here before they put any more distance between you. You can still fix this. All you have to do is explain what's in your heart and be glad to show anyone else who looks too. It's not that hard. And it's definitely nothing to be embarrassed about. Be honest. With yourself. With them. With the world."

Alanso, Eli's husband, reached out and put his hand on Eli's shoulder. Kason had heard about their rocky start. Their wife, Mustang Sally, was even more blunt. "Quit being a coward. Why do you give a fuck what anyone thinks if it's not you or the two people you're in love with?"

"Is it that obvious?" Kason winced.

"Yes," Alanso answered. "So there's no use in trying to cover it up. Then you seem like a phony and an undeserving asshole. It's not a good look on you."

"I thought I was manning up by putting aside my own feelings and doing what I had to for my career and the careers of everyone involved. But I'm starting to think I had it backward. I need to do what's right for myself even if that means giving up everything else or I won't be any good to anybody."

"There you go." Sally smiled at him. "Now you're making sense."

Kason turned toward Van and Kyra. "I'm sorry, guys. I need them."

Kyra stepped closer and hugged him. "You'll be better for it, not worse off. Quit hiding, Kason. Everyone else will love you as much as we do."

"And if they don't, fuck 'em," Sally said with a wave of her hand.

Kason grinned—miracle enough given the situation—then reached for his cell, remembering it hadn't been as lucky as the rest of him. It hadn't survived the crash. "Van, can I borrow your phone?"

Rick elbowed his way through the Hot Rods, Van, and Kyra. "Are you sure you want to do that?"

Sally glared at Rick and said, "Yeah, he's sure. Didn't you hear him?"

"Who are you?" Rick asked, then shrugged her off before she could rip into him. "Doesn't matter. Look, Kason, we both know it was never going to last with those two. You're on the road constantly, you're surrounded by women who throw themselves at you night after night. You're risking your entire career for something that has practically no chance of working out."

Kason looked between the founding members of Hot Rods, standing united, and Rick. One of them might have more possessions, but the other had everything Kason had ever wanted and then some. Team Hot Rods for the win.

"Well, Rick, we both know I like to gamble even when the odds are terrible," Kason tipped his head to each side until his neck cracked, releasing some of the tension there, and said, "I'm going to roll the dice. Who's going to give me a ride?"

"Kason! Don't be stupid!" Rick was about to stroke out.

Every single person ignored his antics. "You're throwing everything away for what? Some dick and pussy?"

Kason's head snapped around, making him see stars again. But still he corrected Rick. "For love."

Their friends gathered around hooted and hollered. Even Van cracked a smile.

"So who's taking me? Let's go. They're getting too far away already. Can someone call Devra? Tell her to turn around."

Alanso volunteered, "I will. But I came separate. All I've got is my bike. It's right there, though..."

He jacked his thumb over his shoulder and Kason realized the other man had parked right by the bus. Perfect.

"They say when you fall off the iron horse you gotta get back on, right? I'm might have crashed and burned with Wren and Jordan, but I'm not giving up. Let's go." Kason came alive again inside. Feeling returned to him in a rush. Although some of it hurt, it was better to feel this than that awful nothing.

He was doing the right thing.

"Okay, now I might agree with Rick on that one." Van held up his hand. "Wait for me to get my truck..."

"Not waiting. Sorry." Kason grinned as he swung the three hops over to Alanso's motorcycle. The bald man sprinted over and got on. Kason dropped his crutches as he climbed behind Alanso, and stuck his leg out to the side, leaning in the opposite direction to balance out the shift of his weight. "Hurry. Please."

Alanso did as he was asked. Kason grinned as they flew down the road, especially when he realized—at a red light—that the bus was following them, though falling farther behind by the second. Kason shouted into the wind, hoping his friends were right and that it wasn't too late.

Someone must have gotten through to Devra. Her sedan was pulled over in one of those scenic-view turnoffs on the side of the road. They rolled to a stop behind her. Wren and Jordan rushed out of the car.

Jordan shouted, "Are you fucking crazy?"

Wren glared even as she helped Jordan brace him so he could get off Alanso's motorcycle without putting weight on his bad leg. As they were arguing about it, Kason's bus pulled up behind them, hogging most of the space in the bump out that overlooked a stunning valley.

"Please. Come inside. Give me a chance to explain. To make it right." Kason didn't care if he had to drop to his knees in the dirt and beg. Whatever it took, that's what he was going to do.

"It's probably better if we take some time to think things over first." Wren shook her head.

Surprisingly, it was Jordan who persuaded her. "It's okay. Let's hear him out. Even if you're not interested, I am. I know you're still upset about what happened back there. But you know what? There was a time in my life when I didn't have the guts to be honest either. A time when I was too afraid to stay with you and risk hurting you more. People change, Wren. They grow. Sometimes they deserve a second chance like the one you've given me."

He dipped his head and kissed her lightly.

Wren blinked, then nodded. "Okay."

"Thank you," Kason said. He turned and nodded at Alanso, who was grinning like a fool. He waved to their friends then headed for the bus before Wren and Jordan could change their minds. His bus driver came off and let

Kason know they had the place to themselves, then grabbed a ride back with the Hot Rides, who were leaving.

It wasn't pretty, but Kason managed to hop up the stairs on his good leg. At the top of them, Jordan was right there to assist. He put his arm around Kason and said, "Where to?"

"My bedroom is at the back. Help me lie down and put my foot up?"

"Does your leg hurt?" Wren asked.

"Not as bad as knowing I let you down. I'm so sorry, Wren."

She shook her head. "It's Jordan you should apologize to."

He turned his head to meet Jordan's stare from a couple of inches away. "I am sorry."

It was probably a bad sign that Jordan didn't respond directly. Instead, he maneuvered through the narrow gap between the band bunks, then got Kason into bed. Wren piled a few pillows at the foot of it and gingerly lifted his leg into place. Kason sighed.

"Damn, I had no idea a bus could be this fancy." Jordan looked around Kason's home on wheels. The marble floor and plush bedding were pretty impressive. "Truth is, Kason. I'm not sure we belong here. With you. Your manager is right, you know. You stand to lose a lot. I don't think I really understood how much until this weekend."

"Yeah, I could." He shrugged.

Wren looked like she was going to knock his head off with the bedside lamp. So he clarified, "What I mean is, if you two leave me, I won't have anything that matters. You're more important than cash or big houses or even the adoration of millions of people. Because you two are the only ones I love, so your opinions matter more than all the others combined."

Both Jordan and Wren froze at that.

Wren whispered, "What did you say?"

"I love you. Both of you." Kason cleared his throat. "When I saw my life flash before my eyes today, the only regret I had was that I hadn't given myself to you completely yet. I'm working on it. I'm not perfect, but I'm yours if you'll have me."

Jordan stepped forward, ready to take anything Kason would share.

Wren put her hand on Jordan's wrist. "It's not that easy. You can't only give yourself, you have to accept us too. I've been so fortunate in my life to be loved unconditionally twice."

"Three times," Kason corrected, unwilling to let them go without a proper fight.

Wren stared at him for a full five seconds before nodding. She believed him! "But that's not enough. Jordan hasn't ever had that from a man, and he'll accept scraps because it's something, which is more than he had before. That doesn't mean it's good enough for him. He deserves everything I've been given and more."

She turned to Jordan then. "You know I love you with my entire heart and soul and I won't let you settle for less from someone else."

"He doesn't have to." Kason pleaded with her, trying to make both of them understand the truth. "I'm all in. With you both. I love you, and I'm doing my best to overcome a lifetime of doubt and fear to show it. I fucked up earlier. It was a reflex. I swear it will *never* happen again, no matter the consequences."

"Damn fucking right it won't." Wren crossed her arms, making her breasts look fuller.

Jordan angled toward her then and cupped her cheek in his palm. He looked down into her eyes with so much devotion that Kason's heart ached. He wanted them to look at him like that someday, when he deserved it. "I appreciate you fighting for me, Wren. But I've got this. Not everything in life is certain and I'm willing to take this chance. It's going to be worth it. I can feel it."

"But what if—"

Jordan silenced her objection with a tender kiss. Then he murmured, "You'll be here to pick me up if I need you to."

She blinked up at him, then nodded. "Always."

This time when their mouths met, they were hungry. Passionate. Everything Kason had ever dreamed about. He could spend the rest of his life watching them and basking in the glow of the love they shared.

But he didn't have to.

Because when they broke apart for a breath, they turned to him as one.

"Say it again," Wren demanded.

"Which part?" he asked.

She put one hand on her hip. "The L word."

Kason grinned. "I love you. I even wrote a song about it. Want to hear?"

Wren shook her head no. It bruised his heart a little, thinking he'd lost them for good. Then she said, "Not until later. First we've got something else to do."

"Like what?" Kason asked.

"Like helping Jordan finish losing his guy-on-guy virginity. Yours too." She flashed them both a wicked grin, and began to undress Jordan, first getting rid of his T-shirt and then his jeans.

Jordan must have liked the idea since his cock was rock hard and jutting out. Kason licked his lips. "Come here."

Thankfully, Jordan didn't hesitate. He stepped to the side of the bed, level with Kason's head and held still when Kason leaned over to take him deep into his mouth with a single long slurp.

Jordan groaned. His thigh quivered where Kason's hand rested.

Wren's tone was sultry when she said, "That's better. I remember that day at Hot Rides, when I walked in on you. I wished I'd gotten to see this part."

Kason did his best to show Jordan exactly how much he'd wanted a do-over by sucking, licking, and fondling his cock and balls. Meanwhile, Wren began to pull down the oversized sweats someone had brought him at the hospital after they'd cut off his jeans. When she tugged his shirt off, Jordan's cock slipped free of his mouth.

"Probably for the best," Jordan panted, his hand stroking Kason's hair, letting him know precisely how much he'd been enjoying the attention. "Otherwise this would be over before we really get started, and there are a lot of things I want to try with you."

Kason squirmed in the bed, annoyed that his bum leg kept him from attacking Jordan like he'd fantasized about.

Wren crawled up on the bed next to him and plastered her naked body against his side. Her skin was soft over her trim figure and the lean muscles beneath it. She told him, "You know during those nights when Jordan and I weren't having sex, while we took some time to get reacquainted and waited for you to come around?"

"Yeah." Kason nodded. "Since we're being totally honest, I was pretty sure that you two were going to get back together and realize you didn't need me. It was only last night that I realized I was wrong. Everything is new and...it's not a good excuse, but I hadn't prepared myself yet for the outside world criticizing what I already know to be true. I love you."

He would never get tired of saying it.

"I love you too." She kissed him then, but only briefly. Her hand wandered down his chest and abs toward his cock, which was lying hard on his abdomen. "And we do need you. We always have, we just didn't know it was you we were missing."

Jordan joined them then, as if he intended to show Kason how much they needed him. He stretched out along Kason's opposite side, bookending him in warmth and comfort. How could he have even thought about throwing this away?

"Anyway, those nights Jordan and I shared our wildest fantasies. Sometimes we talked until we couldn't stand it and ended up masturbating together. But we waited. For you. For this moment, to do anything about it. Want to know one of Jordan's favorite scenarios?" Wren asked, entirely too good at driving him wild.

Unable to speak, he nodded.

"He wants to make love to his soul mate while I watch," Wren told him.

Jordan hissed and began to rock his hips so that his cock nudged Kason's side.

Kason reached for his own hard-on, but Wren slapped his hand away and fisted it herself. "But more than that, he wants to eat me while he's fucking you. And make me come on his face. Then he wants me to ride you so that we're both making love to you together."

"Yes. Do that." Kason was afraid he was going to erupt from listening to them talk about the pleasure they were about to heap on him.

"There are other things." Jordan's voice was husky and raw. "I want to experience it too. To feel your cock buried deep inside me while I'm fucking Wren. Someday, when you don't have a damn broken leg."

Kason had never wished he had superpowers more than he did at that moment. But since he didn't, he said, "Let's do what we can. I can't wait to give myself to you and take anything you want to give me in return."

Wren cooed, "That's a good boy."

Kason settled into his bed, allowing her slowly pumping hand to erase his nerves. He told Jordan, "There's lube in the drawer of the bedside table."

It was all the invitation the other man needed. Jordan dove for it and returned, already slathering his cock as he took his place between Kason's thighs, careful not to jostle his bum leg. Then he hooked one hand beneath Kason's good knee and raised it, opening him to whatever Jordan intended to do.

Jordan paused to kiss the inside of Kason's knee. Then took his slicked fingers and began to explore. When the tip of one nudged Kason's asshole, he moaned.

Wren covered his mouth with hers and sipped the sound from his lips. She traced them with her tongue, flicking it inside and distracting him thoroughly while Jordan inserted first one and then two fingers.

Wonder exploded through Kason. He couldn't believe Jordan was touching him there and that it felt so fucking good. He grunted and bore down, taking the other man deeper inside.

What would it feel like when it was Jordan's cock and not only his hand doing the penetrating?

Kason couldn't wait to find out. "Fuck me. Connect us."

A muscle in Jordan's jaw ticced and Kason realized how desperately Jordan needed the same.

He spread his legs wider.

Jordan was there, aligning his cock. It took several tries, but eventually the fat head began to sink inside instead of slipping across Kason's hole. He shouted Jordan's name.

The man stopped until Wren inspected Kason's expression. "It's fine. You're not hurting him. He wants more."

"More," Kason echoed.

Wren kept his dick stiff as Jordan worked his own deep into Kason's ass. When Jordan stroked across Kason's prostate, Kason twitched. "Right there."

Kason's cock dribbled precome onto his abs. Wren smeared it around and smiled at the proof of his desire. He could relate. "Let me taste you, Wren. Show me that this turns you on."

"It's the hottest thing I've ever seen," she promised him. "You're spread around him, taking him so deep, and he's loving every second."

Jordan cursed, then began to move. "I can't stay still anymore. I need to fuck you."

"Do it," Kason said. His leg might be broken, but his arms weren't. He reached for Wren and lifted her, helping her settle so that she was kneeling over his head, facing away from Jordan. He stretched upward so he could bury his face in her folds and make her feel even a fraction as good as he did right then.

She tipped forward, which exposed her and what Kason was doing to her to Jordan as he put his hands on Kason's hips and began to ride. Then he too leaned in. While Kason focused on sucking Wren's clit, Jordan slipped several fingers from his left hand into her pussy, making her shiver.

Wren shouted their names, giving herself over to the rapture she was sharing with them.

Jordan leaned in, causing his cock to impale Kason deeper. His tongue swirled around the base of his fingers before wandering upward. He rimmed Wren while Kason suckled her clit.

She clawed at the headboard and screamed their names before an orgasm swept through her.

"Fuck, she's so tight on my fingers, Kason. It's going to feel so good when this pussy is hugging your dick and I'm pounding into your ass. Isn't it?"

Kason couldn't respond except to groan. He thrust his hips upward, until Jordan took the hint and wrapped Kason's cock in his hand. He stroked it, though not too much, because they both knew ecstasy this intense was fleeting.

Kason tried to think of every scale he'd ever memorized to give Wren time to recover, but he should have known that wasn't the kind of woman she was.

She'd barely stopped twitching from the aftershocks of her climax when she inched her knees backward. Now, instead of straddling his head, she was spanning his waist. It took some maneuvering and a few tries, but eventually Jordan aimed Kason's cock as she lowered herself over it and her pussy welcomed him home.

Kason's head thrashed on the pillow. He lay there and took their duel advances, knowing he was the luckiest man alive. Wren rode him, massaging his cock with her wet heat while Jordan ramped up his strokes.

Jordan wrapped his arm around Wren's waist, locking them together so they could fuck Kason in unison. She smiled down at him, her palms resting on his chest, before turning her head so she could exchange a frantic kiss with Jordan.

"Is it everything you hoped?" she asked breathlessly when their mouths separated the barest bit.

"So. Much. More." Jordan groaned. "I love you. Both of you. It feels so good I never want to do anything else."

Kason laughed. In the middle of the sexiest, most desperate, and profound moment of his existence, he couldn't help but express the joy bubbling over inside him.

This was it. Where he belonged.

He'd found it and he'd never let anyone stop him from claiming it publicly or privately again.

"Ah, shit." He moaned. "I'm so close. I can't hold on."

"Me either," Jordan rasped as his hips began to bump and grind on both Kason and Wren. He tipped his head and bit the crook of Wren's neck in that possessive trademark she seemed to get off on as much as Jordan did.

Because right then, Wren's pussy clamped down on Kason's cock.

She settled fully onto him and ground her pussy across his torso. He reached between them to rub her clit, and that was all it took. Wren came again. The sucking motion of her flesh around Kason's cock was impossible to resist. He exploded within her, pouring his release as deep inside her as it was possible to be.

And Jordan...

Jordan did the same to Kason. It made him come twice as hard when sticky heat flooded his ass while Jordan's cock tapped his prostate over and over.

It was by far the best and most powerful orgasm of his life.

He might have even blacked out for a moment, high on their love, because when he came to, Wren was draped over him, his cock still buried inside her, and Jordan had collapsed by his side. He roused to Jordan dusting the hair off his forehead before laying a sweet kiss on his lips. "Thank you for making my dreams come true. That was...everything."

Kason swallowed hard. He knew how the other guy felt.

He ran his fingers up and down Wren's spine, loving how she snuggled into him, and whispered, "I was wrong. It wasn't music I was meant for, it was you. Both of you. Please tell me we're good now."

Wren lifted her head so she could smile sleepily up at him and said, "We're fantastic. At least it didn't take you five years to realize you fucked up."

"I deserved that." Jordan grumbled, then thunked his forehead on Kason's shoulder. "But seriously, Kason, why can't it be both?"

He nodded solemnly and took a deep, steady breath. Everything inside him settled for the first time in forever. When he exhaled, it was to sing the song he'd written for them that morning at the mountain house. It hadn't come to him at once. It was while he rode his motorcycle that some of the lyrics filled themselves in.

He hoped they liked it. In his mind, he was calling it "The Real Thing" because it was. "'Sometimes you have to crash, before you can heal. Sometimes you have to bust, before you can make it real..."'"

It was the most important performance of his life. And when he was finished, both Wren and Jordan were sniffling while beaming at the same time. He hoped that when he sang it for the world and showed them his soul, they clapped instead of booing.

Kason finally understood that if they didn't, he'd be okay because he had Jordan and Wren in his life. But it would be so much sweeter if they did.

29

A few nights later, Kason played his first concert since his hiatus.

Wren watched nervously from the wings of the stage, hoping his leg didn't bother him too much. He'd been nervous as fuck before going on, something both Van and Kyra found unusual enough that Wren was afraid he might trip and break his other leg or something. It was no longer funny.

Nothing that could injure him or Jordan was a laughing matter.

They had reached the tail end of the show now, this song and an encore from the end, and he was killing it despite using the rolling scooter the Hot Rods and Hot Rides had made cool for him, even on short notice. The crowd was singing along with every song, dancing, and generally lusting after her man. Well, one of her men.

Wren looked over at Jordan, who was mouthing the lyrics to one of Kason's hits as he danced beside her. He was a different person than he'd been five years ago. Hell, even a month ago.

He caught her stare and grinned. Then he twirled her around before dipping her and coming in for a kiss.

They were so enthralled with each other and the bliss overwhelming their lives that at first they didn't notice the spotlight that flicked onto them as Kason ended one song and a low intro began to play in the background.

"Hey, you two lovebirds," Kason called, snapping their attention to him. "Come out here, please?"

The crowd whistled as they noticed Wren and Jordan making out before shuffling onto the stage awkwardly. Right behind them, Wren heard Rick shouting, "What's going on? We didn't rehearse this! What the fuck?"

She also heard Van intervene, keeping Rick from following them or yanking them back, though she didn't bother to give the asshole much of her attention.

There might have been tens of thousands of people watching, but only Kason and Jordan mattered to her.

"Hey," he said to them as they neared. "Everyone. I want you to meet two of my favorite people in the world. This is Wren, and Jordan, and they're in love."

More whistles and cheers.

"I happen to be the most fortunate bastard in the world, because they also love me."

A crash from the side stage didn't deter Kason. He kept going, putting his heart out there for the world to see and judge. Wren couldn't help herself. She reached for him and kissed him too.

The roar from the crowd was nearly deafening. She had no idea how Kason could stand up there and absorb that every night. The lights, the noise, it was...overwhelming.

She stepped back. Then she looked from Kason to

Jordan—who was standing statue still, as if afraid to say or do anything wrong—and raised a brow. She'd shown him the way—would he take it or halfass this?

Kason didn't disappoint.

He rolled closer so that he could put his hands on either side of Jordan's face and bring it to his. The scorching exchange of their lips and tongues left absolutely no doubt in her heart or in the minds of anyone watching.

Kason loved them too. Both of them.

Wren cheered so loud she probably wouldn't be able to speak for a week. She jumped up and down and clapped while her two men blew everyone in the audience away.

She knew for sure they had, because suddenly, it was so quiet she heard Rick cursing from the other side of the stage.

Kason pulled away from Jordan with a sigh that promised he was saving a lot more of that for later. Then he turned to the audience and spoke to them with a steely certainty that made Wren's heart blossom.

"In life, you don't always know what's coming your way. But when something spectacular shows up, you have to grab it. So for this encore tonight, I want to perform a new song for you. One I wrote for Wren and Jordan. I hope you like it even better than the ones I've written before, because it's authentic and it comes from my heart."

A roadie rushed over and handed Kason the acoustic guitar he'd been playing that day at the cabin. He told everyone, "It's called 'The Real Thing.'"

The music picked up and Kason joined in. "'Sometimes you have to crash, before you can heal.

Sometimes you have to bust, before you can make it real…'"

Wren wished she could look out at the people listening to their love song to gauge their reactions, but she couldn't peel her stare off Kason long enough to see if his words had as much impact on the crowd as they did on her. She'd meant what she'd said. No one else mattered.

But for Kason's sake, she prayed that they loved him as much as she did.

The song was beautiful, and not only because it was theirs.

As Kason played, she noticed a flicker of light and then another as people began to turn on their cellphone flashlights in appreciation. At first it was a few, sprinkled here and there, but as Kason went on they grew more plentiful until it looked like fireflies in a field on a summer night.

Soon, the sparkles became a glow as more and more people showed their support.

And as the last note reverberated around the stadium, the entire place was ablaze.

Kason stood there, staring out at the reflection of his emotions. At acceptance. At love.

He'd earned it.

Wren and Jordan flew to him and crushed him in a hug. If there were tears in his eyes, she knew they were happy ones. "I love you both."

As the house lights came up, Wren could see that not everyone was as euphoric as she was. Some people scowled and one person in the third row even threw a beer at them. Others stomped out of the stadium, unwilling to listen.

Kason had lost some fans, true. But he would gain others.

None of them as devoted as her or Jordan.

Thunderous applause followed as he said goodnight to the crowd, then abandoned his scooter, putting one arm around Jordan's shoulders, the other around Wren's and leaning on them. They would gladly carry him when he needed.

As they reached the edge of the stage, he said, "That was the best moment of my life."

"It was amazing, Kason. They adore you," Wren said, reaching around to pat his abs with the flat of her hand.

"No. I mean the way you stared at me when I was singing." He shook his head. "It was like the day you looked at Jordan the same way in the parking lot of Devra's restaurant. I thought then that I would kill to have someone beam at me with such intense pride. Tonight you did. No high I've experienced was ever as intense as your admiration. Unless it's Jordan's. I love you both so much."

"You deserve it." Wren squeezed him, loving how her arm and Jordan's rested against each other in the small of Kason's back. "And in case I haven't said it enough yet, I love you too, Kason."

"Well, isn't that quaint?" Rick spat, as red as if he had a third-degree sunburn. He looked angry enough to lunge at Kason and might have done it if Van hadn't been restraining him. "You're going to regret this. How could you throw it all away for this?"

"For the loves of my life? Easy." Kason stared straight into his manager's eyes and said clearly, "Rick, meet my future spouses. *Nothing* is worth more to me than them.

Also...you're fired. Van, escort him off the premises, please."

From beside him, Jordan snorted when he heard Van say, "Rick, I think you'll be going now."

The Hot Rods and Hot Rides, who were already partying backstage, roared with laughter. Holden raised his glass and said, "Way to take out the trash, Kason."

Sabra, his wife, was standing beside him. Kason motioned for her to come closer so he didn't have to shout over the din. "You're a reporter, right?"

"I used to be." She smiled. "These days I produce the *Hot Rods* reality show."

"Do you still have contacts in the media?" Kason wondered.

"Hell yeah, she does," Holden chimed in.

"Would you like to interview me about what happened tonight and how insanely happy I am in my new relationship?"

"You don't have to go that far," Wren said softly. "Not to prove to me that you care. I believe you."

"Same." Jordan rubbed his hand up and down Kason's side, making the man shiver.

"I want to. I want the whole world to know that it's okay to love whoever the fuck you want." He looked from Wren to Jordan and then at Tom, who was standing at the heart of them all, celebrating with Ms. Brown. "This could be the perfect opportunity to announce our charity work, too. Let's turn this into something positive so that as many other people can be as happy as I am right now. Maybe that's why I've been given this chance. I want to make the most of it."

Wren was afraid she might crack Kason's rib, she was

clutching him so tight by the time he finished his impassioned speech. She couldn't wait for them to be alone so she could show him, and Jordan, how perfect the rest of their lives were going to be.

It was going to have to wait a little while longer, though, because it seemed like there was always some drama circling around their group of friends. Now that theirs was resolved, it was someone else's turn.

Van stormed back inside. Except, instead of looking pleased that Rick was history, he seemed pissed. Kason asked, "Everything okay? He didn't give you any trouble, did he?"

"Who, Rick? No." Van scowled as he glared at Holden and Sabra. "But that weaselly little traitor of yours? You can take him right back to Middletown. If he doesn't get out of my face soon..."

Ollie interrupted as he caught up, breathing hard, Kyra tagging a few steps behind, her lipstick smeared. "Van, I'm sorry. I know you have a thing for her."

"Then why'd you have your tongue stuffed halfway down her throat? I thought we were friends, asshole." Van shocked everyone gathered by pulling back and popping Ollie right in the face. Guaranteed black eye. Damn!

Kaelyn and Nola, who were closest to Ollie, huddled over him, preventing Van from taking another shot. Kaige and Bryce rushed Van, pinning his arms while trying to force him to calm down. Instead, they only made him a captive target when Kyra rushed up to him and kneed him in the nuts.

Ouch.

"How dare you act like you want me now that someone else is interested? How many times have I thrown myself at you?" She sounded like she might cry or curse; it could go either way. Wren knew that was when a woman was most dangerous. On the verge of destruction. In that place where everything hurt and you wanted to lash out. "You idiot! You don't have the right to say jack shit to me now or ruin this. Fuck you."

Kyra tried again to lunge for Van. This time the women restrained her.

"Hey, come on." Wren wedged herself between Van and Kyra. She held out her hand, leaving Jordan to keep Kason upright. "You're going to be pissed at yourself for this tomorrow. Come with us. We'll eat a ton of that ice cream I saw in your dressing room and figure out how to handle this better."

Devra was there too, speaking in her calm voice, inserting herself between Kyra, Van, and Ollie. Together, they defused the situation.

Ollie called Kyra's name. Though she flinched, she didn't turn around.

Devra and Wren steered Kyra toward her private space, bolstering her with well-meaning lies about how men were dumb and promising everything would be okay once things settled down.

Ollie tried again to pierce the wall of people keeping them safely separated.

Van shouted her name too.

"Stop. Both of you. I just want to be alone," Kyra said loud enough for them to hear.

Wren and everyone else around them winced, because no one who'd ever said so in such a miserable tone of voice really meant it.

· · ·

———

To FIND out what happens with Kyra, Ollie, and Van, check out Hard Ride HERE.

If you missed out on the Powertools: Hot Rods series, you can buy all eight books in a discounted single-volume boxset by clicking HERE.

If you'd like to start at the very beginning with the Powertools Crew, you can download a discounted boxset of the first six books HERE. Yes, know it says complete series but I wrote a seventh book more recently and haven't gotten around to updating the boxset yet, sorry! You can find the seventh Powertools book, More the Merrier, HERE.

CLAIM A $5 GIFT CERTIFICATE

Jayne is so sure you will love her books, she'd like you to try any one of your choosing for free. Claim your $5 gift certificate by signing up for her newsletter. You'll also learn about freebies, new releases, extras, appearances, and more!

www.jaynerylon.com/newsletter

WHAT WAS YOUR FAVORITE PART?

Did you enjoy this book? If so, please leave a review and tell your friends about it. Word of mouth and online reviews are immensely helpful and greatly appreciated.

JAYNE'S SHOP

Check out Jayne's online shop for autographed print
books, direct download ebooks, reading-themed apparel
up to size 5XL, mugs, tote bags, notebooks, Mr. Rylon's
wood (you'll have to see it for yourself!) and more.
www.jaynerylon.com/shop

LISTEN UP!

The majority of Jayne's books are also available in audio format on Audible, Amazon and iTunes.

ABOUT THE AUTHOR

Jayne Rylon is a *New York Times* and *USA Today* bestselling author who has sold more than one million books. She has received numerous industry awards including the Romantic Times Reviewers' Choice Award for Best Indie Erotic Romance and the Swirl Award, which recognizes excellence in diverse romance. She is an Honor Roll member of the Romance Writers of America. Her stories used to begin as daydreams in seemingly endless business meetings, but now she is a full time author, who employs the skills she learned from her straight-laced corporate existence in the business of writing. She lives in Ohio with her husband, the infamous Mr. Rylon, and their cat, Frodo. When she can escape her purple office, she loves to travel the world, avoid speeding tickets in her beloved Sky, SCUBA dive, hunt Pokemon, and–of course–read.

Jayne Loves To Hear From Readers
www.jaynerylon.com
contact@jaynerylon.com
PO Box 10, Pickerington, OH 43147

ALSO BY JAYNE RYLON

4-EVER

A New Adult Reverse Harem Series

4-Ever Theirs

4-Ever Mine

EVER AFTER DUET

Reverse Harem Featuring Characters From The 4-Ever Series

Fourplay

Fourkeeps

POWERTOOLS

Five Guys Who Get It On With Each Other & One Girl. Enough Said?

Kate's Crew

Morgan's Surprise

Kayla's Gift

Devon's Pair

Nailed to the Wall

Hammer it Home

More the Merrier *NEW*

HOT RODS

Powertools Spin Off. Keep up with the Crew plus...

Seven Guys & One Girl. Enough Said?

King Cobra

Mustang Sally

Super Nova

Rebel on the Run

Swinger Style

Barracuda's Heart

Touch of Amber

Long Time Coming

HOT RIDES

Powertools and Hot Rods Spin Off.

Menage and Motorcycles

Wild Ride

Slow Ride

Rough Ride - Coming Soon!

Joy Ride - Coming Soon!

Hard Ride - Coming Soon!

MEN IN BLUE

Hot Cops Save Women In Danger

Night is Darkest

Razor's Edge

Mistress's Master

Spread Your Wings

Wounded Hearts

Bound For You

DIVEMASTERS

Sexy SCUBA Instructors By Day, Doms On A Mega-Yacht By Night

Going Down

Going Deep

Going Hard

STANDALONE

Menage

Middleman

Nice & Naughty

Contemporary

Where There's Smoke

Report For Booty

COMPASS BROTHERS

Modern Western Family Drama Plus Lots Of Steamy Sex

Northern Exposure

Southern Comfort

Eastern Ambitions

Western Ties

COMPASS GIRLS

Daughters Of The Compass Brothers Drive Their Dads Crazy And Fall In Love

Winter's Thaw

Hope Springs

Summer Fling

Falling Softly

COMPASS BOYS

Sons Of The Compass Brothers Fall In Love

Heaven on Earth

Into the Fire

Still Waters

Light as Air

PLAY DOCTOR

Naughty Sexual Psychology Experiments Anyone?

Dream Machine

Healing Touch

RED LIGHT

A Hooker Who Loves Her Job

Complete Red Light Series Boxset

FREE - Through My Window - FREE

Star

Can't Buy Love

Free For All

PICK YOUR PLEASURES

Choose Your Own Adventure Romances!

Pick Your Pleasure

Pick Your Pleasure 2

RACING FOR LOVE

MMF Menages With Race-Car Driver Heroes

Complete Series Boxset

Driven

Shifting Gears

PARANORMALS

Vampires, Witches, And A Man Trapped In A Painting

Paranormal Double Pack Boxset

Picture Perfect

Reborn

PENTHOUSE PLEASURES

Naughty Manhattanite Neighbors Find Kinky Love

Taboo

Kinky

Sinner

ROAMING WITH THE RYLONS

Non-fiction Travelogues about Jayne & Mr. Rylon's Adventures

Australia and New Zealand